THE
WORLD'S
END

THE WORLD'S END

KAREN FITZGIBBON

POOLBEG
CRIMSON

Published 2024 by Crimson,
an imprint of Poolbeg Press Ltd.
123 Grange Hill, Baldoyle,
Dublin 13, Ireland
Email: poolbeg@poolbeg.com

A catalogue record for this book is available from the British Library.

ISBN 978-1-78199-680-5

www.poolbeg.com

Printed and bound by CPI Group (UK) Ltd, Croydon CR0 4YY

About the Author

Karen Fitzgibbon is a theatre and filmmaker based in Limerick city. She has been co-writing, co-producing, acting in and directing plays and short films with community groups and professional groups for over twenty years. She holds a Licentiate in Theatre Studies with Trinity College London. Karen lives in Limerick with her family and much-loved springer spaniel Major. *The World's End* is the first in a series of novels, introducing Private Investigator, Lana Bowen.

Acknowledgements

A few years back, I happened upon the remains of a holiday home leading onto a small beach in County Clare, Ireland. The beach is known locally as Seafields and you have to pass through the ruins and cross a field to reach it. Farm animals roam around the old building and an empty pool overgrown with weeds. And, as the crow flies, the immediate view in front of the house is a small, uninhabited island, Mutton Island. I asked my mother-in-law about the house and she informed me about some time in the fifties when the building was a luxurious holiday home, hosting lavish parties, and that often the revellers would take boats out to Mutton Island. The ruin, the barely visible pool and the magnificent view inspired me to write this book and so began the story of *The World's End*. My visit to Seafields beach was only the beginning though! The story has evolved and grown from that first visit. And so many people have helped me along the way.

I would like to thank you, my two dearest friends Stephanie O'Keeffe and Niamh Bowen, who read this book not long after my first draft. Your incredible support, encouragement and enthusiasm allowed me to keep going and, hand on heart, I don't think I would have continued if it were not for you.

Thanks to my amazing sisters, Marie and Carmel, who also read this book in its very raw state and gave me very different, honest advice as only siblings can. I cherish you both, every day. Thank you to my brother Ger, the stalwart of the family, Michael, Ciaran, William, Chris, Lorcan, Seany and Mia.

A massive thank-you to my son Peter, who sat with me for hours on end, correcting my grammar and giving me solutions to plot holes. It's a lovely feeling when the day arrives that your child is teaching you.

To Julia Droney, my legal eagle, who made me realise my legal errors!

To Ger Nichols from the Book Bureau who has said wonderful things about *The World's End* and gave incredible comments and encouragement.

I would like to thank St. Saviour's, the Northside Misfits, Southill Community Drama Groups, Headway, Adapt Services and Thomond Studio who have allowed me to write with them for theatre and film for many years. For empowering me to be creative, have lots of fun and for trusting me.

A huge thank-you to award winning writer Donal Ryan, who always has a kind word and a humorous story to tell – thank you so much for everything, Donal.

To writers Sam Blake, Patricia Gibney and Roisin Meaney, thank you for your support and kindness.

To my daughter Lauren and son Jonathon who smiled as if to say, "I told you so", whenever something positive happened. You both had faith in me, even when I didn't.

To my husband, Pat, who always has my back, who would pass the living room every now and then while I was typing away on my laptop and comment, "Are you writing your book, you are?" Yes, I was, and I did!

To my dear friends Joy Ferris, Martina McDermot, Louise Campbell, Brídín Ryan, Sharon Kiely, Dawn McCarthy, Helena Enright, Richard Lynch, Niamh Coghlan and Anne Fitzgibbon. Thank you for believing in me.

A huge thank-you to my adorable and very crazy Springer Spaniel, Major, who sits beside me with a very worn-out tennis ball in front of him while I write, his eyes pleading with me to take him out for a walk.

To my editor Gaye Shortland who is far too clever. When reading her edits, the penny dropped, so many times.

To Paula Campbell, who sent me the most wonderful email on the 5th of July 2023, an email that has changed my life, in so far as only then, on that day, did I believe that I could be a writer. Thank you.

To everyone at Poolbeg for making this happen.

Finally, thank you, the reader. No matter the platform, theatre, film, books, TV – the audience is where it's at. Always. Thank you.

Dedicated to Sheila and Michael

Prologue

A lone figure stood outside the bravura summerhouse as Lukasz steered his boat out into the dark waters of the Atlantic. Up late, he thought, finishing his day – not like himself who was up early about to start his. It was just after six. Lukasz loved this time of morning, the quiet of Castle Cove, the small, scenic fishing village sleeping soundly as the sea lapped gently around its shores. In a few hours the pier would be bustling with locals and tourists savouring its beauty but, for now, it was all his to enjoy. He noticed a second figure as he cruised past the house, hands gesturing excitedly, harsh words floating in the air. A fight, he assumed, or a drunken argument.

He navigated his way out to sea. The sun was rising behind Mutton Island, a microcosm of sedimentary rock, pine trees and sand, uninhabited except for a colony of seagulls. He sailed close to the island now, enjoying its tranquillity as the sun peeked over the rocks. He noticed a shape on the sand, a heap or mound of something, he could not be sure. It appeared too small to be a beached whale, but possibly the cadaver of a large fish. Lukasz decided to help the creature – it could be alive and unable to find its way back into the ocean. He drew in close to the pier, disembarked and tied the rope to one of the dock cleats. As he turned, he caught sight of loose fabric billowing around the fish, and then, a flicker of movement beneath the cloth. *A hand.* He hurried up the strand.

A young woman lay on her side. There were beads of moisture on her forehead, drool dripping into a hollow in the sand. Her long, dark, stringy hair was speckled with sand, glittering in the early-morning light. Her lips were cracked at the edges and the right strap of her white sundress was torn. But not to the same extent as her face which had been eviscerated with gashes, especially on the left side. He knelt down to check for a pulse. It was faint, but it was there. Her eyes were closed, moving rapidly beneath the lids. Lukasz thought, she sleeps as if she has a nightmare. He winced when he saw her legs, or at least what was left of them. Glancing up and down the beach, he saw that it was completely empty, save for him and the girl, no boats or cruisers out on the sea. He had to make a decision. He gently lifted the girl and carried her to his boat. With effort he climbed onto the vessel and carefully laid her on the deck. Her breath quickened as he moved, a faint murmur of something he couldn't understand.

"*Spokuj,*" he soothed – *easy.* He removed his jacket to cover her legs.

Starting the engine, he pulled the lever and headed back to the mainland.

There, he jumped onto the pier and shouted for Nora, the harbour manager.

"*Nora! Nora!*" He secured the rope to the mooring cleat and sprinted up to the port cabin. "*Nora!*"

A heavy-set, middle-aged woman with short, spiky red hair

emerged from the cabin, a look of concern on her face. "You're back early, Lukasz?"

"I found something!" he gasped. "A girl. Call an ambulance. *Now.*"

He hurried back down the harbour towards his boat with Nora following, talking on her phone as she moved. He helped a breathless Nora onto the boat, her cheeks pink from the exertion.

"Where did you find her?" she asked breathlessly.

"On Mutton Island. I saw something on the beach. I thought it was some fish, in trouble, you know …" He took a breath, wiped his brow with the back of his hand. "I did not know what to do. If I moved her, I might hurt her. If I left her and come back for help, she might have died. So, I chanced my luck. I carried her onto the boat and rushed back."

"Well, you did good, Lukasz. The ambulance is on its way." She checked her watch. It was just after seven. "I hope it won't be too long."

"I don't think it is a good idea to move her from the boat, she is … her feet, they are bad, there is damage. And her face …" Lukasz grimaced as he stole a glance at the girl.

"Show me?"

"I don't think you should …" he began.

"Show me, Lukasz. I was a nurse for twenty-one years before I saw sense. Maybe I can help her until the ambulance gets here." Her expression softened. "Show me."

Lukasz leaned over the girl and pulled back his jacket. He turned his head away – he could not look at her feet. Not again. Nora's breath quickened beside him.

"*Jesus Christ!*" she exclaimed. "What happened to the poor girl?"

Lukasz replaced his jacket. The girl moved her head so that she was facing him. Her lips parted. He thought he heard her try to say something.

"What did she say?" Nora asked quietly.

Lukasz leaned closer.

"*Waaaaattttt …*" It came out in a whisper, the girl's cracked lips barely moving.

He frowned. "Maybe water, I think she is asking for water." He opened a cooler box and pulled out a plastic bottle.

Nora reached out and took the bottle from him. "No," she said firmly. "Don't give it to her – there might be an obstruction in her throat, she might choke."

"But she is thirsty …"

"I'll pour some onto the bottle top and wet her lips. That's all she needs."

Nora carefully poured a few drops onto the bottle top. She gently held the girl's head in the palm of one hand as she tilted the cap towards her mouth with the other. The girl's breath quickened as she tried to drink the liquid.

"Careful now," soothed Nora, "that's it." She gently pushed the strands of the girl's dark hair away from her eyes.

"Who is she?" Lukasz wondered aloud.

"I don't know. She's not from around here though. I am certain I have never seen this girl before. Having said that, the weekend was busy with tourists. She could be from anywhere."

"She might have died." Lukaz was shaking. He felt Nora watching him.

"You might have just saved a young girl's life today, Lukasz. You must be in shock, but you should be proud of yourself." Nora rested a comforting hand on his shoulder.

"I am alright. Really." He frowned. "I am just confused." He narrowed his eyes. "How did she get to the island?" He glanced up the harbour … something was different about the boats. What was it?

His thoughts were diverted by the alert of sirens. He was worried the noise would frighten the girl. Nora stepped onto the pier and waved at the vehicle. The ambulance pulled to a stop in front of his boat.

Lukasz glanced down at the girl lying in front of him. He didn't even know her name. Suddenly, he felt so sad for her. An image of her mangled feet drifted in front of him. He closed his eyes. He wished Pete or some of the other fishermen had come out this morning. They could have all helped the girl together. To think he almost did not go out on the water himself. He did not want to contemplate what might have happened if he had made that decision.

The paramedics fixed an oxygen mask to the girl's face and carefully lifted her onto a stretcher before rolling her into the back of the ambulance. One paramedic sat in beside her while the other climbed into the front seat. A moment later, they drove away, their lights flashing.

Lukasz stood staring after the ambulance.

Nora patted him on the back. "She is in safe hands now, Lukasz. Go home and get some rest." She turned and walked back towards her cabin.

Lukasz continued to observe the vehicle as it drove past the World's End summerhouse. It was then that he saw the same figure, the very one he had seen earlier, alone this time, standing by the pool at the side of the house, watching.

PART ONE

1

3 DAYS EARLIER

Stephen looped his silk tie through the stiff fabric of his collar. He had gone for a run on the boardwalk flanking the River Shannon during his lunch break before grabbing a quick shower in the basement gym of his office building. He paused to admire his reflection in the full-length mirror as he headed out the door. His face was glowing after his run and his hair was damp against his skin. He stuffed his wet towel and running gear into his bag, slinging it over his shoulder. He then rummaged in his pockets for some coins and fired them into the vending machine along the hall, selecting a bottle of water. Pressing the cold plastic against his skin, he felt immediate relief. He switched on his mobile phone. Five missed calls from Andy. He sighed. *What now?* Flashing a fleeting glance around the foyer, he returned her call. The building housed several different companies and the lobby was busy with office workers milling around during their lunch break. Andy took forever to answer. Grateful, believing he had just won another few minutes of respite, he went to hang up when he heard the dial tone stop. *Shit.*

He took a moment before he spoke. "Andy?" He cleared his throat. The line was quiet. He adjusted his grip on the phone. "Andy? I was just about to call you." Silence. "Andy? You there?"

"Where were you?" Andy's voice was soft, barely audible.

Stephen rolled his eyes as his temper flared. He steadied himself. In an even voice, he replied, "It has been a busy morning. I've been tied up with meeting after meeting – one of those days, you know how it is?" He stopped himself – he was talking too much.

The line remained stubbornly quiet.

He tried again. "I wanted to call you and then the work kept piling up on my desk – it just hasn't stopped, you know?" Still nothing from Andy. He decided to change tactics. "How are you?"

"It's lunchtime." She sounded sharper, more assertive.

Fuck sake. "I know. I had a presentation to finish. Just this minute I sent it through for approval." He hesitated, before looking over his shoulder to see if she was there, watching him. It would not be the first time.

Stephen worked for a marketing company, Jennings Studio 61, based on the seventh floor of the River Point building in Limerick city – his wife's father, Luke Jennings, was the CEO of the business. His eyes rested on a young woman with shoulder-length blonde hair entering through the swivel doors. She was wearing a short red dress, revealing long shapely legs. He was sure he hadn't seen her in the building before and he wondered what company she worked for. His gaze followed her as she strode towards the lifts.

"How was your day?" he asked. He could hear his wife's breath quicken. He was pretty sure she was crying. He dropped his head. "Andy?"

She exhaled slowly, sniffing loudly.

"Andy, what is it?"

"You said you would call." Her breath was unsteady.

"I told you, I was just about to."

"Today has been hard."

"Andy, I ..."

"I thought I saw him."

"Andy ... stop."

"I went for a walk and ..."

"Andy, you didn't see him."

"He was so like him, Stephen."

"Christ sake, Andy, this is all in your head." He gripped the phone tightly.

"Don't you say that." She shot back. "You don't get to say that. You go to work every day so you get to forget."

Now it was his turn to remain quiet. He hadn't exactly chosen to go back to work. It was more like their mortgage depended on it. And, there was the small matter that Andy's father was his employer. Stay calm, he warned himself, do not react.

"I'm sorry." Her anger abated as quickly as it had risen.

That's better, he thought. "Look, Andy, I'll be home later and we can talk then, yeah?" He turned the corner just as the lift was about to close. He put his foot inside the door and it automatically reopened. The blonde woman was leaning against the brass rail in front of the mirror, applying lipstick. She was of average height and sported the kind of figure that went to the gym. She caught sight of Stephen's reflection as she pressed her red lips together. He averted his gaze.

He heard a sigh at the other end of the phone, but he knew that he had appeased Andy – for the time being. He mouthed the word 'sorry' to the woman and pressed the button for the seventh floor.

Andy said, "OK."

"Love you," he just about managed to say before the line went dead.

He shoved his phone back in his pocket and took a deep breath. Andy was driving him crazy. She had become insufferable and he just didn't know what to do about it. It had been three years since … since the event, and he was trying to move on, but Andy was rooted in the past.

"That's so cute," the woman said as she closed the lid of her lipstick and placed it back in her purse.

"Sorry?"

"What you just said to your wife. It's not often you hear declarations of love from a husband to his wife," she nodded at the ring on his wedding finger, "assuming that was your wife?"

Stephen looked at the ring, his wedding ring, a gift from Andy. The lift arrived at the seventh floor and he nodded as the doors opened. He caught a glimpse of the woman's expression as he departed. He was unsure if it was indifference or pity.

He arrived at his desk and checked his email. There was one from his team leader about the presentation due to take place that afternoon. He hadn't been lying about that – he'd just bent the truth to suit him better. He was always bending the truth when it came to Andy, it made for an easier life. He quickly replied that he would head straight to the boardroom to set up.

There was another email from his friend Harry, with the words **What you think?** written in the subject line. He ruminated on whether to open it or not. Harry had a reputation for coming up with flippant business ideas and this was probably another investment plan of his or some other such proposal. Stephen and Harry had been friends since childhood and they'd had some wild adventures together over the years. Harry had been Stephen's best man seven years before. The only difference between them now was that Stephen had grown up. Well, he had no other choice. Happy-go-Harry was still always unapologetically himself. Stephen quickly clicked on the email. Maybe it was some funny story or a meme and he could do with cheering up before he faced into the afternoon. A photo of a magnificent white house facing the sea popped up on his screen. Captioned: **World's End.** The photo must have been taken in the evening – Stephen could see the red sun setting on the horizon. He hit the reply button and typed in several question marks. A moment later, another email arrived in from Harry, announcing that the house belonged to a client and that it was free for the weekend and how did he feel about a trip away, just a few of the lads? There was no mention of Andy in the invitation.

Stephen clicked on the original email and opened the picture again. The house was two storeys in height, painted white with large black-framed windows. The building featured imposing columns, a rotunda, myriad balconies and a wide driveway leading up to the front. He could see what looked like the edge of a pool at the side. Stephen badly wanted to be there, to escape his life, to escape Andy. To be away from her for a short while and just be with some friends, swim and have a few beers and not worry about life. Yet, how could he ever dream of getting away from her?

Another email popped into his inbox from Harry with just one sentence in the subject line: **Small little fishing village called Castle Cove. About two hours' drive down south. Come on, man!!!**

Maybe he could persuade Andy to go visit her sister at the weekend. Cathy had given birth a few months back and Andy hadn't been down to see her since, and she kept saying that she missed her. Given their past, it could be complicated for her, for sure, but she couldn't avoid her sister forever. He decided he would talk to her tonight, at dinner. He would make the suggestion, and he would gently encourage her. She was fragile. He would have to tread carefully, but he was determined to make this happen.

Once again, he hit the reply button, answering, **Yeah, sure, why not? What can I bring?** He pressed send before he could change his mind. Closing out of his email, he collected his paperwork and the USB containing his presentation. He made his way to the boardroom, his step a little bit lighter. This weekend couldn't come fast enough.

2

Grace watched the young family come through the door of the café. The woman was carrying a baby in a pouch snuggled into her chest, the little feet dangling from either side. Two sulky children gathered around her legs as she scanned the café. One of the children, a little boy who looked to be around six or seven, pulled at the woman's skirt and she bent down to whisper something in his ear as she held his hand firmly in her own. Grace glanced at the clock on the wall, quarter to six – the café closed at six. She knew they would leave a mess, even the best-behaved small children always left a mess. She would have to refuse them. Grace sighed as she approached the family.

"Are you still open?" the woman asked.

She sounded tired. In fact, everything about her *looked* exhausted. Fine lines gathered beneath her eyes, the crow's feet had trampled her youth away. Grace was sure she was much younger than she appeared but, undoubtedly, sleepless nights had made her age rapidly. She felt sorry for the woman, and the children. A memory of her own childhood came to mind. She quickly pushed it aside.

"We close at six," she said.

The woman's face dropped. She nodded and turned to leave.

15

"You're just in time," Grace rushed to add, smiling brightly. Her boss was going to kill her.

She directed them to a table close to the entrance, so that she could proceed with her end of closing-up duties. Perhaps they wouldn't stay for long. She handed the woman a menu, informed her that the specials had finished for the day and promised to return in a moment to take their order.

She went to the kitchen to inform her boss, Sue, that a family of four had just sat down. Sue was rightfully pissed off.

"What is wrong with people? We're open since eight this morning and they come in fifteen minutes before we close? Seriously, like?" Sue, a woman in her late fifties, of slim build with short black hair, was the owner of the café Grace had been working in for the past couple of years. The woman worked hard. She arrived early in the mornings, before any of the staff, and she was the last to leave in the evening. She worked six days a week, most of the time without taking a break. But she was a good boss and she liked to close on time.

Grace shrugged. "Beats me. I kind of feel for the mum though, she looks beat." She picked up a clean tea towel and rummaged in her apron for her docket book and pen before heading back out to the dining area.

"Well, I'm fucking exhausted too!" Sue called out after her.

In the end, they only wanted some sandwiches and drinks. Sue would be pleased with how uncomplicated their order turned out to be.

Grace cleaned and polished all around their table while they ate their meal. They finished in record time, in fairness to them. The woman smiled gratefully as they prepared to leave.

"Thank you so much for feeding us, I'm just so tired." She said as she gestured at the bundle she was carrying. Grace smiled as a little hand stirred before resting against its mother's breast.

"How old?" Grace enquired, waving gingerly at the little boy holding onto his mother's hand.

"Two weeks and three and a half hours. I've hardly slept since he arrived." The woman gave a small smile.

Grace cleaned up their table and swept for any loose crumbs. She untied her apron, went back into the kitchen and placed it in the laundry basket. "I'm off, Sue. See you next Tuesday."

"What about tomorrow?" Sue said.

"I'm off for the weekend, remember?" Grace reminded her. "And it's the May Bank Holiday!"

"Oh yeah, sorry, forgot. Well, don't do anything I wouldn't do."

"Sue, there is nothing you wouldn't do!" Grace said laughingly.

"Make sure to turn the sign to closed when you leave. I don't want any more customers," Sue warned. "Much as I love them."

Grace laughed. "Doing it now. Have a great weekend, Sue." Grace waved as she turned the sign and pulled the door shut behind her.

As she headed up the street towards the bus stop, she reached for her phone in her pocket and turned it on – she always kept it off at work. Sue was very kind and as bosses go she was easy enough to work for, but she hated staff looking at their phones during their shift, so good girl Grace always kept hers switched off. Besides, the café was right in the centre of Limerick city, across from the courthouse, with a constant flow of customers throughout the day – there was never any time for scrolling through phones. She checked for messages but there was still nothing from her best friend, Sarah. Disappointed, she rounded the corner as a bus was just pulling in to her stop. Waving her hand at the driver, she sprinted to the bus, and was completely out of breath as she climbed the steps.

"Sure, I would wait for you, Grace love, there's no need to be running yourself to death like that." The bus driver grinned at her.

"Ah thanks, Frank, I couldn't see if it was you or that other fella driving." She smiled sweetly. "You're my favourite."

"Go way out of it, you charmer!" Frank blushed. "Long day for you?"

"Yeah, but finally it's Friday and I'm off tomorrow. Actually, I'm off for the next three days! I do love my job but …" She rooted in her bag for her wallet.

He smiled. "Well, someone's happy."

"I'm going away for the weekend. Hopefully." She handed him money for her fare.

"Who's the lucky fellow?" He accepted the coins. "A pretty young girl like you, you must be beating them off with a stick."

Grace laughed. "No *fellow*, Frank. I'm heading off with my friend Sarah."

"Well, enjoy yourself."

"You can be sure of it," she replied.

The bus was busy, brimming with passengers eager to get home to enjoy the long weekend ahead. Grace managed to find an empty seat halfway down the aisle and settled in by the window. Limerick city whipped by as the bus made its way up the street, with fleeting images of shops and cafés preparing to close for the day. The evening sky was painted in shades of pinks and orange, promising a good forecast for the weekend. She whisked her headphones out of her pocket and closed her eyes while she listened to some tunes, allowing herself to think about her trip with Sarah. Maybe she would meet some cute guy. It had been ages since she'd been with anyone, not since that night in Amber's nightclub when that tall skinny lad from Kerry stuck his tongue down her throat. She swallowed involuntarily at the memory, blaming the dark interior of the club for her poor judgement – he had seemed all right up until the moment he pushed his tongue into her mouth. She stifled a yawn and tried to get more comfortable in her seat. She had best not fall asleep. With all the stops the bus made, her journey home was usually about thirty minutes, but tonight she was getting off a few stops early so she could visit her mam. She wondered what mood her mother would greet her with tonight. She dispelled the thought – she would cross that bridge when she came to it. Her mind drifted as to why Sarah had not been in touch. Surely plans were in place by now? They had spoken the previous night. Grace knew that Sarah had been in college for most of the day, but she said she would text and let her know what was happening. Maybe Sarah didn't know herself.

Traffic was light and she reached her stop sooner than expected. Waving goodbye to Frank, she made her way up the street towards her mother's nursing home. As she turned the corner, she slowed her pace, the usual dread coming over her as she stood outside the building which appeared more like a large bungalow than a nursing home. The property, privately owned, employed a small pool of staff recruited locally. The surrounding flowerbeds were in full bloom, a green wooden bench tucked underneath the front bay window, with the building's ivy traipsing along its arms.

Rosie Doran had just turned fifty-three years when she'd moved into the care home twelve months before. Rosie had a serious stroke two days before her fiftieth birthday, resulting in her being partially paralysed down her left side. Initially, Grace's sister Erin had taken time out from her job in the local supermarket to become their mother's primary carer. Twelve months before, Erin had made the surprise decision that she was not able to care for their mother anymore. Grace had not asked any questions – she was not the one who had been minding their mother after all. Grace knew how difficult the woman could be.

Grace slowly walked up the path towards the front door, her mind on the weekend ahead. Sarah would be in touch with a plan in place and, after this visit, she would go home and pack for their weekend away. She pushed open the front door and signed the visitor's book on the small wooden table, scanning the list of names to see if Erin had been in. But it seemed Rosie had not had any callers all day. She turned to the previous page – someone had been in the day before, but Grace couldn't make out the signature. Squinting, she leaned in closer and attempted to decipher the name.

"Alright, Gracie love?" a voice called from behind.

Grace recognised the speaker as one of her mother's carers, Peggy. She turned the page back to today's date. "I'm grand, Peggy. Just signing in," she lied. "How is she today?"

Peggy hesitated, but that was all Grace needed to realise that her mother's mood was not good.

"She's a bit quiet. Can't get much out of her," Peggy replied. "She didn't sleep that well last night so I wouldn't stay too long." She smiled kindly. "For your own sake."

Grace nodded. "Thanks, Peggy."

She took off down the short corridor, stopping outside her mother's room. She gently pushed the door open. Her mother lay on her side, facing a set of sliding glass doors that opened out onto a small patio area. Outside, there was a round table with chairs around it. A newspaper lay on top, along with a pair of reading glasses and an overflowing ashtray. Rosie had been sitting out at some stage reading the paper and smoking her cigarettes. Or, pretending to read the paper. Her mother's way of ignoring her daughters.

She approached the bed, stalling slightly before reaching the edge. "Mam?"

Rosie slowly turned towards her. She looked haunted. Her eyes were sunken in their sockets, her mouth drooped, snagging at one corner of her dry lips. Her breath hastened when she saw Grace, the uncertainty breathing life into her shell.

Grace took hold of her mother's hand and gently rubbed her thumb across the papery skin.

"It's alright, Mam, it's just me, Gracie."

Rosie became more agitated. She started snarling at Grace like a trapped animal. "*Geeesh oush!*" she spat. Since the stroke, her voice could not pronounce words properly. A mix of fear and urgency fumbled the command. She started gathering the bedsheets with her fingers in bunches around her, her body rigid with terror. With increasing angst, Rosie repeated her cries desperately. "*Geesh oush, geesh oush!*" she groaned.

Tears pricked the corner of Grace's eyes as she gently tried to soothe her mother to no avail.

Over her shoulder she called, "*Peggy! Peggy!*"

Her mother gripped her wrist – she seemed to have incredible strength.

"*Geesh oush, geesh oush!*" she screamed, spittle landing on Grace's face. Her nails dug into Grace's skin.

"Mam! Stop! You're hurting me!" Grace cried.

Peggy came rushing into the room with another staff member that Grace hadn't met before. Together, they restrained Rosie, Peggy whispering words of comfort while they got her back into a lying position. She eventually calmed and Peggy managed to administer her night medication. Grace sniffed quietly as she looked on. When her mother showed the first signs of sleep, the staff member whispered to Peggy that she would stay for a while and so Peggy took Grace by the arm and led her outside.

Grace sniffed as she wiped at her face with the sleeve of her cotton work shirt. "She just started shouting when she saw me. Same as last time. Same as every bloody time."

"I know, pet," Peggy said softly. "It is not you personally, you know that. You just trigger something in her memory. That's all."

"But she doesn't react like that with my sister," Grace said as Peggy rubbed her arm. "I don't know what to do."

"Head off home for yourself and get a good night's sleep," Peggy urged. "I'm on tomorrow then off for the weekend – give me a ring and I'll let you know how she is."

Grace thanked her and left the nursing home. It was just two bus stops to her apartment, but she decided to walk the rest of the way instead of waiting for one. She needed to clear her head. She felt hurt and alone. Most of her visits with her mother ended badly but still she forced herself to go, repeatedly, her guilty conscience pushing through.

She was still shaking a few moments later when her phone rang. Sarah's name flashed across the screen. Finally, she thought. Wiping her face with the back of her hand, she answered. "Hey, Sarah – I was wondering when …"

"Pack your bags, Gracie! Time to apply that fake tan!"

3

Sarah pressed down on the cover of her overnight carrier. She had been packing for the past hour and she had to sit on the case to fasten the zip. She had crammed too much into the small bag. Black skinny or baggy boyfriend jeans? She packed both. Pink bikini or blue? She had decided on both. Red heels or green? Both, obviously. It was not a crime to have choice after all, and now her bag was bursting with it. She justified her decisions with ease. A girl can never have too many outfits on a trip away, she thought. Prepare for all eventualities. She glanced around her small bedroom, a frown creasing her forehead. Even though she was sure she had packed everything she needed, she still felt that she was missing something. She should have made a list. Sarah liked making lists. That way, you don't forget. She'd had an overwhelming morning, as two assignments had been due for submission for college. She'd had to get them in, having already asked her supervisor for an extension. She'd been up at the crack of dawn, literally. Then there was the matter of her four-year-old son to keep entertained – Zack, a ferocious bundle of energy. And he had been quite a handful, demanding her attention up until his dad, Alex, had pulled up outside her ground-floor flat. She barely had time to pack her son's bag, never mind her own. But now she was almost ready.

She was looking forward to this weekend, and nothing was going to stand in her way. Perching on a stool in front of her dresser, she pulled her black silky hair back, fastening it with a clip. Then she began to apply a light foundation with a brush.

She had been waiting all week for *him* to call and then when he did she stilled herself to remain calm and poised. She wanted to appear casual, a *chill* girl. When he asked if she was still up for travelling down to the coast for the weekend, she had to stop herself from shrieking down the phone. Keep cool, she told herself. She had chipped at her pink nail polish while he spoke, a distraction to keep her voice normal. "Yeah, I am … if you are. I don't think I have anything on."

"Great," he replied. "I am heading down tonight with one of the lads."

Sarah pulled a hangnail clean off the cuticle. "Lads? What lads?" she had asked, wincing as a trickle of blood spread across her skin.

He laughed at that. "Just one or two of the boys, Sarah. What? I told you to bring a friend?"

"One friend, you said bring one friend." She stopped. *Whatever happened to keeping it cool?*

"Yeah, well, the more the merrier, right?" he said. "What does it matter? We have the most amazing house for the weekend. With a pool and our own island to travel over to. We can hire a boat during the afternoon and have some food and drinks on the beach. It's going to be great."

She thought about it for a moment before replying. She didn't want to appear too eager. She had made that mistake before, many times.

"I told the boys that the bedroom with the sea view is mine. I mean, ours," he corrected. "We have our own private balcony, Sarah – we can watch the sun set tomorrow evening."

Sarah had smiled slowly. Her black hair fell forward over her brown eyes and she pushed it back behind her ear. "What do you think?"

"Sounds good, I guess." She was still determined not to appear too keen.

"So, is your friend coming? What was her name again?" he had asked.

"Grace. Yeah, I think so. I'll call her later."

"Make sure you do. And, ah … I can't wait to see you. I've missed you."

There, he said it. Her heart did a funny flip.

"OK, gotta go. Text me the arrival time of your bus tomorrow, yeah? I'll come pick you up." Before she could reply, he had hung up.

Sarah leaned in closer to the mirror, outlining her lips with a burgundy-coloured pencil. She liked him, *a lot*. He was somewhat immature, maybe a bit wild or something, a little bit edgy. They had only been on a couple of dates, but it wasn't as if she was going to marry him or anything. *Well, not yet*, she thought as she smiled at herself in the mirror. He was fun and carefree and exciting, something she wanted, no, *needed*, and it kind of helped that he was really good-looking. So, what of it, she was childfree for the weekend. She was taking a few days off from her college lectures and assignments and she was going to have a good time. No, she was going to have a great time. She pressed her lips together. OK, she was kidding herself, she did really like him. She would have to play it cool though – she didn't want to drive him away.

A car horn sounded outside her flat. She peeked out the window. The sky was clear blue and the sun was shining brightly, lighting up the whole street. Despite the early hour, it already appeared warm.

She could make out her friend Grace in the back of a red taxi across the street, laughing at some story the driver was telling her. Sarah rolled her eyes, amused, as she watched her friend throw her arms up in the air as he continued his chat. What could be so funny, she wondered? Taxi drivers weren't that funny, were they? Grace liked people and people liked Grace. She had one of those engaging personalities, bordering on irritating at times, she was so *nice*. Stop it – she told herself, you are being a bitch. Grace was her closest friend – they had met at a house party while in college a few years back. Sarah was fond of wine, especially rosé, and unfortunately she didn't know her limits back then. Feeling sick, she had escaped the party through the back door, hoping to be alone, but somebody was already there throwing up their insides. Grace Doran. They had sat on the grass afterwards and chatted and found that they had something in common: they despised their chosen courses, Computer Science and Biochemical Engineering respectively. Subsequently, they both dropped out, for different reasons. Eventually, Sarah gave the old college a try once more and enrolled herself into a course that appealed to her – Law Plus – and she had been excelling. Grace was still uncertain about her own path, but she was much happier working in the café and gaining confidence.

Grace had been more like a sister to Sarah these past few years. She had been there for her through every shitty little thing that had happened since she fell pregnant. Her break-up with Alex long before the child was even born, the birth, and the lonely months that followed when she was living on her own as a single parent with little or no money. The flat had been small and badly in need of a deep clean and a bit of modernising when she had moved in with Zack. She had barely turned the key in the lock when Grace had arrived with tins of paint and brushes. She had brought throws and brightly coloured cushions and they turned the dull empty space into something resembling a home. Yes, Grace was a very good friend.

At that moment, Grace glanced out the car window. Sarah waved and Grace beckoned her to come on. They were catching the eight o'clock bus. If they missed it, there wasn't another one for two hours.

She threw her handbag over her shoulder and grabbed the handle of her overnight case. She had her keys in her hand when she spotted the sun cream. That was what she had forgotten. According to the weather forecast, the weekend was due to be a scorcher and Harry had said there was just one supermarket in the village. Sarah figured sunscreen in these small touristy towns would be expensive and so she had picked up a cheaper brand. Money was tight. *Money was always bloody tight.* She caught a glimpse of the pile of outstanding bills on her dresser – she had no clue when she would get around to paying them. She stuffed them into her drawer and closed it shut. Out of sight, out of mind. She wasn't going to think about money this weekend.

She checked the sunscreen bottle was sealed and tipped it into her hand luggage. She left the apartment, locking the door behind her.

She crossed the road and said hello to a grinning Grace.

The driver got out and put her suitcase in the boot. "Jaysus, love, what have you got in the bag?"

Sarah laughed as she eased into the back seat beside her friend. She took two small bottles of sparkling wine and two straws out of her handbag and handed one set to Grace.

Grace shook her head. "Sarah? It's, like, half past seven in the morning!"

"We're on our holidays, Grace!" She unscrewed the cap of her bottle, clinked Grace's, and took a long drink. "Oh my God, this is amazing!"

The two friends laughed as the driver smiled his amusement into the rear-view mirror. He put the car in gear and took off.

4

Lukasz pulled on the thick rope and hauled the nets onto his boat. Beads of sweat formed across his brow as he continued to tug until the last of the fish cleared the water. He checked the nets, smiling when he saw what he had caught – the local hotels and restaurants were going to be happy with him that night. He cinched the net with the drawstring and dragged it on board, the fish secured safely. Then he stored the fish in boxes of ice. He didn't have much time to get his catch out to clients so he hastened his pace as he gathered the nets. Once he had finished, he tossed the trawl onto the back of the boat to untangle later, before turning towards the mainland.

Lukasz approached the harbour just as the sun was coming up behind him, the blue sky emerging above the fog, creating a light mist hovering over the dark water. He glanced over his shoulder and he could just about make out the shape of the small island on the horizon. There was still a slight chill in the air for the time of morning, but there was one thing he was sure of – once the fog lifted completely, it was going to be a glorious day. It was a long weekend and the start of the season and Lukasz expected the small coastal town to be brimming with tourists come lunchtime.

He slowed his pace as he steered his small vessel towards the waterfront, observing the hire boats lined up along the harbour for tourists to take on day trips to the island. He could see the boat-hire guy, Gary Duke, and his nephew preparing for the weekend ahead. When the weather was good, the hire boats booked out fast. He noticed there was a nice bit of activity already around the harbour, even for the early hour. On the other side of the harbour there was a path leading down to a sandy beach, safe for swimming.

He steered close to the pier and found a free space beside his friend Pete's boat. There was no sign of Pete – he was probably still in the bed sleeping off his hangover. They had necked back a few beers and gambled away playing poker, in a quiet, dimly lit corner of the local pub, McKeogh's, with some of the villagers the night before. Lukasz knew there was an opportunity for a bountiful catch the next morning and so he had retired early, long before closing time. And, besides, he couldn't put away pints like the other lads, about three Guinness in and his stomach was full. But Pete and his friends could keep supping away for hours. He had left them behind him, looking very settled with their pints, their animated features glowing as they solved the problems of the world.

He anchored the small boat and jumped onto the pier, looping the rope around one of the bollards. He stopped to breathe in the fresh spring air. He loved this place, he felt at home here. He was fond of the people too and was content with his life. Every day he reminded himself how lucky he was to live in a serene place like this. Not only because of the people and the lifestyle, but also the scenic coastline, so very different from where he grew up. And soon he would have enough money saved to buy his own trawler. A sadness crept over him as he thought of his home, his mother, his family and the life he had to leave behind. He turned towards the ocean and noticed the fog had lifted revealing the tiny rocky structure of Mutton Island. Nobody lived there but many visited. The sandy beach was gently sloping and it was a beautiful spot to spend an afternoon. But, if you stayed too long, there was a dangerous undercurrent to pass through on return, so the hire parties were always advised to sail according to the tide, especially the inexperienced sailors. Gary Duke had a set of guidelines for the tourists – all boats must be home before sunset. Lukasz didn't know whether punters stuck to this rule or not – he was generally gone from the harbour by lunchtime.

His mouth was dry, he could murder a cup of coffee and a cigarette, but first he had to offload his catch. He spotted Nora Hanley's head of short red hair bent over her desk inside the small port office. Nora managed all the craft navigation, both in and out of the harbour. She looked up as Lukasz approached, waving him inside.

"Morning, Lukasz, you're up with the lark," she observed.

"Lark?" Lukasz had left his native Poland four years ago and moved to Ireland and his English had improved greatly since then, yet he still didn't understand some of the colloquialisms.

Nora rolled her eyes in amusement. "The lark – the bird, Lukasz. Up with the lark means you're up early." She chuckled.

Lukasz nodded smiling. "Up with the lark, up early. Yes! There is lot of fish out there this morning. You have to be up early to catch them. Up with the lark!" He laughed at the sound of the word rolling off his tongue.

"And you caught them all, I would say? Nothing left for anyone else?" Nora winked.

Lukasz's face reddened. "No, no, there is a lot of fish for everyone. The ocean – it is big." He gestured with his hands.

31

Nora laughed a deep throaty laugh, followed by a wheezy cough. "I'm only codding you, Lukasz. Sure, the ocean is huge."

Codding? Lukasz had no idea what she meant by *codding*.

She glanced at the phone on the wall. "I suppose you want to use the telephone to ring Tommy Ryan?"

Lukasz nodded yes. Tommy Ryan would be out to the port in fifteen minutes and he would take the fish from Lukasz and give him a fair price. Tommy would then distribute the produce to the restaurants and hotels in Castle Cove and the neighbouring towns.

Nora held the phone out to Lukasz and he made the call, and sure enough, Tommy answered on the first ring. The distributor confirmed he would be out straight away. Lukasz would be his only source today. He thanked Nora and hurried back to his boat. He quickly loaded the boxes onto the quay. He had just stacked the last one when he heard a van pull up. Tommy Ryan, a skinny man, late fifties, with grey sideburns, climbed out of the driver's seat. "Well, fair play to you, Lukasz! Sure, if it wasn't for you, there wouldn't be a fish in the restaurants for the weekend. I heard the rest of the yobbos were sinking pints until all hours?"

Lukasz smiled at Tommy. "Yes, it was good morning for fishing."

Tommy didn't waste time. He opened the back of his van exposing a walk-in freezer compartment. Methodically, he loaded the boxes one by one. They negotiated a price and Tommy promised to return with the containers later that afternoon. Lukasz was grateful – he planned to go out again first thing the following morning. Tommy pulled away and Lukasz set about untangling the nets on his boat. Depending on the currents, the job could be tedious – the more the net was bashed around in the sea, the more tangled it became. Luckily, that morning the sea had been calm and he wasn't long meshing out the knots.

He felt his stomach rumble and realised he had not eaten since the previous evening. Once he had his work done, he stored away the nets and locked up the boat. Waving goodbye to Nora, he headed up the harbour towards his van. When he switched on the engine, some guy on the local radio station was reporting about the weather for the weekend and warning about wearing sun protection. Lukasz agreed with him – two things that he had learned about Irish people: they were friendly and always up for a laugh, but they were foolish when it came to protecting their skin.

As he drove out of the harbour, he noticed the windows in the World's End summerhouse had been pushed wide open, meaning the house would be occupied for the weekend. There was a blue van with a cleaning-company logo printed on the side parked in the driveway outside the front door. A man dressed in a black T-shirt and pants was carrying a bundle of what looked like white bed linen or towels into the building. Lukasz slowed his pace as he observed the house. The property hadn't been occupied in a while and he wondered who was letting the luxury house. Probably one of the rental agents in the next town. He had heard that some executive from Limerick city now owned the property. Sometimes he came down for weekends and held parties, and there were rumours about the kind of clientele who attended the gatherings. Lukasz had heard his friend Pete and some of the locals talking about them in the pub – drug-fuelled all-night bashes with girls hired in for extra entertainment. The locals were not happy about it, though the bars and restaurants were eager to take their money.

The man emerged from the house, followed by two middle-aged women, also dressed in black. He locked the front door of the house and all three climbed into the van and drove off down the road.

Lukasz smiled. He was pleased with his morning's work and, with holiday homes like the World's End occupied, no doubt the restaurants would be busy. He felt the crisp notes in his pocket. Satisfied, he put the van in gear. Yes, it was going to be a wonderful day.

5

Stephen felt the hot water trickle down his back and he finally began to relax, just a little. The strong shower-jet prodded his skin as his body adjusted to the heat and he allowed himself to enjoy the sensation. Closing his eyes, he tilted his head back as the warm water poured over his face. He was packed and ready to go, once out of the shower all he had to do was get dressed, climb into his car and drive for a few hours down to the south coast.

He needed this – and so did Andy. When he had first brought up the idea of her visiting her sister for the weekend, she had just stared at him, confused, her expression one of disbelief. Her reaction was quickly followed by paranoia and suspicion. *Why did he want her away? Why this weekend? What would he do while she was gone? Why didn't he want to go with her?* He didn't dare mention the fact that he was planning to head away himself. He told her he would hang around their apartment for the weekend and tackle some work that he kept putting off. She was suspicious of that too. She was distrustful of everything he said and did. He had to show her the proposed plan for his upcoming presentation, what his team leader had outlined for his role in the staging. He pointed out that there was a stack of preparation to do and her sister lived in a rural area with poor Wi-Fi. What he omitted to tell her was that the presentation had been postponed until the following week, a modification of the truth. With Andy's father the CEO of the company where Stephen was employed, it wasn't easy to lie about his day-to-day work schedule, but the man was at a conference in London for the weekend. Stephen knew he was covered.

In the end, she agreed with him, that it would do both of them good to have a short break from each other. So, he had dropped her at Limerick's train station earlier that morning and, once she was on the train, he had practically sprinted back to his car, driven home and packed in record time.

He dried himself with the towel, dressing quickly in a pair of faded blue jeans and a grey T-shirt. The cat pushed the bedroom door open and slipped past his leg. *Shit*. Milo, he had completely forgotten about bloody Milo. He had hoped Andy would take him, but her sister didn't want a cat coming into the house with a new-born baby. He pondered what to do. He could leave him on his own, couldn't he? Though that was probably a bad idea. He had taken a break in Dublin with Andy the previous year, leaving out plenty of food for Milo, only the stupid cat had eaten the whole lot in one go and thrown up all over their bed. If it happened again, how could he explain it to Andy? There was always Mike across the hall – he could ask him to look in on Milo and put some food out for him later in the day, couldn't he? And Andy never talked to Mike, she just did not *get him*, she said, she thought he was too much a macho man, so she would never know.

Crossing the hall, he tapped on Mike's door. He could hear a TV playing on the other side, and then the sound lowered. He heard footsteps before the door opened. Mike looked like he had just rolled out of bed, his hair was dishevelled, his feet were bare and he wore a faded purple dressing gown tied messily around his waist. There was a yellow stain on the white T-shirt he had on inside the robe. Mike just nodded at him to come in.

Stephen stepped inside, noticing the almost empty bottle of whiskey sitting on the counter. "Late night?" he asked.

"Two seasons of that new documentary about saving our planet." Mike stopped mid-pace, put his hand on his extended stomach, releasing a loud burp. "Excuse me."

Stephen grimaced. "Charming."

"Do you want some coffee?"

Sometimes Stephen and Mike hung out. Mike, like Stephen was a big football fan when he wasn't watching documentaries, and they would while away a few hours chatting about players and clubs and old matches, enjoying a coffee or a cold beer. But not today. Stephen needed to get going.

"No, thanks." He hesitated. "Actually, I was wondering would you look in on Milo and give him some food? There's a couple of unopened cans beside his bowl in the kitchen."

Mike poured steaming coffee from a cafetière into a cup. "Sure, like, later this evening?"

Stephen nodded. "Yeah, and again in the morning? Just a small amount, like, half a tin each time. He tends to overeat. Would that be OK?"

Mike stopped pouring. "You two going away for the weekend?"

Stephen paused. He didn't want to lie to Mike, but he didn't want to tell him the truth either. "Yeah, just for the night. I'd really appreciate it."

Mike sipped his coffee, observing him over the rim. "No problem,

I'm not going anywhere. I have another couple of seasons of that documentary to watch."

Stephen relaxed. "Must be interesting?"

Mike smiled. "Yeah, well, it's something to watch, right? The planet needs a lot of saving." He drank some more of his coffee as he studied Stephen. "Things are better then?"

Stephen knew what Mike meant by *things*. They'd had a couple of beers together a few months back and Stephen had confided in Mike that all was not well across the corridor. He hadn't told Mike everything that had happened before they moved into their apartment – he'd just mentioned that Andy had become difficult to be around. Mike hadn't responded. He'd not given an opinion either way. He had just listened and he never brought it up again. Stephen had wondered if Mike even remembered their conversation – he'd a lot to drink. But clearly, he did. Again, he hated to lie to him but …

"Yeah, better." Stephen pulled at the loose skin around his fingernail. "It will be good to get away. On our own, you know?"

Mike took a moment to reply. He looked like he was about to say something and Stephen braced himself for what might be coming. Mike was all right, but sometimes he could be a bit strange.

Thankfully, he just smiled and nodded. "Milo and I will be good – I'll look in on him and make sure he gets his dinner. Go – enjoy yourselves." He gestured. "You deserve it."

"Thanks, mate." Stephen dropped a spare key on Mike's kitchen counter. "I'll text you later. Thanks again, mate, I owe you one."

He went to grab his bag from the apartment. Milo lay on the bed staring up at him – it was as if he knew that Stephen was lying. *Fuck you, Milo.* He had never liked the bloody cat. He locked the apartment behind him and instead of taking the lift, he took the stairs. He had left his car parked on the street when he had arrived back from the train station, instead of going underground. Opening the boot, he threw his bag in before easing himself into the driver's seat. He looked at the wedding ring on his finger for a moment, and he thought about Andy, the lie he had told her. The *lies* he had told her.

Stop. Get a grip, man, you are staying with an old friend, he reasoned. You're doing nothing wrong. Switching on the engine, he put the car in gear and took off.

6

"You get it, Grace," Erin whispered. *"You're smaller than me. She won't see you."* Erin lifted Grace over the wall. *"Go on!"*

Terrified, Grace crawled across the cemented patio to retrieve a tin of beans that had toppled over the wall during their game. The door opened and a woman with long black hair with hints of grey stood, her eyes narrowed, her smile crooked. She reached for Grace.

"No!" Grace screamed, *"No! Get away!"*

She scrambled back over the wall. Her mother was waiting for her, hand raised …

She woke, confused, wondering where she was. Her head ached.

Sarah was slumped in her seat, asleep too. When they had finished the small bottles of sparkling wine in the taxi, there was yet another couple in Sarah's bag and they drank those too and, an hour into their bus journey, Grace leaned against the window frame and fell into a deep sleep.

"What the hell was that?" Sarah yawned.

"What was what?" Grace's mouth was dry – she pulled a bottle of water from her bag and took a long drink. She really needed to use the bathroom.

"You were shouting something, like *'no, no, get away!'*?"

Grace realised that some of the other passengers were staring at her curiously. She gave a small smile, embarrassed. "I don't know – probably a dream or something." She knew that Sarah was watching her. Sometimes Grace would get nervous about stuff and she knew it irritated Sarah. But Sarah didn't push her this time and Grace was grateful. She hadn't told her much about her childhood. She would rather forget.

She had dreamt that she was in her family home, the one she had grown up in – an end-of-terrace townhouse with a small enclosed garden to the rear. Their mam had been very strict when the girls were growing up, never allowing them out the front to play with the other kids on the road. There were a lot of rules. Their school had been a short five-minute walk from their home and so they used to leave the house every morning five minutes before their classes started and they had to be home five minutes after the school closed in the evening. They could never be late. *Rules.* Their mam would sit in the kitchen, smoking her cigarettes, reading the paper, though she never turned the page. Every now and then, she would glance down the hall towards the front door, a look of dread in her eyes – she always had the same expression of fear in her eyes. After a moment, she would light another cigarette and go back to staring at the paper, only leaving her spot to prepare meals, do the laundry or buy groceries. She rarely engaged with her two daughters, unless she had reason to, like for school or a meal.

Oftentimes Grace and Erin had to make their own fun in the evenings and weekends, and in the summer they would play out in the garden for hours and hours, avoiding their mother's moods, making up games of shop or school. Erin as the eldest always got to play the role of the shopkeeper or the teacher, while Grace just did what she was told.

In her dream, Grace and Erin were playing a game of shop in the little back garden.

* * *

Their mother was sitting in the kitchen reading her newspaper and smoking her cigarettes, the only sound coming from a clock ticking on the wall. A row of tinned food lined the top of the low wall that divided their garden from the house next door. The neighbour, an elderly woman, lived alone, and their mother said she suffered from her 'nerves', rarely leaving the property. They hardly saw her from one end of the year to another, but they had been warned that if the woman ever did try to speak to them, they were not to engage with her. And they must *never* enter her back garden. Under *any* circumstances. The girls didn't mind – it was just another place they were forbidden to go. *Rules.*

Erin had advised Grace that she should buy the beans. "How are you today, Grace?"

Compliant as ever, Grace replied, "I'm fine, thank you, Erin. Could I buy some beans, please?"

"Well, it's your lucky day, Grace!" she said, beaming. "My delivery has not come in yet, so I am a bit low but I think I have one tin left. I will check for you now." She reached behind her, swinging her hand, and knocked the can of beans clean off the wall. The tin toppled onto the neighbour's patio. The girls watched in horror as it rolled until it stopped just outside the back door.

Erin pulled at Grace's arm, whispering, "You go and get it."

Grace looked up at her sister in alarm. *"Me! Why me?"*

"Because you're smaller!" Erin hissed. "If you crouch down really

42

low and crawl across the patio she won't see you from her kitchen window. I am taller than you are, so I'll keep cover from this side. I'll keep talking so Mam won't notice. Go on!"

Grace was so scared. "But what if Mam comes out and sees me? She will get really mad, Erin." Her bottom lip trembled.

"She will get madder if we don't bring everything back in!" Erin whispered. "She warned us, remember? I will block you, Gracie, I promise. Now go on quickly!" Erin gave her a gentle shove.

Reluctantly Grace climbed over the wall, hunkering down low, scraping her knees as she crept along the hard ground until she reached the back door. She could hear Erin continue her narrative behind her, chatting happily about her stock and her deliveries.

Just as Grace reached the tin of beans, the back door opened. Grace looked up to see the next-door lady staring down at her. Grace had never seen the woman up close. Her dark hair was long and greying at the edges and the skin on her face was bright pink and heavily lined. She smiled as she extended her hand, bony fingers reaching out to touch Grace. Grace screamed and fell backwards.

Erin stopped talking. Grace scrambled across the yard and mounted the wall as quick as she could. When she landed on the other side, her mother was there to meet her, the expression on her face telling her she was in big trouble. There was no sign of Erin. Grace thought about climbing back over the wall – the neighbour was less threatening than her mother, somehow. She heard the neighbour's door close softly behind her.

"*You are a stupid little bitch, Grace Doran!*" her mother hissed. "*What did I tell you? Get into the house!*"

Grace ran into the kitchen, her mother marching in after her, slamming the back door.

Grace stood on the cold tiles shivering as her mother came towards her. She raised her hand.

* * *

"You sure you're OK?" Sarah was watching her, her expression amused.

Grace cleared her throat. "Yeah. Too much wine."

"Not enough, you mean!" Sarah grinned.

"How long more?" Grace asked.

Sarah glanced at her phone. "About ten minutes I would say. I am so hungry."

Grace laughed. "You packed wine and no food?"

Sarah grinned. "Of course! I'm sorry now though, I really need to eat something."

"I really need to use the bathroom."

"That too!" Sarah grimaced.

Grace looked at her friend and smiled. "Thanks, Sarah."

"For what?" Sarah raised an eyebrow.

"For suggesting I come away with you for the weekend. You didn't have to."

"I wanted to."

"But this new guy? I know you like him. You probably want to be left alone and have some one on one time, and not have your boring friend tagging along."

"Ah, we are not at the 'holding hands and gazing into each other's eyes' stage. Yet!" She laughed. "If ever. It's just a bit of fun, Gracie, honestly."

"Still. Thanks. You're a great friend."

Sarah smiled and squeezed Grace's hand. "Well, so are you, Grace. The best a girl could have."

The bus driver announced that they were pulling into the small village of Castle Cove. Grace stretched as she took in the picturesque little town, if you could call it a town. They passed a scattering of pretty white cottages facing the sea as they drove in, along with a small supermarket with two fuel pumps on the footpath out front, a couple of restaurants, one pub and a boutique hotel. That seemed to be it. There was a man outside the pub shifting barrels, its front doors wide open. Good, she thought as the bus came to a stop, she would be able to use the facilities.

She noticed a tall man with dark hair and sunglasses leaning against a shiny and expensive- looking black car close to the bus stop, his white shirt open at the neck, sleeves rolled up revealing muscular arms folded across his broad chest. When he saw Sarah step down from the bus, he sauntered towards her, a grin spreading across his face. Sarah ran into his arms and he swung her around before kissing her full on the mouth.

Grace looked on, amused. *Just a bit of fun, she says. Yeah, right.*

She decided she would have to make herself scarce for a few hours. She looked out at the beautiful blue sea framing the small town of Castle Cove. She sniffed, taking in the sea air. She knew exactly what she was going to do.

7

Stephen had stopped to top up on fuel and had bought a coffee. The steaming hot liquid burned his lip. He contemplated turning back to pick up some water but he decided to push on – he had been on the road for over two hours and he felt sure it wouldn't be long before he reached Castle Cove. Despite the hot coffee on a very warm day, he felt good, he felt free, and the most relaxed he had been in a long time, away from his wife and her controlling father. The sky above was clear blue and the passing countryside was a welcome sight after the busy city.

Harry had called to say that the house was amazing, that the pictures didn't do it justice. He'd mentioned he had packed some food to barbeque later but had forgotten burger buns – he asked Stephen to pick some up on the way. He confirmed that the beers were on ice and told him to get his ass down as soon as possible. Stephen didn't need to be told twice.

Stephen hadn't realised how much everything had been getting him down lately. Work was always busy, there was always a deadline in the marketing department and there were plenty of people to step into your shoes if you slacked off. Having said that, he liked the challenge of a new pitch and, if he was being honest with himself, his work wasn't really the problem. The problem was Andy. His mood dipped as he thought about his wife and the guilt he felt about lying to her came to the forefront of his mind. He did not know why he felt so guilty – he wasn't doing anything wrong, was he? Just spending a night away on the coast with his best friend. He just wanted to go for a swim, have a few drinks and some nice food and hang out with his friend – there was nothing wrong with that, was there?

The only problem was that he had lied to Andy about what he was doing, but he couldn't have told her the truth, could he? If he had, she wouldn't have travelled to her sisters and he wouldn't be out here on this motorway. A white lie for her own good, he reasoned.

He indicated left at the exit and followed the slip road until he saw the sign for Castle Cove. The road narrowed considerably, the hedges intertwined with flowers the colour of burnt orange on either side. He drove for two more kilometres and then he could see the sign on the left-hand side of the road: *Welcome to Castle Cove.* He slowed his pace as he took in the small village, realising he needn't have worried about stopping for fuel as he spotted the two pumps on the path outside the one and only grocery store on the main street. Pulling in, he switched off the engine. He hesitated before leaving the car. He had to ring Andy, and he thought it better to do it now and get it out of the way before arriving at the summerhouse. He dialled her number and, for once, she answered immediately.

"Hi."

"Hi." He paused for a moment, trying to gauge her mood, waiting for her to say something else. She didn't. *Christ, he hated these awkward phone calls.* Neither of them knowing what to say to each other. "How was the train journey?" he finally asked.

He heard her sigh.

"Long and boring. I slept and read. I hate trains, you know that. I don't know why you couldn't have just driven me to Cathy's."

"I have a lot of work to do. I told you."

"Yeah, you told me." Her tone suggested she didn't believe him.

He decided to change the subject. "How is your sister? And the baby?"

"They're both great." Her tone had softened, a little. "The baby, Izzy, I can't believe how much she has grown – I mean it's incredible. And I think she smiled at me earlier. In fact, I'm sure of it. I'm just in love with her."

"Andy?" he warned.

"No, Stephen, it's OK. I'm OK, honest," she reassured him. "It's good to be here with them both and I'm fine about it."

"That's good." Stephen noticed a young woman emerge from the grocery store. She had an ice-cream cone in her hand. Her long dark hair had been pulled back into a ponytail that swung from side to side as she strolled down the road, concentrating on the path in front of her. She adjusted the strap on her pink backpack and headed in the direction of the beach. Maybe he could get a swim in before arriving at the summerhouse. He would have to pick up the burger buns first.

He could hear Andy talking to someone in the background.

"Stephen, I have to go. Cathy is going to town for a while and she asked me to keep an eye on Izzy – she has hardly left the house since the birth. She needs to go through some things with me before she leaves. The weather is so nice today – I think I might take Izzy for a walk while she's gone."

"Yeah go, go. It sounds fun." He opened the car door and

stepped outside. It was warmer than earlier and he felt the fabric of his T-shirt sticking to his back.

"She's so beautiful. She's so like …"

Neither of them spoke.

"How is Milo?" she said then.

Stephen hesitated. "Fine. Sure, you know Milo, easily pleased."

"I'll try to call you later?" she offered. "If I can get away."

"Don't! I mean – you'll be busy with the baby. Don't worry about calling me. I'm just going to finish my presentation and I might go across the hall and have a beer with Mike."

"I don't know what you see in that guy. He gives me the creeps."

"Ah, he's harmless."

"OK, I really have to go. I'll send you a photo of Izzy."

"Do. I'd like that."

"Right, well, I gotta go."

"OK." He hesitated. "Love you."

"Love you too." She hung up.

He entered the grocery store and selected a few packs of burger buns. Harry hadn't said how many he needed – it would be better to have too many rather than not enough. As he queued at the counter, he spotted the freshly whipped ice-cream cone machine. Feck it. He was going to get one and then head to the beach for a swim. He paid for his purchases, left the shop and threw the bread into the back of his car. He grabbed his swim shorts and a towel and headed in the direction of the beach.

8

Grace ploughed into the cold Atlantic swell. Rising to the surface, she quickly inhaled before plunging and rising again, each time taking a breath. After a few minutes, her lungs began to burn and she slowly eased her pace. The initial shock of the cold water was gone as she gently smoothed the waves around her to keep her head above water. She took in her surroundings while allowing her breathing to return to normal. The white sandy beach was long and wide. She'd had to trek down a worn path to reach the strand, much further than she envisioned from the top, and she wasn't looking forward to climbing back up. There were only a handful of people on the beach – a family of four playing Frisbee with their dog, a woman walking alone and a man with a towel wrapped around his waist, juggling with a swimsuit no doubt. Another brave soul. Over to the right she could see a pier lined with boats.

She turned back towards the sea. The Atlantic Ocean stretched far and wide, the only obstacle a small piece of land in the distance. She remembered Sarah had mentioned something about an island close by and that Harry wanted to hire a boat to travel over for a day trip. She wondered whether anyone was living there. It didn't look like much of anything.

Feeling cold, she decided to swim back to shore. On reaching the shallow area, she waded out of the water. She arrived at her bag and searched for her phone. It was just after half past four. She decided she had better get going. She'd promised Sarah that she'd be out to the house by six at the latest and she had to hike up the cliff first.

When they had arrived at the bus stop earlier and she saw the way Sarah greeted her so-called *friend* or boyfriend or whatever he was, she'd decided she would go for a swim and let the couple spend the afternoon on their own. Sarah had begun to protest, but Harry had nodded his approval. Grace took the hint. She stuffed a towel and swimsuit into her pink backpack and, after using the toilet facilities in the pub, she had dropped into the shop and bought herself an ice-cream cone.

Now she pulled her towel out of her bag and began to dry her long hair. The beach was quiet, the only sound coming from the ocean as the waves lapped over each other. Suddenly she felt uneasy. She had the prickling feeling that she was being watched. When she looked around the beach, she noticed that it was empty now, the family with the dog and the Frisbee and the woman walking unaccompanied were gone. But the man she had seen changing earlier was standing at the edge of the water, his back to the sea, looking straight at her. Grace was aware that she was completely alone, and she didn't know why but the way he was staring at her made her feel uncomfortable. She wrapped the damp towel around her waist, grabbed her bag, swung it over her shoulder and made her way up the beach towards the road – she would dress once she got to the top.

She was at the edge of the cliff when she heard pounding in the wet sand. *Shit.* Why had she stayed so long in the water? It had seemed perfectly safe when there were other people around, but now she was on her own. There was no way she could run up the cliff path – her fitness levels were not up to it. She pulled the towel tighter around her and quickened her pace.

"*Hey!*"

The man's voice behind her was much closer than she had first thought – he must have sprinted up the beach.

"*Wait up! I just want to ask you something!*" He sounded out of breath. "Is this yours?"

Grace turned and the man was now right in front of her, dripping wet and breathing hard. He held a silver charm bracelet in his hand. The bracelet had five charms: an elephant, a toad, a ha'penny, the letter G and a love heart. She knew each charm on the bracelet, without having to take a closer look, because the bracelet was hers. Her mother had given it to her when she turned eighteen. She had said it belonged to her own mother, Grace's grandmother, who was also called Grace. She had given a gold necklace with a diamond-encased rose drop to Grace's sister Erin when she had turned eighteen. Grace knew the necklace had a much higher market value than the charm bracelet, but she didn't care. It was a rare expression of warmth from a woman who was made of stone.

Grace felt like a fool. "I – yes. That is my bracelet. Where did you find it?"

"There at the edge of the water." He gestured towards the sea. "It was just lying there. At first I thought it was a bunch of shells or something." He handed Grace the bracelet.

"Thank you." Suddenly she felt tears prick her eyes. Embarrassed, she swallowed hard, willing them to stop. God, this was just mortifying. First, she ran away from the poor guy and now she was crying. She told herself to get a grip.

"Are you OK?" The man looked concerned.

"Yes, I am fine. I … it is just sentimental. I would hate to lose it." She draped the bracelet around her wrist, fumbling with the clasp. Her fingers were cold and unable to grasp the small hook.

"Here, let me," the man offered.

He stepped closer and fastened the bracelet around her wrist. He smelled of the sea. His skin was warm as he touched her and she felt a flutter in the pit of her stomach.

She stepped back. "Thank you," she said, her words catching. She cleared her throat. "I'm very grateful."

"Happy to help. Though you didn't make it easy for me." He gave a small smile.

Grace noticed how tall he was. His dark-brown hair was cut short and his eyes were a deep shade of blue.

"Well, nice to meet you." He turned to leave.

"Wait!"

He turned, a question on his face.

"Thank you," she said. "I'm sorry for running away from you. I thought … well, there is nobody here and I'm not from the area …"

He laughed now. "You thought I was going to murder you or something?"

Grace smiled, uncomfortable. "Yeah, something like that. I have an active imagination."

He didn't respond for a moment. "Stephen. And you're welcome."

He extended his hand and she took it. His skin was cooler this time.

"I'm Grace."

They just stood there, smiling at each other.

She dropped his hand and secured her bag over her shoulder. "Right, well, I'd better get up the cliff." She backed away.

"I'd better go back to my swim." With that, he turned and ran down the beach.

Grace watched as his long muscular legs sprinted along the sand. She shook her head at her own stupidity. What the hell was wrong with her? She glanced at the charm bracelet on her wrist and wondered how it had ended up in the sea. The clasp was strong, or at least she thought it was. She should have taken it off when she went into the water. She was so lucky that guy had found it. She made a mental note to get it checked by a jeweller when she returned to Limerick.

Suddenly, she felt cold. She shivered as she retrieved her clothes from her backpack and dressed quickly. Taking one last glance towards the beach, she could just about make out the guy's shape as he swam in the sea, his strong arms slicing through the surf. She wondered if he was local. He hadn't mentioned where he was from.

Her phone pinged in her backpack. She pulled it out, and saw that there was a new message from Sarah. **Where the hell are you? You said a quick swim. You must be halfway across the Atlantic by now!** Grace laughed and quickly replied that she was on her way. She stuffed the wet towel and swimsuit into her backpack and made her way up the cliff. Harry had mentioned he was preparing a barbeque. Great, she thought. The sea air had given her an appetite.

9

Stephen changed into his clothes. His fingers fumbled with the stiff fabric in his jeans. Despite the warm weather, he felt a chill when he left the water after he found the girl's bracelet and no matter how hard he swam, he could not warm up. His fingers were rigid as he fastened the buttons. But, it was worth it. The icy Atlantic sea was just what he needed. Adrenaline surged through his body and he felt cleansed, and more alive than he had in a very long time. He eased into his trainers, shook the wet out of his hair, and started up the cliff path.

His thoughts turned to the girl with the pink rucksack. She was the same girl he had seen leaving the grocery shop with the ice-cream cone earlier. She had that carefree energy about her as she strolled down the road towards the beach, her long dark hair tied loosely in a ponytail as it swung from side to side, her cut-off denim shorts revealing lightly tanned legs. She looked like she didn't have a care in the world and all Stephen had wanted to do was grab his gear, lock up his car and join her.

She was swimming while he was changing and by the time he was ready to enter the water, he was disappointed to see her leaving. It must be cold, he had thought. And it was. Then he had found the bracelet and as there had been nobody else around, he thought it must belong to the girl. When he had caught up with her, he was taken aback by how pretty she was. Her damp hair had been pulled to the side of her heart-shaped face, and her dark eyes gazed at him under long lashes. She had been cautious when he first approached, and then she had seen the bracelet in his hand and her expression had softened. She had the loveliest smile. Stephen wondered where she was from. She had said she wasn't local. Maybe she was a tourist, just like him. Down for the long weekend.

He checked his watch and decided he had better get a move on if he wanted to shower before dinner. Harry had probably started the barbeque and Stephen had promised he would be out to the house with the bread – Harry would lose his shit if he didn't get there soon. Harry was Stephen's closest friend, but he liked things to go his way and he had a short fuse if they didn't. Having said that, he had invited a girl down for the weekend, his latest squeeze, so hopefully he was distracted.

Harry always had a new girl in his life, and there had been so many over the years that Stephen had lost count. It had been awkward having him over for dinner because he regularly brought a different girl with him and, more often than not, either he or Andy would get mixed up with their names. Of course, that was before everything had gone to shit. Andy hadn't wanted guests after … she would just retreat to her room and Harry, or whoever had called to visit, would only stay for a short while. Eventually, their friends stopped calling. Stephen would go out to meet people instead – it was easier. He decided he'd better give Harry a quick call and let him know that he was on his way with the bread. He pulled his phone out of his pocket and dialled Harry's number. He answered on the first ring, and Stephen could hear loud music in the background. The party had already started.

"*Stephen. Wait. Hold on a minute*," Harry shouted over the noise. "*I can't hear you, bloody music is too loud. Wait until I go inside!*"

Stephen heard the sound of footsteps moving and a door close, the music becoming a distant beat.

"Mate, where are you? I thought you would have been here hours ago. Sarah and her friend are upstairs getting ready and the beers are well and truly flowing."

Sarah must be Harry's new girlfriend. And she had brought a friend? Harry hadn't mentioned that. "I went for a quick swim."

"Tell me you got the burger buns?"

"I got the burger buns. I'm on my way back up the cliff path to the car. How far is the house from the village?"

"It's the big white house. You can see it from the harbour." He laughed. "Trust me, you'll know it when you see it."

"Great, I'll be out there shortly. Have a cold one ready for me."

"You bet! And, Stephen? Just wait until you see this place. It's unbelievable. I mean, it is *unbelievable*."

"You must have made him happy." Stephen's calf muscles began to ache as he pushed his way up the sandy path.

"Made who happy?" Harry sounded confused.

"The client? You said one of your clients lent you the house for the weekend."

Harry didn't reply.

"Harry? Are you there?"

"Oh, yeah, that's right. Well, he owes me – he might be out to the house over the weekend actually, with a few mates. I played golf with them a few times. You'll like him."

"Great." Stephen reached the top of the cliff and found his car. So, Harry had invited more people over. It didn't bother him – he could only stay the one night – Harry could invite whoever he wanted.

"Right, well, I'd better go," Harry said. "Someone has to make sure the barbeque is still lighting."

"I'm on my way."

Stephen hung up and unlocked his car. He opened the boot and threw his wet gear in the back. He would have to leave early the following afternoon to get home before Andy, so that he could wash his gear and stuff, hide the evidence.

Andy.

Something dawned on Stephen as he drove towards the World's End. He hadn't thought about his wife since he arrived.

10

Sarah flung her phone onto the bed. She was seething. *"Bastard!"* she roared, the loud beat of the music by the pool drowning her out. Zack's dad, Alex, had just texted informing her that he had been called in to work and he would be bringing their son back a day earlier than originally planned. Meaning that Sarah would have to get an early bus in the morning in order to get back on time. The shit. The useless piece of *shit*. He was always letting her down. He was always letting Zack down. She sighed as she sat on the edge of the bed. And, where in the bloody hell was Grace? She had been gone for hours. Sarah picked up her phone, but there was nothing new from her friend. She should be back by now and Sarah really needed her. She fired her off a quick message. She decided she better call Zack, make sure he was OK, otherwise she wouldn't be able to enjoy the one and only night that she had. If he were upset or missing her, she would be miserable.

She dialled her ex's number and walked out onto the balcony. This place was incredible – Harry hadn't exaggerated about that. Which made it all the more depressing that she had to leave a day early. Painted a brilliant white, the building looked impressive. There was a pool and a BBQ area at the side of the house overlooking the sea. Peering out over the balcony, she could just about see Harry and one of his friends down by the pool. Beers had been opened and loud music pulsated. Sarah had met the lad earlier, Donal or Declan or something like that. She couldn't remember, but he seemed pleasant enough, didn't say too much. Harry told her they both worked in the same line of business, whatever that meant. He hadn't elaborated. Sarah still didn't know what Harry did for a living, but his car was luxurious, really classy, so she guessed he was doing OK for himself. He also mentioned that another friend was on the way. So much for a quiet romantic weekend away together. Harry was stoking the fire on the barbeque pit and it was beginning to redden. He had a bottle of beer in his hand and he was laughing at something his friend was saying. His broad shoulders were swathed in a white T-shirt. Sarah blushed at the memory of their afternoon together, in this same room. Harry had been very attentive.

Alex finally answered. "Hi, Sarah, look, it can't be helped, I'm afraid. I'm on call this weekend, I think I told you." His tone was curt, confident and a little bit condescending. "There was always a chance this would happen."

She re-entered the bedroom and closed the balcony door. "No, Alex, no, you didn't tell me." Her manner was even, assertive. She could play his game.

"Didn't I? Sorry, it must have slipped my mind. I've been very busy and one of the doctors in the emergency department just called in sick. So I have to cover tomorrow night's shift. Can't be helped, I'm afraid. Life and death."

Life and death, everything was always life and death – *his* work was so important. Arrogant piece of shit. Zack's dad was a medical student on placement in the emergency department of one of the hospitals in the city. And you would swear by the way he carried on that he was the president of the United States. He was so freaking serious. Sarah didn't reply as she watched Harry and Declan through the glass. The two men were wrestling with each other at the edge of the pool, each trying to throw the other into the water. Harry was winning.

"Sarah? Are you there?"

"Yeah. I'm here."

"I'm sorry, OK?" There was a pause. "Look, I'll make it up to you, I promise."

Sarah sighed. What could she say that she hadn't already said to him over the years? There really was no point – Alex was a selfish man – that was the bottom line. He would never change. She wished things could be different though, just for once in her life. She hadn't told Harry about her son, Zack. Now, she would have to make up a story or tell him the truth – that she had a child. And something told her that Harry Reddan would disappear when he heard that piece of information.

"Do you want to talk to Zack?"

"What about your mother?" Sarah resented having to ask but Alex's mother had recently shown an interest in her grandson. It had come out of the blue. For the first four years of the boy's life she had wanted nothing to do with him.

"Ah, I think she has tennis …"

She knew Alex was lying. He hadn't bothered to ask her. It was easier to put her out than his mother. She was the one funding his education and she hadn't exactly been pleased when she found out about the baby. For Christ sake. He was afraid of upsetting the woman's routine at the tennis club.

"Do you want to talk to Zack?" he repeated, his tone superior.

Prick. She wasn't one of his patients.

"Yes, put him on." She wanted to get Alex off the phone. She heard Alex call out to Zack and then she heard the sound of her son's little feet running down the hall.

"Mummy!" he squealed.

Her heart melted. "Hi, sweetheart! How are you?"

"Mum, we had pizza for lunch and then we went to the zoo, Mum, we went to the zoo! I saw elephants and tigers and monkeys. Mum, the monkeys were so funny, they were tickling themselves in the part under their arms – it was *soooo* funny!" He roared laughing.

Sarah smiled. Her little boy always managed to cheer her up.

"That's amazing, Zack. The zoo? How cool is that?"

"Mum, can we go sometime? It's the best place ever!"

"Well, I did take you when …" Sarah stopped – he obviously didn't remember. "Yes, sure, love, I can take you there. We can take a picnic."

"*Yes!*"

She could picture Zack's fist pumping the air, his latest reaction to anything that pleased him.

"Thanks, Mum. I gotta go, Dad's cousin is here. He is playing football with me in the garden and he is like super-good."

"OK, Zack, I miss you."

"Miss you too, Mum. I love you." He made a kissing sound into the phone and then he was gone.

"Hello? Sarah?" Alex was back on the line.

"He sounds happy," she offered.

"We had a good day so far." He hesitated. "I'm sorry, Sarah, about you having to cut your trip short."

Sarah sighed. "It's OK. I'll get the early bus. I should be up by the afternoon."

"I'll drop him off on my way to work. See you." He hung up.

"Yeah, see you." She shoved the phone into the back pocket of her shorts and opened the sliding door. She breathed in the sea air as she leaned over the balcony. Harry glanced up at her, a smile spreading across his face. Again, she remembered their afternoon together and her stomach did a funny flip. *Careful, Sarah.* He beckoned for her to come on down and she gave him the thumbs-up. As she turned to go back inside, she caught a glimpse of someone on the road disappearing past the corner of the house. She leaned over the other side of the balcony to get a better look at the front of the property. The girl was searching in a pink backpack for something. Grace. About bloody time. Sarah's weekend had been cut short and she was damn well sure that she was going to make the most of their time.

11

Grace read the words *World's End* etched in white italics onto a large boulder rock at the foot of the driveway. Loud music mixed with splashing water and laughter came from somewhere around the other side of the property. Judging by the vivacity resonating around the building, it sounded like the party had well and truly started. She stopped to take in the house, painted a brilliant white, framed by a clear blue sky – the building looked magnificent, enveloped in the late evening sun. Harry's flashy car was parked at the side of the house, the one he had collected Sarah in earlier. Grace whistled her appreciation. The image in front of her was one of luxury and extravagance. She advanced towards the house. She climbed the steps and tried the handle on the front door. It was locked – which meant that she would have to go around the back. Suddenly she was nervous. She had only met Harry briefly, and other than Sarah, she didn't know anybody. What would she do if Sarah wasn't out by the pool?

She was just about to pull out her phone and call her friend when the front door opened and there she was.

"Welcome to my gaff!" she said, her dimples deepening as she smiled.

She looked gorgeous. Her shoulder-length glossy black hair was styled to the side, hanging loosely over her bare, lightly tanned shoulder. Her make-up was minimal – just a light touch of rose-pink tinted lipstick and mascara subtly darkening her long lashes. She was wearing a pair of tailored white denim shorts, revealing long, evenly tanned slim legs and bare feet. Not a fake tan streak in sight.

"Oh, thank God you answered! I didn't want to walk out the back on my own. It sounds like there are loads of people out there."

Sarah held the door back. "I know, it sounds like loads, but it's just Harry and one of his mates. Messing around the pool – that's it, honestly."

"Sounds like about fifty people!" Grace laughed.

"Don't be so shy, Grace." Sarah rolled her eyes. "Come on in."

Grace followed Sarah into the house and then she stopped. To say the front hallway was impressive was an understatement. It was pretty enormous – the biggest hallway in a private house that Grace had ever seen, with a wide staircase that curved its way up towards the landing. An ornate chandelier with dozens of tiny crystals hung from the ceiling.

Grace's mouth dropped open. "What the …?"

Sarah grinned. "I know! It's unreal. You should see the view from the pool. You can see all the way to America," she declared.

Grace pushed past her friend playfully. "Friends in high places, *huh*?"

Sarah shrugged. "It's some client of Harry's. Not even his friend." She made a face. "Well, that's what he told me, but I don't care who owns it. It's all ours, Grace."

"Very generous," Grace observed.

Sarah's smile faded. "Grace, I have to tell you something."

"What?" Grace looked at her, concerned.

"I have to go back tomorrow. Zack's dad was on call at the hospital. He omitted to tell me." Sarah looked crestfallen. "He got called in to cover for someone."

"Ah, Sarah, what?"

"I know, I know. But there's nothing he can do about it."

Sarah looked so let down, and so was Grace. They had only just got here. The swim and the cliff walk had been so refreshing, Grace had already decided she was going back to the same beach the following day. But when she saw the disappointment on Sarah's face, she pulled herself together. It wasn't Sarah's fault that they had to leave early and, anyway, they were here now, at least that was something.

"Never mind, Sarah. Look, we have this amazing house for one night. Let's make the most of our time, yeah?"

Sarah brightened. She pulled Grace towards the stairs. "Come on, you need a shower. You smell like the sea. I will get us some wine from the fridge in my room. Did I tell you there is a fridge in my room, with wine in it?"

She took the stairs two at a time, her bare feet disappearing in the soft carpet. Grace stepped out of her flip-flops and followed her up, taking in the artwork as she climbed. Several paintings mounted the walls, the pictures grotesque fanciful murals, a mixture of animals and humans, twisted limbs and bulging eyes staring out at her. There was something unnerving about the images and she wondered who had chosen them. The upstairs carpet must be at least three inches deep, she thought, she could barely see her feet as she padded across the landing.

Sarah pointed towards a closed white door. "That's your room.

You have an ensuite, no less. Don't lock the door, I'll just be two seconds." She disappeared into the room three doors down.

Grace was just about to enter her room when she heard a car pull up in the driveway out front. A door slammed and heavy footsteps ran up the steps to the front door, followed by a male voice.

"*Jesus Christ, what now?*"

He sounded angry, annoyed.

She crept across the landing and saw a pair of male legs and the hem of a pair of shorts standing to the right of the front door. Sarah had said it was just Harry out the back by the pool with one of his pals. This was a new arrival.

"*Tell me what happened?*" she heard the man say. His voice sounded familiar.

He disappeared back down the steps, out of earshot.

Sarah came out of her room, the stems of two wine glasses hanging between her fingers and a bottle of white wine tucked under her arm.

"I can't believe you, Grace. I thought you would be in the shower by now." She marched across the landing and herded Grace into her room. "Get the hell ready, girl! *Every moment we spend here is precious!*"

"*OK, OK!*" Grace stripped as she climbed into the shower.

12

Stephen gripped the wheel of his car, his knuckles white. Andy's sister had just called – his wife had one of her episodes. He slammed his fist into the wheel. *Fuck sake*. Cathy's call came in as he got out of his car in the driveway of the World's End. She had been crying hard when he picked up and, in that moment, he knew he should not have come here. He should never have persuaded Andy to go see Cathy and her new baby. She wasn't ready. At least, not on her own without his support. He had desperately wanted some time on his own for a day or two. Now he knew that he had been selfish. He leaned his forearms on the wheel and rested his head as the memories flooded back to him.

Three years earlier, they had lost their baby. A boy they had christened Luke after Andy's father. Luke had been six months and two days old and he had been perfectly healthy. There was no rhyme or reason to his sudden death, the doctors had said, he had just stopped breathing in his sleep.

They had been married for over four years when Andy announced that she wanted to start a family and what did he think about it. Stephen remembered that he had been indifferent about having children – he assumed that he would want to have kids at some point, but he wasn't particularly pushed about doing it anytime soon. He had gone along with it anyway, thinking it wouldn't happen for a while. As it turned out, it happened quite quickly. Andy had only stopped taking the pill for two months when the nausea started. Other than feeling a little queasy at the beginning, there had been no problems during the months that followed – even the birth had gone relatively smoothly. Stephen fell immediately in love with Luke, and they had brought their little boy home and their life had been as close to perfect as humanly possible. For six months and two days.

Stephen had been at work when it happened. It was a Wednesday and Andy was still on maternity leave from the art gallery. She had been downstairs preparing dinner while Luke was upstairs taking his afternoon nap – the baby monitor was set up in the kitchen and she could hear him breathing softly as she sliced vegetables. It was just a *normal* day.

Andy blamed herself, of course. She kept saying that she had not become aware of the monitor going silent. Why hadn't she noticed? When Luke didn't wake at his usual time she went to check on him. He was already cold. He must have been dead a little while. If she had been listening to him properly, she would have realised he had stopped breathing and she might have been able to save him. Even though the doctors told her that there was nothing she could have done – a fact that Andy refused to believe.

An autopsy was performed, standard when there is an unexplained death they had said. But there was nothing new to report, no undetected heart defect, no bleed in the brain. Sudden infant death syndrome. There was no other explanation – a perfectly healthy baby had just stopped breathing. Luke had been in their lives for six months and two days and then he was gone, erased – it was as if he had never existed.

Those first few weeks were a blur for them both. They barely functioned. Andy stayed in bed most of the time while Stephen got up every day, looked after the house, and tried to feed them both. The doctors said they could try again for another child. Soon. But neither of them was ready. And besides, Andy had refused to talk about it, about him. Their son. Luke.

They sold their house in the countryside – the memories of the short time Luke had been in their lives was too painful to bear. They bought a small apartment overlooking the river in Limerick city, the one they were in now. Eventually, and strongly encouraged by his father-in-law, Stephen returned to work and tried to move on. But Andy didn't.

Then he slipped. An intern at work started paying him attention and he liked it. They began an affair. A few months in, he got careless and Andy found a message on his phone but he managed to explain it away – *She's an over-eager intern, has a crush on me, it's nothing*. She believed him. But her father found out about the affair and made threats. That if it happened again, he was out on his ear. While at the same time he dangled a carrot in front of him. *When I retire, Stephen, I want you to take over the company. But you have to keep your nose clean*. Passive aggressive bastard. Andy became watchful. Stephen ended the affair but Andy was already wary, mistrustful and paranoid. He would get up and go to work every day and she would ring him incessantly, up to twenty times a day, fearful that he was never coming back. And he would reassure her that he would be home that evening, as he had been the evening before and the evening before that. It was exhausting and, even though his team leader and colleagues were sympathetic, the constant calls started to irritate everyone. But there was nothing he could do about it. The phone would ring and he would look at the screen, see Andy's name, smile apologetically, and leave the room to take the call. Every day he left the apartment and went to work, Andy would phone him persistently and he would reassure her that he would be home that evening, the very same as the day before.

Then her sister and only sibling Cathy announced that she was pregnant. Stephen fretted that this would make everything worse, but he was wrong. Andy was really pleased for Cathy. She started to get her focus back, returning to her job at the art gallery part-time. She was excited about the arrival, even buying gifts long before the child was due.

Cathy gave birth to a beautiful, healthy baby girl, Izzy, and Andy's reaction was good, considering everything. There were no warning signs of any of the behaviour she had exhibited after Luke had died. She was pleased for her sister and she adored Izzy. Until a couple of weeks after the birth when her old insecurities resurrected. What if she was on her own with the baby and something bad happened? Dark thoughts cultivated inside her head, no matter how much Stephen tried to persuade her otherwise. They went to see a counsellor, but that didn't accomplish much. Andy was too vulnerable, she had regressed. She left the art gallery and she started calling him at work every day. *Again.* She was right back where she had been when their son had died.

He should have known that their earlier conversation was too good to be true. When Cathy had left to go shopping, Andy had taken Izzy for a walk in her pram and on her way back to the house, the child fell asleep. Andy immediately panicked. She woke the baby, to make sure she was breathing. The child started crying, she wouldn't stop, so Andy lifted her out of the pram and pushed the stroller back to the house while holding her – too frightened to place her back in the buggy for fear she would stop breathing. When Cathy arrived back from town, she had found Andy slumped on the sitting-room floor, leaning against the sofa, tears streaming down her face, a screaming Izzy squirming beside her.

Cathy said she kept repeating over and over again, *"What if she stopped breathing, Cathy? Then I'll have killed two babies."* Cathy was distraught. She hadn't realised the extent of Andy's grief, she had thought things had improved – otherwise she never would have left them on their own. Stephen had asked Cathy to put his wife on the phone but she said Andy was resting. She had taken a sedative and it was best to leave her be for the night. She would wake her later and try to talk to her. Stephen knew it was useless. What could change now? It was always going to be like this, wasn't it? His wife would be forever damaged by what had happened. He had lost a child too, but it was as if his grief did not matter. His grief wasn't important. In addition, the worst thing was that they were bound together by their mutual anguish, for eternity. He could never leave her – she would not survive.

He lifted his head off the steering wheel and wiped his face with his hands. They were wet when he pulled them away. He was both sad and angry. *Why him?* Why had this happened to him? He glanced at the ring on the forefinger of his left hand, his wedding ring from Andy. He could hear the faint sound of music coming from the house and he knew the boys were getting stuck in. Stephen looked up at the building – he could see a girl leaning over one of the balconies at the side. She held a towel together under her bare arms with one hand as she brushed her long dark hair with the other. The girl looked vaguely familiar, but he couldn't get a proper look from where he was sitting. He knew there would be girls in the house, Harry had said as much. Earlier he had not cared, but now … He slipped his wedding ring from his finger, opened the glove compartment and carefully placed it inside. Glancing at the phone in his hand, he hesitated. *Decide. You deserve to live your life too.* Andy would be staying with her sister tonight. He placed the phone in the glove compartment beside the ring and shut the cover. Andy was safe with her sister – he would call her in the morning.

He checked his face for tears in the interior mirror before climbing out of the car, thinking he could do with a quick shower. He grabbed his overnight bag from the boot and advanced towards the house, the music louder with each stride. To hell with his shower – he would go without. He continued around the side of the house and the first person he saw was Harry.

"*Finally!*" his friend called out, a little leaden – he had started on the beer already. "*Hey, Declan, Stephen is here!*" He thrust a beer in Stephen's hand.

Stephen accepted the cold bottle from his friend and took a long drink as he observed the view. *Wow*, this place was something else.

"You look like you needed that," Harry observed, a grin spreading across his face.

Stephen wiped his mouth with the back of his hand. "You have no idea."

Stephen felt a strong hand on his shoulder. He turned and Harry met his gaze. There was something in his expression that Stephen couldn't quite read, something mischievous, something very Harry-like. "The night has only just begun, mate." He gave a small smile. "Come on, you have a lot of catching up to do."

Beer in hand, Stephen wandered around the building and stole a glance up at the balcony. The girl was gone.

13

"Come on, come on, come on!" Sarah was pulling Grace out of the bedroom.

"Patience is a virtue, Sarah," Grace pointed out.

"Well, Patience didn't have much fun, did she? Come on, Grace!"

"Hold on, I forgot my phone." She turned to go back into her room.

"You don't need your phone! Come on, will you?"

"Ah, photo opportunity? I was out on my balcony just now. Have you seen that view?"

"True that, true that. But hurry." Sarah straightened her black halter-neck top.

Grace grabbed her phone from the locker and checked her appearance in the full-length mirror. Her long dark hair had curled up at the ends after her shower. She had forgotten to bring her hair straightener with her. Grace liked to keep her hair straight – it was easier to manage, especially at work, but it was naturally wavy and people she didn't know very well were always surprised by it when she didn't straighten it. She pushed her hands through the curls and decided she didn't look half-bad. She had caught the sun today – her shoulders were a little red. It must have happened while she was walking back from the beach. Her skin felt warm under her black sleeveless playsuit.

"You look gorgeous! Come on, will you? We're wasting precious time!"

"Coming." She closed the bedroom door behind her and followed Sarah down the stairs.

The music was louder now. The hall led them towards the back of the house into a large open-plan kitchen with cream marble tiles and a dark-grey marble-topped island taking up its centre. French doors opened out onto a white decking area. There was a pool at the side of the building, its water a beautiful blue. Following Sarah outside, Grace noticed a guy in the pool doing headers with a soccer ball. A couple of empty beer bottles sat on the tiles surrounding its edge. She smiled hello as she walked past and the guy grinned and waved back, clearly happy to see newcomers. Harry stood beside the barbeque, flipping burgers. He was chatting with someone who had his back to them.

Sarah walked up behind Harry, reaching up to cover his eyes with her hands. "We are finally here!" she announced. "Don't blame me – Grace took forever to get ready."

Harry turned and so did his friend. Grace's heart skipped a beat as she realised who it was. The guy from the beach, the one who had found her bracelet, the one she had run away from. She felt her cheeks redden.

"Finally, is right. The night is almost over!" Harry announced.

"Ah no, not if I have anything to do with it!" Sarah smiled as Harry leaned in for a kiss. A look passed between them, a memory perhaps, of the afternoon they had shared.

Harry gestured to the guy at his side. "This is my friend, Stephen. Stephen, this is Sarah."

Stephen nodded towards Sarah politely and kissed her on the cheek before turning to look at Grace, a small smile playing at his lips.

"This is my best friend Grace," Sarah declared. "Grace, this is Harry, I might have mentioned him." She grinned and again that look between them. "And this is Stephen who I am meeting for the first time."

"Nice to meet you, Grace." Harry grazed her cheek. "Wine?" He got busy pouring.

Stephen said nothing. Harry noticed and frowned at him.

"Is everything alright, mate?"

Stephen nodded and smiled. "Yeah, yeah, it's just, we've met." He gestured toward Grace. "Earlier on the beach today." He turned to Grace. "I didn't know you were staying here."

"I didn't know you were staying here either."

Sarah looked on, amused. "Sorry? Did I miss something?"

"Remember I went for a swim earlier?" Grace said. "Well, I forgot to tell you I lost my bracelet." She motioned to Stephen. "Stephen found it at the edge of the water." She shook her head. She couldn't believe he was here. In this house. She couldn't take her eyes off him.

Harry pushed a cold glass of wine into her hand.

"Good thing you did, Stephen! Grace loves that bracelet," Sarah said.

"What are the chances, eh?" Harry replied, grinning at Stephen. Fat hissed and fire flew out of the barbeque. "*Shit!*" He grabbed the tea towel hanging over his shoulder and waved it at the flame.

There was a loud cheer from the pool. "*Wasn't banking on burned beef for dinner!*" Declan roared.

"*Yeah alright, shut up! Meat tastes better when it's a little bit scorched!*" Harry shouted back as he turned the burgers over and the flames relaxed. "These are nearly ready, guys."

Declan got out of the pool and gave Stephen a clap on the back. "How are you, mate? Everything OK?"

Stephen glanced at Grace before he answered. "Yeah, everything is fine. Good to see you, Declan."

"It's been too long." Declan grabbed a towel from one of the loungers. He turned to Harry. "The sooner we eat this charred food the sooner we can really let loose."

Harry gave Declan a playful dig. "Watch it!"

Declan dropped the towel, ran back to the pool and jumped in, twisting and turning his body, making dolphin noises, his eyes bulging. Everyone laughed. Harry shouted "*Nutter!*"

Grace sipped her white wine and felt herself relax as she watched Stephen chat with his friends, his easy manner. Every now and then, he would turn and catch her eye and they would both smile. She turned to look at Sarah who was helping Harry serve up the food. She seemed cheerful, engaged, included, and just happy.

Grace looked out at the sea and the small island. The sun would set soon and the sky would change colour. She took another mouthful of her wine and she forgot about her life back in the city, her job, her mother in the nursing home, her sister Erin, and the childhood that continued to haunt her. She might have to go home tomorrow with Sarah, but she had tonight. She continued to sip her drink as she looked out at the incredible view.

And, she knew he was watching her.

14

"Grace, you look like shit!"

Grace flushed the loo and threw cold water on her face. Tentatively, she walked back into the bedroom and eased her body onto the mattress, pulling the duvet up to her chin. Her head was hurting and there was a terrible taste in her mouth. She felt like she had swallowed something dead, the mere thought making her gag. Closing her eyes, she groaned aloud. She could hear Sarah walk across the room, pull back the curtains and open a window.

"This room smells like a brewery," Sarah observed.

"No, Sarah, I can't do daylight. Not yet," Grace protested. She pulled the duvet over her head.

"Grace, you cannot lie in bed on this glorious day. The weather is amazing, and we have to get the stupid bus at lunchtime. Do not waste the morning in bed. Come on!"

"I will, I will. Just give me an hour to wake up properly," she pleaded. "I'm afraid if I move that I'll throw up."

"Grace, hangovers don't get any better if you stay in bed. You should get up and move around, have a shower, drink some water. Or try some yoga? Yoga is good."

Grace opened one eye and peered out at her friend from under the duvet. "Who the fuck told you that?'"

"Come on!" Sarah persisted. "You will start to feel better much sooner if you just get out of that bed."

"Sarah, I have never felt this bad in my whole life."

Sarah sat on edge of the bed. "Yeah, well, if you're going to knock back as much wine as you did, you're asking for trouble. Just saying …"

"Don't judge me, Sarah. I wasn't the only one."

Sarah grinned. "Yeah, I noticed that."

Grace narrowed her eyes. "What do you mean?"

"Just that you seemed to be getting on well." Sarah nudged her. "With Stephen?"

"He's nice. That is all it is!" Grace shot back. "The conversation is easy. And he is funny."

"Sounds like the perfect partner!"

Grace threw one of her pillows at Sarah. "Well, what did you expect me to do? You were kind of occupied yourself."

"I know, I'm sorry." Sarah stretched her arms.

And there it was again, that secret smile. Sarah was smitten.

"Don't be sorry. You deserve to have some fun." Grace pulled the pillow over her head. "Oh God, I am hanging, this is the worst I have ever felt. *Ever.*"

"What time did you call it a night?" Sarah asked.

Grace shrugged. "No idea. But at least I made it to bed," she defended herself. "I just don't remember how I got here."

"And alone." Sarah raised an eyebrow.

"Shut up, Sarah."

"What? He is nice. And he clearly likes you. I asked Harry if

Stephen is in a relationship and he just shrugged. That means no, or, nothing exclusive. You should go for it."

"Is everybody up?" Grace changed the subject. She was too ill to deal with the interrogation.

"Harry and Stephen took off to the beach for a swim. I spotted Declan out by the pool opening a bottle of beer."

"Seriously?"

Sarah nodded.

"I think he was still up when I went to bed. I think so anyway."

"What is he like? Declan? I didn't really get a chance to talk to him."

Grace considered her answer, choosing her words carefully. She hadn't taken to Declan, but he was Harry's friend and Sarah was clearly mad about Harry, so she didn't want to insult anyone. "He seems alright, I guess.

"What?" Sarah quizzed.

Grace shook her head. "What do you mean, what?

Sarah laughed. "Come on, Grace, I know you. It's rare that you don't like someone, and when you do you are shit at hiding it."

"I don't know." She shrugged. "He was a bit quiet, you know, after you guys left. Didn't say much, but kind of watching everything. And the more we drank the soberer he got – that always makes me nervous. He talked a bit about his business deals, his obsession with the gym. He was kind of boastful, and, I got the impression he is loaded. Maybe he was trying to impress, I don't know. I wasn't interested." She leaned against the headboard and closed her eyes. "I don't think that Stephen has much time for him."

"Why do you say that?"

"I don't know. Declan made a few sarcastic comments." Grace

shifted her position on the pillow. "Ah, it was probably the wine."

Sarah's phone beeped in her pocket. She glanced at the screen.

Grace watched as her friend covered her mouth with her hand, her eyes widening.

Grace sat up in bed, alarmed, the sudden movement hurting her head. "What is it, Sarah? Is it Zack?"

"*No!*" Sarah shrieked. "*Well, yes, but it's good!*"

Grace slowly lay down again. "OK, you're not making sense and my brain is not able to compute too much today."

"Zack's dad, he just texted. His mother came to visit and she wants to take care of Zack while he goes to the hospital. She has offered to stay over." Sarah scrolled down through the long message. "She's playing tennis early on Monday so I can stay for an extra night if I want, as long as I can get an early bus back home to collect Zack." She narrowed her eyes. "What time is the first bus home on Monday?"

"I don't know. Take a look at the website."

Grace looked on as Sarah pinched the screen on her device.

"*Em,* there is a bus every morning at seven thirty except for weekends and bank holidays." Sarah looked at Grace. "Monday is a bank holiday." She glanced down at the message again. "She has to be on court by noon. It is a two-and-a-half-hour drive on a bus. So, the seven thirty would've been perfect. *Fuck sake!*"

"Except it doesn't run on a bank holiday." Grace stated the obvious.

Sarah scrolled down and frowned. "The earliest bus is at ten. We won't make it back in time." She sighed.

"There might be another service," Grace suggested.

"There is nothing else. This is a small village." Sarah sounded exasperated. "Damn, what should we do?" She grabbed Grace by the arm. "Oh, Grace, we have to make this happen!"

"What time is the last bus back to Limerick leaving tonight?"

"Seven thirty."

"Why don't we get that one? We could spend the whole day here. The boys were talking about hiring a boat to sail to the island for the afternoon. We can go with them now."

Sarah didn't look that impressed by the suggestion.

"Come on, Sarah, it's better than having to leave at lunchtime today, isn't it?"

"Yeah, but it would be so cool to have one more night. Harry said the guy who owns the house is coming by later with some friends. He's throwing a big party."

"What time is Harry going back tomorrow?" Grace asked.

"He didn't say."

"He might be leaving early. Maybe he could drive us. If you ask him?"

Sarah shook her head. "I'm not asking him. I don't want to ask him for anything." She glanced around the room. "I mean coming here, that's different. It's not his house and he isn't paying for it, so it's not as if I feel under compliment, you know? But asking for a lift, that would be different. If this ..." she shrugged, "if this thing that we have, if it turns into a relationship, I want to be independent. I won't be making that mistake again."

"I get you," Grace replied. Sarah's relationship with Zack's father had been controlling. *He* had been controlling. "Look, this is better than nothing," she reasoned. "We can have the whole day on the boat. Then get the late bus. You can stay at mine tonight. We can get take-out and drink wine." The thought made her feel sick. "Well, you can drink wine."

Sarah smiled at that.

"That's better. Now come on, I need to get ready."

Sarah laughed. "What happened to your hangover?"

"Oh, it's still there, but you're right – it's better to get up. Lying in bed isn't going to fix it." Grace threw back the duvet and walked over to the window. Slowly. "Text him back. Tell him you'll be there to collect Zack tomorrow in time so his mam can play her game of tennis." Alex's mother was a nob. Grace had met her once and the woman screamed pretension. Grace could see the beach from where she stood, two figures running into the surf. She couldn't make out whether it was Harry and Stephen.

She smiled when she thought of Stephen and felt a warm flush circle her neck. He had paid her a great deal of attention the previous night, without making it too obvious. Though Sarah seemed to pick up on their mutual attraction, flirtation, whatever it was. He had sat beside her at dinner and she was very aware of his closeness. And she thought he felt it too because every now and then he would lean in to her. By the end of the night, their bodies were close.

She watched the figures on the beach diving into the waves. The day was beautiful, boasting another clear blue sky.

"We need sun cream today," she noted. "Especially if we're going on a boat."

"I packed it," Sarah replied.

"Right, that's settled then," Grace said. "We stay until this evening."

Sarah slipped off the bed and made for the door. "I'm going for a swim in the pool before the boys come back. Do you want to join me?"

Grace looked back out the window. A swim might help her hangover. "You bet. Give me five minutes to get ready."

Sarah ran out of the room. *"Five minutes?"* she shrieked. *"Ah, come on, Grace? Five minutes!"*

Grace laughed as she changed into her swimsuit. God, she loved that girl.

15

Stephen searched his bag for his phone. He found it in the side pocket and checked for any new messages or calls – there was nothing new from Andy, or Cathy. He took this to be a positive thing – the sisters must have talked things through. Well, good, he thought. Yes, Andy was his wife, but she needed the attention of her own family too. Following the initial expression of support, the burden was all on him. Still, he thought, he'd better fire off a quick text, just in case.

Hey, are you OK? Call me when you get a minute.

He hit send and stuffed his phone into his back pocket. He had a terrible hangover earlier, but the swim in the cold sea with Harry had cleared his head and he felt much better. He was starving though, he needed to eat. He flung his bag into the boot of Harry's car and sat into the passenger seat beside his friend. The interior had that distinctive smell of a new car and the black leather interior design sported many special features. It was a high-spec model and must have cost a great deal of money.

"So, when did you get this one?" He ran his hand over the smooth and glossy dashboard.

"Last month." Harry glanced over at Stephen, frowning. "I told you, didn't I?"

"Nope. Must have slipped your mind that you had traded in your ten-year-old Honda Civic for a brand-new BMW?" Stephen observed his friend. "Quite a leap. Business must be good?"

Harry grinned as he started the engine. The car barely made a sound. "It has been better recently. Got a few new clients."

"Like the one who owns World's End?" Stephen quizzed. He noticed Harry grip the wheel a little tighter.

"Yeah, he's one of them." Harry shrugged. "I just got lucky with some investments. One good deal led to another, you know the way it is. The commission has been generous on return. The client is happy, I am happy." He shifted the gear into first and moved off.

Stephen could still barely hear the engine. Harry relaxed his hands on the wheel. The vehicle appeared to drive itself.

When they finished college, Harry had started working with an investment broker for a large company in the city. A few years back he'd decided to venture out on his own and things seemed to be working out for him. For a brief moment Stephen wondered if dishonesty was at play – it wouldn't be the first time. Harry seemed to be doing very well for himself, with flash cars and friends in high places. He pushed the thought aside. Don't be so resentful, he told himself, be happy for your friend.

"Glad you came down?" Harry said, changing the subject.

Stephen sighed. "You can say that again. I needed a break. Quite badly."

"How are things with Andy?" Harry asked casually, though Stephen knew what he meant.

"Ah … they had been better for a while, but ever since her sister had the baby she has just regressed, you know? It seems to have brought everything back to the surface."

"Well, you are here now, so put her out of your head."

Stephen grimaced at this. Harry really had no idea. Harry never had any time for Andy. He thought she was too clingy, even before Luke had come into their lives. Clingy, Stephen could handle.

"I'm trying," he said. "It's not that easy." He leaned against the headrest and closed his eyes.

He felt Harry looking at him.

"I didn't tell Sarah, you know?" Harry said. "That you are married. She asked me if you're seeing someone and I kind of didn't say anything."

Stephen opened his eyes and regarded Harry as he drove. "It makes no difference, Harry. I'm not interested in anyone else."

Harry laughed. "Yeah, right!"

"What do you mean by that?"

"I saw the way you were looking at her last night." Harry grinned. "Grace. You couldn't take your eyes off her."

"That's not true."

"Mind you, I don't blame you. She is gorgeous." He whistled softly. "If it wasn't for Sarah, well …"

"I hadn't really noticed."

Harry laughed again. "Oh, come on, Stephen? You were sitting beside her all night. And I think the feeling might be mutual by the way."

Stephen was silent. He was uncomfortable with the conversation.

"Stephen, you've been through a rough time. I know that, mate. So, if you want to get to know Grace a little better, nobody is going to talk about it, OK? Don't worry about Declan – he doesn't know much about your personal life. So, relax."

"What time have you booked the boat hire?" Stephen changed the subject.

Harry checked his watch. "Midday, I think, Declan made the booking. A cuddy boat, has its own cabin below deck. We have an hour to get ready."

"Are you sure you know what you are doing?"

"What? Why?" Harry sounded confused.

"Have you ever steered a boat before, Harry? Out on the sea?" Stephen laughed. "It's not like driving a car."

"You have little faith, my friend!" Harry grinned. "Besides, Declan says he knows a bit about boats. I hope he means it."

Now it was Stephen's turn to laugh. "Declan is only useful if he stays sober. He was uncapping a beer when we left for a swim this morning."

They turned the corner of the cliff road and Stephen could see The World's End up ahead. He marvelled at its beauty. It looked even more majestic in natural daylight.

"No sign of your client last night?" he said.

Harry frowned. "Who?"

"The owner of World's End?" Stephen offered. "You said he might be coming over to the house on the weekend."

Harry shifted in his seat. "Oh, yeah, he texted to say he couldn't make it last night. I was relieved, to be honest. Nice guy, don't get me wrong, and very generous, but if he came over it would be more like work for me, you know? Last night, I just wanted to chill, settle in and that."

Stephen knew exactly what Harry meant. He never enjoyed mixing business with pleasure. And you would have to give the impression that you were having a good time, while making sure you didn't have too good a time.

"He is coming over tonight, with a few friends." Harry's phone rang as they pulled into the drive.

"I won't be here, I'm afraid. Heading back this evening."

"What?" Harry looked alarmed. "No, no, no, you can't do that! Come on, man! We said the weekend!"

Stephen hesitated. He would love to stay another night, but how could he with Andy losing her shit? And Cathy mentioned that Andy was talking about cutting her own trip short. He registered the disappointment in Harry's face. "I'll see what I can do."

Harry's phone continued to ring. He looked at the screen and nodded to Stephen that he should take the call. Taking the hint, Stephen climbed out of the car. He strolled around the side of the house towards the pool area, not ready to leave the warm sunshine. He noticed that someone was swimming, a girl, her long strokes synchronised as she broke through for breath. *Grace.* Clad in a black swimsuit, her lean body sliced through the water, her long dark hair sleek on her back. She lifted her head on the turn, smiling up at him. She had the most beautiful smile. Stephen tried not to look as she smoothed her wet hair back from her face. She climbed out of the pool and wrapped a towel around her slim waist. She padded across the decking until she stood in front of him. She squinted up into the sun.

"Hi."

"Hi."

"Nice swim?"

"Yes. And you?"

"Yes."

"*Grace! Come on, food is ready!*" Sarah called from the house.

"Sarah has cooked for everyone," Grace said. "I'm starving."

"Me too ..."

"Right." She went to go around him and he moved at the same time, causing them to bump into each other.

They smiled.

"Sorry!" she said.

"No, I'm sorry." He held on to her arm. Her skin was wet beneath his touch.

Neither of them said anything.

He released her arm. "Better get going."

"Yeah."

She tightened the towel around her body and disappeared into the house. Stephen's heart was pounding. What the hell was he doing, he asked himself. Even though he knew the answer. His phone vibrated in his pocket. He checked the caller ID. *Andy*. He hit answer.

16

Lukasz cupped his hand around his mouth and lit his cigarette. He leaned back against one of the bollards on the dock and watched the water lapping gently around the boats in front of him. He would sit here for hours if he had the choice. The tranquillity always stopped him in his tracks, leaving him immobile at its beauty.

"Hey, Lukasz!"

It was his friend Pete, calling out from his boat which was moored up beside his own. Pete had been up early that morning, like Lukasz. *Up with the lark.* Pete knew he had missed out on the previous morning's catch and he was not going to let it happen again. There was plenty of fish in the sea for everyone and Tommy was only too happy to take it off their hands. "There wasn't a morsel of fish to be had in any of the local restaurants after last night, so give me everything you have!" Tommy had said that morning. The distributor had been delighted when Lukasz had called him from Nora's phone in the cabin. So, Pete was up and already out on the water when Lukasz pulled up in his van earlier that morning.

"Will you help me with this?" Peter asked. "I can't get the knots out. I need someone to hold the other end." Peter's black curly hair hung loosely over his brown eyes. He was dressed in his usual attire

– a pair of faded blue jeans and a white T-shirt. Lukasz marvelled at how effortlessly handsome the young Irishman looked on any given day, despite the many pints he sank in the pubs.

"Sure."

Lukasz pulled on his cigarette one more time before stamping it out with his boot and tossing it into the metal bin. He carefully climbed onto Pete's boat and took hold of the other end of the net. He held strong as Pete weaved the net in and out until finally the knot came loose. "Thanks. I would be here for another few hours if it wasn't for you."

"No bother."

"You're picking up the Irish lingo at last, Lukasz!" Pete grinned. "Fair play to you – it only took you four years."

"I am a good listener!" Lukasz beamed as he rooted in his pocket for his tobacco. He began to roll another cigarette.

Pete reached into a cooler box, took out two cans of beer and handed one to Lukasz. "You won't say no to a cold one?"

Lukasz accepted. "I will not, but just the one. We have one more day to catch fish and I don't want to miss it."

Pete laughed as he drank. "Off with you! I caught enough in one day to keep me going until next weekend. I won't be getting up at the crack of dawn tomorrow. *You* can feed the tourists and their fancy palettes."

Lukasz nodded. *The crack of dawn?* What did that mean?

The fishermen around Castle Cove only went out on the water to catch enough fish to survive until they ran out of money and then they would drink their earnings in the pub every evening. Lukasz wasn't long living in Ireland when he had learned what "*one more for the road*" meant. Not Lukasz. He was determined to go back out onto the water first thing in the morning – it was the last night of the long weekend and he was making good money.

"Hey, the whole town is talking about the noise from the World's End last night," said Pete. "Right shower of townies. I heard they were partying into the early hours. They were making a right ole ruckus when I was leaving. Did you hear anything?"

Lukasz often slept on the boat when he went out early to fish. He often witnessed the tail end of a party as he steered his boat past World's End. "I went to bed early," he said. "I set my alarm for five in the morning and I heard them when I was leaving the harbour. There was only a few of them out by pool. The music, it was loud. But I have heard louder from that house. So, it was not the biggest party in that house."

"Saving themselves for tonight, I would say." Pete nodded out to sea. "I saw them going out to the island on one of Gary's rental boats a while back, the *Karina*. They were swigging back bottles of beer to beat the band. In this heat, they'll be lucky to steer the boat back."

A memory came to Lukasz as he observed the sea. "The sea is calm. *Niech Bog strzeze cie.*"

"What you be saying there?" Pete grinned.

"My mother would say it when I went out fishing," Lukasz replied. "*Niech Bog strzeze cie.* May God keep you safe."

Pete's expression appeared serious for a moment. Lukasz felt he was about to say something, and then he seemed to change his mind.

"You better hope so!" Peter laughed. "And may God be keeping me safe after knocking back a rake of porter in McHugh's."

Lukasz smiled but he didn't respond, aware that Pete was watching him closely.

"Do you miss it?" Pete asked.

"Miss what?" Lukasz took a mouthful of his beer.

"Poland. Your homeland? You must get lonely sometimes – for your family?"

Lukasz shook his head. "No and yes. I miss my family, but I come from a quiet town. No restaurants, bars, tourists, not like here." He gestured towards the village. "There is little opportunity in Poland for me. I like it here. Castle Cove is my home now."

"Ah, but you must get lonesome sometimes? You work non-stop," Peter persisted. "Are you pining for some young one back in Poland, is that it?"

Lukasz glanced away from Pete, uncomfortable at the questions about his personal life. When he had pints with the lads, they talked about fish, cards and local news, and they were always joking around about women, but nobody took it seriously.

"I am OK," he said.

"But you wouldn't say no to a bit of female company if it came along?" Peter asked. "Or male, whatever you're into."

"No, Peter. I have my boat to think about, my work. Maybe you should do the same, instead of drinking pints every night." His tone was firmer than he intended.

Pete did not reply. He finished his can and tidied around the boat.

Lukasz had been harsh in his reply and he regretted it. Pete didn't know anything about him, not really. And he could never tell him the truth.

"I'm sorry, Pete," he apologised. "I didn't mean to sound like a teacher."

Pete laughed. He was always giving out about his mother to

Lukasz. He said that whenever she was annoyed with him, she sounded like a teacher. "Ah, you're grand, boy. Sure, I'm only messing with you. And you are right, I do drink too much." He glanced at his watch. "Speaking of which, I'm off to the pub. Are you sure you won't join me?"

Lukasz smiled, relieved that the tone of their conversation had returned to normal. "Not tonight. Tomorrow I go to the pub. After one more night of fishing."

"Right you are, and I have to admire your discipline. Well, I hope you get some sleep with that lot." He nodded towards the boat heading towards Mutton Island. "See you, Lukasz."

Pete got into his van and drove off down the harbour. Lukasz considered the small island in the distance. He could just about see the boat Pete was referring to in the distance, bobbing in the water. He looked up at the sky and shielded his eyes from the sun. There wasn't a cloud to be seen. The sun was very hot. What is it Nora said the Irish call it? A scorcher? He hoped the people on the boat would not be scorched.

He finished his beer and decided he needed to eat. Tonight, he would sleep, he was tired. One more morning on the boat and then he would rest. He got into his van, switched on the engine and drove away from the harbour.

17

Grace tied the string of her bikini at the nape of her neck and slipped a white halter dress over her head. She had bought it in a sale at the end of the previous summer, but the weather had turned and she never got a chance to wear it. She ripped off the tag attached to the label and smoothed the dress down over her body. Slipping her bare feet into a pair of pale-pink trainers, she checked her appearance in the mirror. She wanted to look nice, but she didn't want to appear as if she was trying too hard. She shook her head in annoyance – just who was she trying so hard *not* to impress? Why did she care so much what he thought about her? She didn't know one thing about him, having only met him twenty-four hours ago. Before that, he hadn't existed in her life and she had not existed in his.

Relax, Grace, she told herself – it's just a random guy that you happen to get along with, nothing will come of it. Come this evening, you will be on your way home on a bus and you will probably never see him again. Somehow, the thought crushed her good mood a little. She sighed as she checked her phone. There was a message from her sister Erin asking where she was. Grace hadn't mentioned that she was going away for the weekend, only finding out herself at the last minute.

Grace read the full message. Erin had called to see their mother the evening before. She had spoken to Peggy who had explained what had happened when Grace had visited Rosie. Now Erin wanted to know what Grace had said to their mother to cause her to react like that. Grace shook her head in disbelief. She was annoyed. Why did Erin always think that she was the one who provoked their mother? They had grown up together, under the same roof and they had shared the same experiences, a few that both of them would prefer to forget. Why did Erin not remember?

Grace had not called the care home the day after her visit as she had promised. She couldn't bear to think about her mother, or to listen to Peggy's reassurances that she was not the problem. Grace knew it had everything to do with her, and the constant rejection was beyond upsetting. She had suffered her mam's unpredictable, hurtful behaviour her whole life, but she would never get used to it.

She checked the time on her phone and decided she had better call Peggy at the care home now before the boat trip. Sarah said they were leaving in ten minutes and she had already used up five of those getting ready. She dialled and her call was answered after the first ring, but Grace didn't recognise the female voice so she asked to be put directly through to Peggy on her mother's floor. She was informed that Peggy was on a day off. *Shit.* Grace had forgotten that Peggy had said she was only working the next day and was off for the rest of the long weekend. Thanking the woman, she hung up. She contemplated ringing Erin. She knew her sister would be worried about her – she was always worried about her, playing the big sister role – she couldn't help herself.

"Grace! Come on! You have exactly one minute to get out here or the boat is leaving without you!" Sarah called from downstairs.

Grace would not have time to call Erin, and if she was being honest with herself, she did not really want to talk to her sister after her latest accusation. She decided to send Erin a quick text instead.

I'm with Sarah. I said nothing to Mam, Erin. She just did her usual thing when she sees me. I walked in, she saw me and she screamed. I did nothing. But thanks for thinking I was at fault.

She pressed send and immediately regretted it. She knew deep down that Erin didn't mean to point a finger at her, but did she have to keep saying shit like that? Why didn't she take Grace's side when it came to their mother, just one time? She knew what their mam was like and she also knew that she could be particularly hard on Grace. It had been part of Rosie's cruelty over the years, playing one sister off against the other with her spite.

"Grace! Come on!" Sarah called again.

Grace threw the phone on the bed. Erin would reply and Grace did not want to have to deal with a back and forth *but-you-said* match between them both. Not today.

She quickly ran a brush through her hair before tying it up in a ponytail. Closing her bedroom door, she walked straight into Stephen on the landing – he appeared to be in a rush too.

They both laughed.

"Jesus, the pressure!" she said. " I thought we were supposed to be on a break, relaxing!"

Stephen grinned down at her. "Yeah, right!"

They smiled at each other, excited about the afternoon ahead.

"Come on, before they lose their shit." He took hold of her hand and led her down the stairs.

18

Stephen hadn't felt this happy in years. He felt like a young man again, as if he hadn't a care in the world, and he figured that Grace Doran had something to do with that. He rested his arms on the back of the long seat at the rear of the boat, enjoying the spray from the sea. His call with Andy had not gone well. She had wanted to come home and he had spent most of their time on the phone trying to persuade her not to. If he hadn't succeeded, he would be on his way back to the city right now instead of drinking beer on a boat with a beautiful girl sitting beside him. In the end, Cathy had persuaded her to stay. He had fired off a quick text to Mike to say that he would not be home until late and could he please feed Milo again. He didn't mention the fact that he wouldn't be back until the following morning. He didn't need to, the cat would survive.

Declan was sitting on the other side of Grace trying his best to chat her up, but every now and then she would steal a glance Stephen's way and he knew by the glint in her eyes that Declan was wasting his time. Still, the chase was on, and Stephen was enjoying the challenge. Declan would eventually give up and Stephen would be ready to make his move.

He knew what he was doing was wrong. And, even though

things were pretty bad between himself and Andy, and had been for some time, he shouldn't even be thinking about getting with somebody else. He knew that but he deserved a little fun, didn't he? Just one weekend would not harm anyone and Andy would never know. He smiled to himself – he was jumping the gun. Nothing had happened yet and maybe nothing would happen, though his gut was telling him otherwise.

He glanced across at Harry who was leaning over the wheel of the boat, having taken over the steering from Declan. He was pointing at something in the distance while Sarah rested her hand on his shoulder. Harry was quite competent. He must have decided to take it easy on the beer. Now he was waving his free hand about animatedly, telling some story and Sarah was laughing at whatever he was saying. He appeared happy with Sarah but, then again, Harry was happy with whomever he was dating. In recent years, Stephen had envied Harry and his easy way with women, his relaxed lifestyle, a lifestyle that had become lucrative recently if his new car was anything to go by.

Harry turned and caught Stephen watching him. He nodded towards Grace, a cheeky grin on his face. Stephen gave a half smile and glanced away. He knew Harry would never mention this weekend to anyone, but he wasn't comfortable with him encouraging anything with the girl, and he wasn't too keen on Declan knowing his business either. He would have to be discreet.

"Anyone ready for another beer?" Declan shouted over the noise of the engine. He stood and dropped his bottle into a bucket.

Stephen looked at his almost empty drink. "Sure, thanks, Dec."

Declan didn't reply.

"Is that alright?" Stephen asked.

Declan nodded. "Sure it is." He turned to Grace. "Grace?"

"Yes, please. Thanks, Declan."

Again, he gave a small nod and nearly fell as a wave rocked the boat. There wasn't much standing-room on the vessel and he almost toppled overboard. He grabbed on to the edge of the boat for support.

Grace reached out to him. "Shit, are you OK?"

He steadied himself. "Yeah, I'm fine. Stupid fucking sea," he slurred. He unsteadily made his way to the steps leading down into the cabin where the drinks were chilling.

"Is he alright?" Grace looked concerned as she watched him disappear below deck.

"Yeah, he's OK," Stephen said. "There isn't much support, is there?" He nodded at the seating area. "You'd want your wits about you. And clearly he had a few beers for breakfast so he's ahead of everyone else."

"Oh God, I couldn't face alcohol this morning, I felt so sick when I woke up."

"Yeah, me too. If I hadn't had a swim, I probably wouldn't be here now."

"Same!" She clinked her bottle against his, smiling. "Cheers!"

"Cheers!"

They both sipped their drinks.

"So, what do you do?" Stephen asked. "When you're not drinking beer on boats with random strangers?"

She smiled. "I work in a coffee house, been there a few years now. In Limerick city, the one across from the courthouse?" Stephen nodded. "It's busy all day with a very diverse clientele. I like it. I was in college, but I didn't connect with the course, so I left halfway through my second year with the intention of starting fresh the following year. You know, a new course." She rolled her eyes. "That was five years ago."

"What were you studying?"

"Biochemical Engineering."

Stephen winced.

Grace laughed. "I know, I know. So boring. I don't know why I chose it to be honest, but you have to pick something, and nothing stood out for me at the time. Some of my friends were doing that so I put it down as my first choice, never expecting that my application would be accepted. It was. Two weeks into the term I knew I had made a mistake, but I stuck with it until the middle of my second year. Then everybody was preparing for their co-operative interviews, work experience and that. I just couldn't do it anymore. It was bringing me down. I was really unhappy."

"How did your parents take it?"

Grace turned away. "*Em*, it's just my mam actually." She shrugged. "She wasn't bothered." She played with a charm on her bracelet. "I don't think college is for me, to be honest."

"But maybe it would have been different if you had chosen another course?"

"I'm sure it would, but I wasn't crazy about the college environment either. I felt like I didn't fit in or something. Students can be so pretentious, people trying too hard to be outrageous, you know? It was as if everyone was in competition to outdo each other with their opinions on climate change or racism or sexual orientation or whatever and, yet, we were all living together in this fish bowl, discussing the problems of the world but never actually experiencing *real* life." She sighed. "I just got bored with it all. I remember there was a girl in school who didn't want go to college so she travelled and worked in hospitality in different cities around the world, and I would meet her when she came home to visit her family, and she was far more interesting than my fellow students." She smiled at the memory. "Anyway, I like the café. You meet some interesting people. And plenty of dickheads too, don't get me wrong." She laughed. "But I think I would like to stay in catering, or some form of it. Maybe invest in my own place at some point – a bar or a restaurant. I don't know, it's a pipe dream now, but some day, maybe." The knot on the string of her bikini had come loose and she reached behind her neck to tie it. "Though some of the customers do annoy me." She laughed. "Maybe I'll move to Christmas Island or something. Set up business over there."

"Christmas Island? There is such a place?"

"In the Indian ocean," she replied. "There's a very small population so I can't imagine there would be much competition."

"Sounds like you have it all worked out," he observed.

"How about you?" she asked.

He smiled. "I worked all through college so there was little time for deep and meaningful conversations about the world's problems. But I do know what you mean. I studied Marketing and I loved it right from the beginning." He nodded towards his friend. "Harry took the same course as me but after college we went in different directions professionally. I love marketing, preparing for the pitch. I work with a very creative team and every day is exciting. Harry went down the investment route." He shrugged. "I wouldn't be able for that kind of pressure, but Harry seems to thrive on it and we have remained friends, nonetheless."

"Sarah likes him."

"I can tell." He looked over at them as Sarah reached up and smoothed Harry's hair. "I hope not too much."

Grace frowned. "Why do you say that?"

Stephen shrugged. "Because Harry doesn't do serious relationships. The minute he notices a girl getting too close, he cuts all ties and moves on. He has always been like that." He turned to look at her. "And he won't mind me saying it either."

She held his gaze for a moment. She had the most beautiful eyes.

"And you?" she asked.

"Me? What about me?"

"Do you do serious relationships?"

Before Stephen could answer, Declan emerged from the cabin carrying several bottles of beer. Harry cheered and Declan passed around the drinks.

Harry pointed towards the island. "We are nearly there, guys. I'll set up the portable barbecue. We can eat al fresco on the beach."

"Who's playing Mr. Domestic this weekend, *eh*? Trying to impress someone, Harry? That's not like you." Declan laughed, but his joke didn't quite land. He stood there, scowling, beer in hand.

Stephen watched the small island as they approached. It wasn't inhabited. The guy hiring out the boat had informed them earlier that the currents could be dangerous at certain times of the day, depending on the tide. But on this particular day, they would be safe if they returned before the evening. There was a jetty lined with bollards projecting into the sea but, other than that, the island appeared to be in its natural form. Harry steered the boat close to the jetty.

"*All hands on deck!*" he shouted. Everyone laughed. "Seriously, someone needs to jump out and catch this rope when I throw it."

"Yeah, I'll do it." Declan was unsteady as he tried to climb over the side of the boat.

Stephen stood up. "Let me give you a hand, Dec mate."

"I thought you were busy, Stevo *mate*?" Declan's speech was a little more slurred than earlier.

Stephen ignored the jibe and climbed over the side of the boat, until he hit the rough jetty. Harry threw him the rope and he pulled as Harry steered until the boat moored parallel to the quay. Stephen looped the rope around the closest bollard. He glanced up and caught Declan watching him as he drank his beer. He had his arm around Grace's shoulder and, even though she was smiling, she appeared uncomfortable. What was up with the guy? Maybe he just had too many beers and it was getting hot now that the afternoon sun was up. It would probably do him good to take a nap.

Stephen wrapped the rope around the bollard a second time and tied a knot. He pulled on the rope to check that it was secure. When he looked up again, he saw Grace watching him, her white dress flattering against her lightly tanned skin, her hand reaching up to stop her hair billowing around her face. She really was a beautiful girl. They continued to gaze at each other for a moment, and he knew the attraction was mutual. He also knew that something was going to happen between them. That it was inevitable. He would have to be careful though. One weekend, that was all he could do.

So far, this day had been perfect. So far, this whole weekend was perfect, and nothing, not even Declan's arrogance or Andy's paranoia was going to change that.

19

"I don't know, Sarah. I'm getting a bad feeling. We don't know these guys at all and *now*…" Grace paused, unsure how she sounded, "now we're on a deserted island with them?"

Sarah carefully applied fresh lipstick and pressed her lips together. They had come down to the indoor toilet in the cabin to freshen up. "Grace, I don't understand. You were fine with everything this morning?"

"Yeah, but that was when we were over at the house, on land. It's different here on the island. Like, I thought there would be other boaters spending the day here, but there's nobody else around. It's completely deserted. It's just a bit eerie, don't you think?"

Sarah turned to look at her friend. "But, it's just Harry. I've been seeing him for a few weeks now and I think I know him a little. Also, these guys, they're his friends." She shrugged. "What's the problem?"

Grace didn't want to tell her friend what Stephen had said about Harry. It wouldn't help anything for her to know that he was not the type to commit and that she was probably wasting her time. Initially, Sarah had been playing hard to get, but Grace knew that Sarah really liked Harry, and now she wasn't exactly holding back.

"I just feel uneasy, that's all. And that guy Declan is really drunk. He was OK last night, just a little bit arrogant and bragging about his business, but it was the first night for everyone so I didn't pay him much attention. But today he's acting really weird around me. When Harry and Stephen were securing the boat, he put his arm around my shoulders and he kept rubbing my neck with his thumb. He's beginning to creep me out, Sarah, and he's acting strange with Stephen too. Like ... kind of hostile. Something is going on between them."

"But Stephen is into you?"

"I don't know. I think he might be, but ..."

"But what?" Sarah asked.

"Something is off, I don't know what it is, but I can feel it. We just don't know these people and now we are on an island with them. And you have to admit, we are outnumbered. Two girls, three guys?" She checked her pocket for her phone and realised she had left it back at the house. "I don't even have my phone."

Sarah closed her lipstick and tossed it into her purse. "Grace, relax. We are only here for the afternoon. Harry is going to cook some food, and then we head back, you and I get on a bus and we go home. No fuss. So just relax, OK?"

"Maybe you're right." Grace wasn't so sure. "But I think I'm going to take it easy with the drinks for the rest of the afternoon. I want to keep my wits about me."

Sarah sighed. "Suit yourself."

They heard a shout, followed by a loud splash, and then more shouting. Grace narrowed her eyes as they listened. "What was that?" Someone was yelling and he sounded angry, but it wasn't possible to decipher what was being said.

Sarah grabbed her hand. "Come on!"

The two girls ran up the steps just in time to see Declan throwing fists at Stephen in the water, his face like thunder. Harry was trying to intervene, their shoulders barely above water level. Grace and Sarah looked on in disbelief as Harry dragged Declan away from Stephen, arms thrashing wildly in the air, shouting profanities at him the whole time.

"*You fucking prick. Mind your own business, you fucking prick!*"

"That's enough, Declan," Harry warned. "Come on, mate. You're drunk. You need to sleep it off."

Declan appeared to have a fresh cut on his forehead. He released himself from Harry's grip and trudged out of the water. He wandered along the pier and unsteadily climbed onto the boat. He stumbled past Grace and Sarah before disappearing below deck into the cabin.

Harry followed closely behind. "Everything is OK, girls. Dec had a little too much to drink, he just needs to sleep it off." He nodded at Sarah. "Sarah, will you get me the first aid box? It should be stored under that seat." He pointed towards a storage unit before running down the steps into the cabin. Sarah found the kit and followed Harry.

Grace could see Stephen wading out of the water. He sat on the edge of the long pier and pulled off his trainers. His top and swim shorts were soaking wet. She grabbed a towel from her bag and climbed down off the boat, walking along the pier towards him. She handed him the towel. He accepted, nodding his appreciation. He pulled his T-shirt over his head and dried off. She moved away and sat on the beach. A minute later, Stephen came to sit beside her. Neither of them spoke for a moment.

Grace picked up a twig on the sand. "What happened?"

"I don't know." He shook his head. "I was tying up the boat and the next thing he was throwing punches at me and I ended up in the water. Then he jumped in after me, but he could barely stand up. I put my arm around his neck and started to swim in and the next thing I know, he's thumping me in the water. At some point, he must have hit his head. The guy has had too much to drink."

"But what is his problem with you?" Grace asked.

"I don't know, Grace," he said, sounding impatient.

They both fell silent. Grace glanced up the beach – it was completely deserted. Harry and Sarah were still in the cabin attending to Declan's wound. She had that uneasy feeling again. Something felt wrong. She shivered involuntarily.

"You cold?" Stephen asked.

"A little, I don't know why. It's really hot today." She started drawing lines in the sand with the twig. Her heart was beating a little faster than normal. She took a deep breath to try to steady it.

"Grace?"

She turned to look at him. His face was so close now. "Yeah?" she barely managed.

He reached up and gently caressed her cheek. He kissed her then, a tender kiss. He tasted of beer and salt. She kissed him back, gently pressing the palm of her hand against his bare chest and realised his heart was beating as fast as her own.

20

There was no sign of Declan.

It was time to leave the island if they wanted to avoid the currents changing, but Declan hadn't returned and they could not leave without him. They had been on the island for over four hours. They had swum and drunk and eaten and swum some more, and now it was time to pack up and head back to the mainland. Where the hell was Declan?

Nobody had really missed him. For the most part, it had been Sarah and Harry, Grace and Stephen, and each couple had been absorbed in each other. Declan had resurfaced about an hour ago and he sheepishly apologised to Stephen for his earlier behaviour. Stephen had shaken his hand, laughed it off and said not to worry, it was just the sun, the hangover and a few too many, happens to us all. Declan had stared at him for a moment, his expression unreadable. He had then nodded in agreement and asked Harry if there was any food left. Stephen ignored his rudeness. After Declan had eaten, he took off for a walk and they hadn't seen him since then.

Stephen scanned the beach, but there was still no sight of him. Where the hell was he? They guessed he had fallen asleep somewhere on the island and would eventually make his way back but time was rolling on. "Harry, do you want to try ringing Declan again? It's really time we started heading back."

"I've tried several times. Maybe he has no signal. I'm going to have to go search for him." He glanced up the beach.

"I hope he gets back soon," Sarah said. "Grace and I have to catch a bus."

Harry turned towards Sarah, a question in his eyes. "When?"

Sarah hesitated. "Tonight," she replied. "Didn't I tell you? Tomorrow's bus is leaving too late."

Harry glanced away, but not before Stephen caught the look on his face. He wasn't sure if Harry was disappointed or annoyed. One thing was clear, judging by Harry's reaction he didn't know the girls would be leaving tonight. Neither did Stephen for that matter. He turned to Grace, stretched out on her towel fast asleep, her tanned legs crossed at the ankle.

"What about the party tonight? I thought you were staying?" Harry's tone sounded hard. What the hell was wrong with him? Was he disappointed? Harry usually didn't give a shit about the girls he dated. Did he actually like Sarah?

"I just have to get back, OK? By noon tomorrow," Sarah replied, indignant.

"It's a bank holiday tomorrow. For work, is it?" Harry challenged her. "Thought you said that you're a student? Some part-time job, is it?"

She nodded and looked away quickly. Whatever it was that Sarah had to get back for, it definitely was not work, Stephen was pretty sure of that.

"And your bus is what time?" Harry continued his questioning. His mood had shifted. He appeared tense, edgy.

Stephen thought that Sarah looked disappointed herself now, let down in some way.

"*Em*, seven, I think." Sarah narrowed her eyes. "Maybe seven thirty? Grace knows the time. Grace!"

Grace stirred on the sand – she sat up, rubbing her eyes. She seemed momentarily startled, as if she didn't know where she was. "What?"

"It's getting late, we need to head back," Sarah said abruptly. "The tide should be changing soon, and we have to catch that bus, but Declan is still up the beach, somewhere."

"He still hasn't come back? But he's been gone for a while, right?" Grace shielded her eyes as she scanned the empty beach.

"I'll go look for him." Harry started up the beach.

"Wait. I'll come with you," Stephen offered.

Harry looked back and shook his head. "Help the girls clean up the picnic area and be ready to go!" he said over his shoulder, then increased his pace.

He seemed angry, and something else. Nervous? What was up with him, Stephen wondered. He had been in great form all afternoon. Had Sarah annoyed him when she announced that she had to head home tonight? Maybe he *did* actually like her.

Sarah started loading their picnic things into a bag. She didn't look happy either.

Stephen turned to Grace. "Were you planning on heading back this evening?"

Grace nodded.

"Why didn't you say? Earlier? I thought that we could spend some time together, tonight."

Grace smiled slowly. "Well, I wasn't thinking that far ahead, to be fair."

Stephen smiled back. "I was."

"*Hey, you guys, can you give me a hand over here?*" Sarah called out from the boat. "*Someone has vomited all over the toilet!*"

Stephen turned to Grace. "Must have been Declan." He looked back towards the boat. "I don't know if I can handle Declan's vomit. His verbal is enough."

Grace laughed. "It's OK. I work in a café. Our customers vomit all the time."

"Remind me never to visit your café." Stephen grimaced.

She laughed. "It's not the food. Just, people they vomit sometimes. Especially kids. And babies, babies are the worst. They spew up all the time."

Stephen didn't reply. He wrapped one of the towels around his hand and carried the barbeque tray to the water's edge.

"You OK?" Grace called after him.

"Sure." He nodded towards the remains of the BBQ. "I'll clear up the rest of this stuff and then I'll help you on the boat, alright?"

"Afraid of a bit of vomit?" she teased as she walked towards the boat.

Stephen watched her go, her long dark hair grainy from the seawater. Andy had been convinced that Luke had choked on his own vomit. There had been no evidence in the cot, but she wouldn't let it go. She wanted, no, *needed* a reason for his death so badly, a logical, genuine reason. But in the end, there had been none. The child had simply stopped breathing. Andy kept obsessing about it when she would revisit what happened that day, over and over, like a broken record, she always talked about the possibility that Luke had choked on his own vomit. Luke had just started solids and she was worried she hadn't blended his lunch properly. It was the same narrative, her trauma dump on repeat. *"He can't have just died, he can't have, I did something wrong, it is my fault, it's my fucking fault, Stephen!"* As humans, we try to find reasons for the unexplainable but, sometimes, bad things just happen.

He glanced up the beach. He could clearly see Harry, just standing there, his hand on his forehead shielding his eyes from the sun. Stephen watched him for a moment. What was he looking at?

He sighed as he gathered up the towels and blankets and headed towards the boat. The wind had picked up and he held up the bundle to protect his face from the sand sweep. He hoped that Harry would find Declan soon, like in the next twenty or thirty minutes. He took another quick look over his shoulder. That's when he noticed a small boat edging towards the island.

21

Grace tossed the bucket of dirty water over the side of the boat and refilled it from the hose. She rinsed and squeezed the mop and ran down the steps to the toilet to wash up the last of Declan's vomit. His spew had travelled everywhere, all over the walls of the small restroom, the floor and the lavatory seat. Grace was pissed off – like, anyone could get sick, that wasn't what annoyed her – but to leave it there for someone else to clean up? It was just disgusting.

"Here, use this, should get rid of the smell." Sarah leaned against the door, a bottle of air freshener in her hand.

"You think?" Grace raised an eyebrow. "Unfortunately, this smell isn't going anywhere. I have bleached the loo five times and it still stinks down here. What an idiot!"

"Ah come on, Grace! The lad had a few too many and got sick. Don't tell me you haven't thrown up after a few drinks? In fact, I remember holding your hair back on more than one occasion while you leaned over a toilet bowl."

"Alright, Sarah, point made. But I remember aiming towards the toilet bowl, not all over the bloody walls. It's as if he did it on purpose and then just walked away. Classy guy."

Sarah shrugged. "The boat moves a lot in the water, he probably lost his balance."

"And you think he lost his eyesight too? Why didn't he just clean it up?"

"I don't know, Grace. Look, it's spotless now. Let's just forget about it."

Grace shook her head, took the air freshener from Sarah, and held her nose while she twisted the nozzle and sprayed it into the air. She hoped the boys were on their way back, because she really needed a shower before catching the bus. Sarah started tidying up around the cabin. Grace wondered what had got into her friend. Was she actually trying to justify that idiot's behaviour? Grace recapped the spray and tore a piece of cardboard from the wine box to stick under the toilet door to enable the air to circulate. She leaned against the doorframe, observing her friend.

After a short while, Sarah stopped what she was doing. "What?"

Grace folded her arms. "Why are you being like this?"

"Like what?" Sarah frowned.

"Just, disagreeing with me?"

"What do you mean, Grace?" She shook her head. "I'm not disagreeing with you."

"Yes, you are. You did it earlier and you are doing it again now."

"Don't be silly. I'm just saying you should stop being so judgemental and cut the guy some slack!" Sarah snapped. "He's away for the weekend with his friends and he got a bit drunk – what is the big deal, Grace?"

Grace was taken aback – Sarah had never spoken to her like this before. "What's got into you?"

Sarah continued to wipe around the surfaces, avoiding making eye contact. "Nothing. You are just …" She faltered.

"I am just what?" Grace asked.

Sarah looked at her now, eyes narrowed. She seemed to be carefully choosing her words. "You are just on edge. Since we got to the island." She paused. "And at other times too."

Grace was incredulous. "What does that mean?"

Sarah sighed. "Look, I love you, Grace, I really do. But, sometimes you are, I don't know, uptight. I just want you to relax and go with the vibe – maybe Declan is a bit of a dickhead, but so what? Stephen is into you, so focus on him and stop fretting about Declan and this island and everything else you worry about all the fucking time!" She went back to cleaning the countertops.

Grace stared at her friend, angry and hurt, and wondering where in the hell this outburst had come from? Sarah was the one on edge. Ever since she had woken up on the beach, Sarah was jittery and abrasive. Grace wondered if something had gone down between herself and Harry, but the two had seemed very happy together earlier in the day. Better not say anything, she thought, there was no point in starting an argument. Sarah was clearly in a mood about something and, whatever it was, she would tell her in her own time. "OK, fine," she muttered.

Grace climbed up onto the deck once more and emptied the water over the side of the boat. Again, she rinsed it out with the hose. She could see Stephen cleaning up the barbeque equipment, methodical as he moved, scraping the charcoal onto the sand and putting the utensils into Harry's gear bag. Every now and then, he would glance up the beach in the direction Harry and Declan had gone. She followed his gaze. There was still no sign of them but she could see a small boat, close to the edge of the island. The sea appeared calm right now, but she knew the riptides were unpredictable. They had been warned. And there was also a bus to catch. The journey home was going to drag if Sarah maintained this sour attitude. She decided she would sleep during the trip – she was still feeling the effects of her hangover from the night before.

She wasn't sure what time it was, but they had been on the island for over four hours now so it must be around five or maybe closer to six. Perhaps Sarah was right and she should chill out a bit. She decided to have a drink while she waited for the others to come back. The last alcohol she had was on the way over to the island with Stephen, having drunk water while they were on the beach all afternoon. Now that they were preparing to head back to the mainland she might as well relax. She was anxious to get back to Castle Cove, but once the guys returned they would be on their way. Maybe Sarah had calmed down and might join her for a drink.

She descended the steps to the cabin. She washed and dried her hands, glancing around for her friend. The cabin was empty. Sarah must have gone back up on deck. But how had she missed her? Surely she would have noticed her. She peered into the cooler box hoping to find white wine, but there was only beer. She didn't fancy beer – the thought made her stomach turn. Peering around the cabin, she spotted some red wine in a cardboard box. She didn't like red wine much, but the choices were slim so she opened the bottle, found a glass and poured a small amount. She took a sip and found it wasn't half-bad. Filling her glass, she climbed the steps towards the deck. She looked around the beach – there was no sign of Stephen anywhere. The barbeque area had been cleared away, there was no evidence of their picnic from earlier. Stephen had done a good job.

Grace sipped her wine, watching the waves roll over each other. When they were kids, her sister Erin had always wanted to go to the beach. They both had, but Erin talked about it the most. Every summer, the sound of the other children's voices in the neighbourhood quietened and they were well aware that the other families had travelled to the coast. They would beg their mother to take them, but she always refused.

Erin had been quite the academic in school, much smarter than Grace. She had determination and dedication, scoring the highest in her final year exams and she had even been offered the opportunity to further her studies at a prestigious university in England – a scholarship, with all expenses covered. Erin had always dreamed of studying marine biology. With the scholarship, her college fees would be paid for, including her accommodation and travel. She would want for nothing. But, Erin would not leave Grace alone with their mother. She knew Grace had a harder time with their mam and so she waited, deferring her course. She got herself a job in the big supermarket in town and waited for Grace to do her final exams two years later. Their mother didn't seem to care either way. By the time Grace finished school and prepared to go to college, their mother had had her first stroke.

Erin never left. She continued to live in the same house she had grown up in, working part-time in the same job since she had left school. When Grace left for college, Erin looked after Rosie Doran until something happened to change her mind. She arranged for their mother to go into a care home and she never told Grace why she had made such a decision right out of the blue. She never once mentioned college to Grace again, her missed opportunity. Instead, she showed her disappointment in other ways, like earlier when she accused Grace of provoking their mam at the care home.

Grace carefully stepped down from the boat onto the jetty. There was still no sign of Stephen. Nor could she see Sarah for that matter. What the hell? Where was everyone? A cold chill spread up the back of her spine as she sipped her drink. Could it be possible that she was alone on this island? And, if that was the case, how had it happened? She told herself she was being ridiculous. She had cruised over with four other people, on a boat, and that boat was right in front of her. So, unless everyone had swum back to the World's End, they were still here, on the island.

She ambled back along the jetty and climbed up the ladder onto the boat. She tried to get a better view of the island's coastline. The beach wrapped around the island so that she couldn't see any further from where she was and there was no sign of the small boat from earlier. She looked in the other direction, noticing nothing but a mound of great big rocks. The hire boat man had advised that the rocks were uneven and too dangerous to climb so the guys couldn't have taken that path.

Grace sensed, rather than heard, that there was someone behind her. She slowly turned around. She relaxed when she saw who it was.

"Jesus! You scared the crap out of me!" She laughed in relief. "Where have you been?"

"Sorry, I didn't mean to frighten you. God, it's so warm today! I need a glass of water. Do you want a glass?"

They descended the steps to the cabin.

22

Grace observed the plane gliding through the sky. The vessel appeared to float as it moved effortlessly through puffs of white clouds in acres of blue. She wondered about the people on board, who they were and where they were going. Whoever they were, she was sure they couldn't see her on the beach below. She could not feel her feet anymore. She must have blacked out, but she had no clue for how long. She felt a sharp pain as she tried to lift her head and she closed her eyes tight, gritting her teeth to silence the scream.

What had happened? She had been on a boat, she knew that much, and she had been drinking red wine. Grace didn't like red wine, but she knew that is what she'd been drinking. And there had been a lot of laughter. One of the men had been telling a story, she couldn't remember the details, but the others had roared with laughter. There had been food. A barbeque? She remembered falling asleep on the sand, and then she was back on the boat. And there was a guy, wasn't there? He had been watching her intently. He had made her feel nervous. Had he moved a little closer to her, whispered something in her ear? Or had he touched her neck? She had pushed him away, maybe a little too harshly. But she hadn't meant to be harsh. She had walked away from him. An image came into her mind and then it was gone. But she felt sure that someone had been watching her.

She was surrounded by sea, everywhere she looked. How the hell was she going to survive this? She tasted the bile in the back of her throat and she inhaled as much air into her lungs as she possibly could to alleviate the sour taste. She was going to die out here, she was sure of it. And nobody would know where she was or what had happened to her.

Tiredness took hold and she closed her eyes. Just for a few minutes, she told herself. She remembered reading somewhere that if you are overtired, you should just close your eyes for a short while and the rest revitalised you. It gives your energy levels a boost, she had read. She promised herself that's all it would be.

She found herself drifting. *Drifting.*

Her eyelids grew heavy.

An image of the people on the boat danced in front of her, like actors in a play.

PART TWO

One Year Later

23

"Ah, for the love of Jesus? What is wrong with some people?" Lana turned over her shoe to find that the heel was smeared with dog crap. It was freshly made too and the pungent odour was already rising up to meet her. *Damn*. She couldn't arrive at a new client's house smelling of dog shit. She noticed a grassy verge running along the side of the footpath and she rubbed the sole of her shoe over and back to clean it off. Her tailored white trousers had escaped at least. She smoothed her short hair behind her ears. She had recently got it cut and changed its colour from blonde to brunette, something she was still getting used to when she passed a mirror. But she had grown to like the new look, though her mother was horrified. It made her feel less obvious, and Lana was all about blending in right now.

Lana was late. She had decided to walk from her office to the client's house instead of taking her car. Google Maps told her it would take twenty minutes on foot and she guessed walking would be faster than juggling Limerick city's one-way traffic system. Besides, her new assistant, Ella, was driving her nuts with her constant chatter – she needed to clear her head. But the indicated time was incorrect and now she was running behind. What was wrong with her that she couldn't be on time for her clients? It wasn't something that she purposely set out to do. She was efficient in all facets of her professional life but, somehow, she struggled to manage her time.

Lana hastened her pace as she crossed the street at the lights and continued until Google Maps told her to turn right at the next junction, announcing that she was just five minutes away. She checked the street sign fixed onto the wall, just in case she was wrong about the route. Lana didn't have the best sense of direction and she relied heavily on the app to find the homes or work places of new clients. She passed a small shop as she turned the corner and contemplated buying some tobacco. She hadn't smoked in a couple of weeks, but today was Friday and she was meeting some friends for drinks later and she knew she would want a cigarette at some point during the evening. She didn't really want to go out, but her mother had warned her that she worked too hard and she insisted her only daughter form some semblance of a social life. Lana knew she was right and she would do just about anything to please her mother, and so she was *trying*. But she might need tobacco to get through it. The group she was meeting weren't really friends as such, more like ex-colleagues from her time working in the Department of Public Prosecution. She didn't know anybody, besides Ella, and there was no way she was going out socially with the girl. Checking her watch, she decided against the tobacco – she was already a few minutes past her pre-arranged meeting time.

The streets grew quieter as she walked through the residential part of town. It was mid-morning in May and most children were in school at this time of the day. A woman wheeled a buggy on the other side of the road as she chatted on her phone but, other than that, the area was pretty much deserted.

Lana's laptop carrier hung heavy over her shoulder and she shoved her hands into the pockets of her jacket to keep it in place. She took a right and the Google Maps lady informed her that she had arrived at her destination. A row of two-storey redbrick terraced houses lined the narrow cul-de-sac on both sides. She looked at the address she had typed into her phone: the house number was twenty-three. She slowed her pace. The young woman on the phone had said her house had a red door, and that the number was missing. Glancing up and down the quiet road, Lana could only see one red door – that had to be the house.

Lana knocked and took a step back while she waited, taking in the small Georgian-style buildings. The area had been redeveloped in recent years and many of the old houses had been demolished and replaced with apartments and offices. Only a few of the old buildings remained, like the ones on this road and the design looked out of place in the new modern-built neighbourhood.

She heard footsteps and the door opened wide, revealing a young woman of slim build, maybe in her early thirties. She had bright red hair that fell in ringlets down to her waist, the longest hair Lana had ever seen on a woman. Her pale complexion was free of make-up and her green eyes shone bright. The rims around her eyes were faded pink – she looked like she had been crying. She wore a yellow apron over a long blue floral-patterned dress. Pulling a used tissue from the front pocket of her apron, she patted at her nose.

"You're late," she said, her expression blank. Lana couldn't tell if the woman was annoyed or simply stating a fact.

"I'm so sorry, traffic wasn't going my way. Lana Bowen." Lana extended her hand.

The woman looked out at the scatter of parked cars on the road.

In a small neighbourhood like this, she probably knew the owner of every vehicle and most likely knew that Lana was lying. If she did, she kept it to herself.

"I'm Erin. I won't shake your hand, I have allergies. In the spring they kick off no matter how many antihistamines I take." She smiled and took a step back. "Don't worry, I'm not contagious. Come on in, we are out on the terrace." She hesitated. "I must warn you, today's not a good day for her – she's in a lot of pain. Well, she has pain every day, but today she's quite vulnerable with it."

Lana stepped over the threshold and Erin gently closed the front door behind her. The narrow hallway was papered in a dark-green design – big leaves swirling around each other making the space appear even smaller. The paper was peeling at the edges. A small table stood inside the front door at the bottom of a staircase. There was an old red telephone and a small diary positioned neatly beside the phone. Lana followed Erin down the hall, passing a closed door on the left. The hallway led to a jaded, sparsely furnished kitchen. A large clock ticked loudly on the wall. A brown door with a glass panel opened out onto a small garden area. From the kitchen, Lana could see a wheelchair, and the back of a head with black shiny hair, leaning to one side.

Erin washed her hands and wiped them on the front of her apron. "Would you like some tea? I was just about to make a pot?"

"Yes, tea would be nice. No milk or sugar, thanks."

"Sure, won't take a minute."

There was an old cream AGA range, with brass tubes sticking into the black tiled wall behind. The AGA looked huge in the tiny kitchen. Erin lifted one of the stove coverings and shoved the big silver kettle onto the stone hob where it began to spit and whistled almost immediately.

Lana noticed a tray with three patterned cups, saucers and a sugar bowl pre-set on the kitchen table. She watched as Erin poured milk into a small jug of the same pattern. She cut thick slices of currant cake – Lana was sure it was homemade – and placed the portions onto a plate, again of the same pattern. Lana felt like she had stepped back in time to visit her grandmother.

"Thank you for coming." Erin lifted the tray, but didn't move.

"Can I help you with that?" Lana offered

"No, no, I can manage." She hesitated. "It's just that, you need to be prepared. You are not the first investigator to call here. The last one got a shock. It was my own fault. I hadn't warned him, you know, mentioned her appearance and that. I am so used to looking at ... just, don't be too alarmed, OK?" Erin said gently. "And try not to stare."

Lana nodded her understanding.

Again, Erin didn't move.

"Was there something else?"

"*Em*, about money ... my mother passed away recently and she left me some funds in her will ..."

Lana held up her hand. "Let's talk about money later, yeah?"

Erin gave a small smile. "Thank you." She lifted the tray and turned towards the back terrace. "Follow me."

Lana felt her heart hammering in her chest. She had to check herself to calm down. She had dealt with all sorts of personalities and situations in her line of work, after all. She took a breath and forced herself to relax and focus on the reason for her visit.

She followed Erin out onto the back terrace. Erin carefully laid the tray on a small glass table and leaned over to whisper into the young woman's ear. Lana watched as she gently smoothed her hair back from her face, revealing a jagged scar. The wound ran the length of the girl's face, from the side of her eye to the base of her chin. The cheek appeared sucked in, right at its centre, it was as if something had cut deep into the flesh and inserted a zip in its place. She turned her head towards Lana. Her mouth sloped a little. The other side of her face featured a high cheekbone, an oval hazel eye and creamy skin. It was like two halves of two different faces. Lana could tell this young woman had been beautiful once and her face would have been perfectly symmetrical. Her left leg was held together with a brace from hip to ankle, stretched out in front of her, as it lay rigid on a chair. A tartan blanket was draped over her lap. Her right leg appeared to be missing. Lana swallowed and tried not to look at the girl's scar.

"Lana, this is my sister Grace," Erin said, her tone measured.

Lana sensed the young woman was watching her closely.

Lana reached out a hand to touch Grace's arm. The girl flinched. The sound came from nowhere. Lana peered around the small garden to see if there was some creature hiding in the undergrowth only to realise it was coming from the girl sitting in front of her. It sounded animalistic as she whimpered in pain, or fear, Lana couldn't tell.

Erin tried to calm her with soothing words as she rubbed her silky hair. "There now, Gracie, it's OK, this lady is here to help you. Come on, sweetheart, we talked about this – she is not going to hurt you, I promise."

Grace stared into her sister's eyes, silently pleading with her for something. Then she spoke, slowly, as Erin continued to gently stroke her face. "I can't, Erin, don't make me ..."

"You can, Grace, you can do this, you are strong. I am here with you. I am not going to leave you, OK?"

The girl's whimpering faded and Lana looked on as Erin wiped a little drool from her mouth. Erin poured tea into a cup, adding a drop of milk and carefully placed it in Grace's hand.

She offered a cup to Lana which she gratefully accepted, thankful for something to wash down the dryness in her mouth. They all sipped in silence as Erin held her sister's hand. Every now and then, she reached up to wipe her sister's mouth when some liquid escaped.

Right, Lana, take control of the situation, do your job. Lana placed the cup on the glass table, opened her bag, and pulled out her laptop. She fired up the screen and selected a new blank file document. Both sisters watched her every move.

Lana smiled at Grace. "Are you ready, Grace?"

Grace looked towards her sister for reassurance. Erin nodded encouragingly. Grace swallowed and slowly placed her cup on the table.

"Tell me what happened, right from the beginning, OK? From the minute the bus pulled into the village of Castle Cove. Do not leave anything out, however small. Every detail counts."

24

Stephen hauled his golf clubs from the boot of his car and slipped into his spikes. Grabbing a windbreaker jacket from his gear bag, he pulled it down over his shoulders and zipped up the fine material. He quickly scanned the carpark. There was no sign of Harry's flashy car. Good, he thought – he wanted to grab a quick drink in the clubhouse before they went out on the golf course. They would probably spend a couple of hours on the green and he didn't think he could wait that long. He was thirsty *and* he was nervous.

He dragged his clubs behind him as he strolled across the carpark towards the entrance. It was quiet inside the clubhouse, just one guy sat at the bar nursing a pint and nibbling on a bowl of crisps as he watched a football game on one of the big screens. Stephen smiled as he glanced around the bar, a few memories flooding back. He had been inside the clubhouse a few times with Harry over the years and the décor had never changed – dark mahogany wooden floors, to hide the dirt, faded patterned fabric on stools, to hide … God knows what. There were dozens of framed photographs on the walls displaying past and present club members proudly exhibiting their trophies or enjoying nights out with their fellow golfers, their hairstyles changing as the years advanced. The members were not interested in aesthetics, and so the interior remained the same.

A barman Stephen didn't recognise was stacking shelves as he approached. "How can I help you, mate?" he called over his shoulder.

"Pint of lager, please, whatever you have on draft?"

"Sure thing." The barman poured and placed the drink on a beermat on the counter in one fluid movement.

Stephen offered his debit card. He idly checked his email on his phone while the barman tapped the card and handed him a receipt. Stephen picked up his pint and drank half of the cold beer as he opened his inbox – there was nothing new. Relieved, he tucked his phone into his back pocket, and, taking his pint outside, sat at one of the wooden tables.

He thought about Harry's earlier text suggesting they meet for a game of golf. Followed by another message saying: **We need to talk.** Apart from the short text message Harry had sent him a few months back, Stephen had not seen, nor heard, from his friend in almost a year. He wondered what was so important now that they couldn't talk over the phone and, somehow, the thought unnerved him.

A small group of Americans passed him as they headed towards the bar dressed in bright clothing, reds and yellows and greens, displaying big, white toothy grins. They were loud as they jostled and joked with each other about their playing techniques, and whether they might get an espresso martini in the clubhouse. They'd be lucky. Their accents were garish and vulgar, interrupting his thoughts.

He checked his watch. Harry was ten minutes late. If they didn't start soon, they wouldn't get to finish their game. The hire out time just about covered the full course and regardless of when they started, they would still have to finish on schedule. The thought didn't particularly bother Stephen – he had never cared much for golf. He had only bought his set of clubs so he could use them if an opportunity arose to entertain clients. Many strong working relationships were formed on the golf course. Deals were made. The odd time, Stephen would play with Harry. Harry had been a member in this club for years and he was pretty good. Unlike Stephen, he took the game seriously.

Stephen looked up as he heard a car pull into the carpark. Harry had arrived. A moment later, he waved as he took his clubs from the boot of his car. Stephen finished his pint and met Harry at the starting point. Harry appeared tired, dark circles shaping the space under his eyes.

"Hey, Stephen, long time no see?" His tone was formal. "How have you been?"

"Yeah, it's been a while."

Harry offered a small smile that didn't quite meet his eyes. He appeared a little awkward as he avoided looking directly at Stephen. Selecting one of the clubs from his carrier, he started walking towards the putting area. He appeared anxious as his eyes darted around the carpark.

Stephen didn't follow. Instead, he called after him. "Harry, what is it? Why did you want to meet like this?"

Harry kept up his pace, ignoring Stephen who now followed him.

On reaching the teeing area, Harry took a golf ball from his pocket and placed it on a peg. Taking a back swing with his putter, he hit the ball, hard. They both watched the golf ball as it moved high up in the air. When it landed and came to a stop, he turned towards Stephen.

"Let's get a little further out, shall we?" He motioned for Stephen to take his position. Stephen placed the ball on a peg and swung back. The ball flew into the air and landed close to Harry's, near the first flagpole.

"Good shot," Harry said, his tone flat, monotone. He pulled his clubs across the putting green and Stephen followed him.

"So, how have you been?" Stephen attempted to make small talk as he caught up.

"Oh, fine, busy with work, you know how it is."

On reaching the position of his golf ball, Harry placed his feet together and bent his knees slightly. Narrowing his eyes, he concentrated hard, judging the distance. He gently tapped the ball and it moved slowly across the smooth grass and into the cup.

"You haven't lost your touch, clearly." Stephen observed. "Been playing much?"

Harry reached down to pick the golf ball out of the hole. "Most weekends. I try to get out when I can."

Stephen nodded, watching him closely. "Who do you play with?"

Harry stared directly at Stephen now, for the first time since he arrived. "Does it matter?"

"Well, it's not me, is it?" Stephen regarded his friend. "I haven't heard from you in a year. Since we got back from …" He looked away. He walked towards his own ball and feet together, knees bent, he took a hit. Too hard. It missed the cup by a couple of inches.

"Hard luck, mate." There was sarcasm in his tone. "You should get it the next time."

Stephen swung around to face Harry. He had enough of this charade. "*What do you want, Harry?* Why did you ask me to come out here? What is so important that you couldn't just send me an email or talk to me over the phone? Why do we suddenly, right out of the blue, after twelve bloody months, *need to talk?*"

Harry glanced around the course. There were a few golfers up ahead on the third putting green, well out of earshot. He turned his attention back to Stephen, a grave look on his face. "The girl, Grace Doran … she's hired a private investigator."

25

Lana tapped her pen against the edge of her desk, while quietly observing the small robin with a grey belly and red neck as it perched in the gap of the redbrick wall opposite her office window. A similar bird had sat in the same spot a few evenings before, remaining perfectly still as it rested at its post, encircled by the sounds of city life. She remembered a story her mother had told her not so long ago, about a bird that flew onto her patio each morning while she sipped her coffee. The little bird would land on the grass, before making its way up the patio steps, where her mam would feed it tiny pieces of her toast and, then, satisfied, the bird would fly off into town for the day, before returning later in the evening. Lana had laughed, dismissing her mother's story – saying that it couldn't possibly be the same bird. But her mother was insistent that it was. *"It is the same bird, Lana. Don't I see it every morning and evening, and birds come back you know, if you treat them well."* Lana wondered now if her mother was right, as she observed the little robin. *So delicate.*

Her thoughts drifted to Grace Doran and the story she had told Lana that afternoon. *"I have a sense of dread in my heart, every morning, every day, Lana."* Sometimes, people got themselves caught up in bad situations, Lana thought, and, it seemed, Grace was one of those people. Not that she had gone looking for trouble – she hadn't. She was a young woman who had taken off to the coast with her best friend for a weekend of fun, and she had paid the ultimate price.

The robin flew away and Lana stood and pulled the blind over her office window, almost knocking the potted plant sitting on the ledge. A plant that had not been there when she had left the building that morning. Her assistant, Ella, must have put it there. Lana sighed. She had hired the young administrator a couple of months back, at her mother's insistence, to alleviate the mounting paperwork. "You cannot do everything on your own, Lana," her mother admonished at the time, and Lana knew she was right, but she had never been one for delegating, she liked to work alone. Five years in the Office of the Director of Public Prosecutions had taught her that. *It was safer.* Her mam had informed her that she knew someone whose daughter had just moved back from the UK – "*Highly efficient,*" she assured Lana. "*You need someone.*" So, Lana had hired the young woman and, though the girl was very sweet and enthusiastic, every day she was finding another reason to dislike her – potted plants were now added to the list. Lana didn't like plants that needed attention, particularly in her office.

She glanced at the stack of files on her desk – she would have to leave them, she decided. Grace's case was at the forefront of her mind now, and everything else would have to wait. She left a note for Ella to go through the pile and call her if she found anything that needed urgent attention. Lana glanced around the pokey office she rented from the family that owned the pharmacy downstairs, with its brown, shabby carpet and walls that could use a lick of paint. The office was quite depressing, she thought. No wonder Ella was buying plants, a vague attempt to brighten the place up.

Lana had worked as a prosecutor for the State until just over a year ago when, out of necessity, she had made the decision to go into private practice. She had rented a tiny workplace in the centre of town, but recently she wondered if she needed the space at all – most of the time she met clients at their homes or venues convenient to their location.

It was late, just after eight. Grabbing her laptop, satchel and jacket, Lana left the office, taking the stairs to the underground carpark. It was empty except for one other car, and, though Lana was used to leaving her office in the evening, the vacant car park, the echo of her shoes on the hard surface, always unnerved her. Throwing a nervous glance over her shoulder, she caught sight of a shadow moving behind one of the pillars. A knot of fear gathered in the pit of her stomach. Before she could stop it, she felt the panic reverberate in her chest, her heartbeat started to race, the palms of her hands became clammy and her legs started to lose their strength. She grabbed at her throat as she stumbled forward and reached for the door of her car, her bag slamming into her side. She ordered herself to breathe, to push the ugly images away. *Clear your mind, and breathe.* A dog barked behind her before running through the carpark, tail pointed as it chased something Lana could not see. Then, it was over, almost as quickly as it had started, her heartbeat slowly returning to normal. She unlocked her car and sat inside, resting her hands on the steering wheel. *Do not cry,* she told herself, *it is over now.* She waited for her breathing to return to normal and, with a shaking hand, she inserted the key in the ignition, silently praying that the old engine turned over without a hitch. She got lucky and, after a little resistance, she was driving through the busy Limerick city streets, heading towards her apartment. *Don't come in, Lana* ... The warning reverberated inside her head. She was furious, and devastated at the same time. She hadn't had a panic attack in a while and she was beginning to think that she would never have one again, that she had turned that corner and moved on from what had happened. But how could she ever move on? A young girl had died because of her incompetence. She switched on the radio to catch the early evening news, an attempt to distract herself from the images spiralling around in her head. But nothing could shake the feeling that she had somehow failed in her recovery, the months of therapy, the breathing techniques. Sudden onset panic attacks were crippling and she had no control over their arrival. Her head felt heavy as she manoeuvred her way through traffic.

Twenty minutes later, Lana was standing in her kitchen piercing the cover of the packaging of her frozen lasagne dinner. She placed the container in the microwave and set the timer. In six minutes, she would eat. She took a bottle of white wine from the fridge and poured herself a large glass. Taking a sip, she sat at the small kitchen table and waited for her dinner to heat up. She positioned the glass in front of her and placed both her hands on the table, still slightly shaken from the event in the carpark.

She had rain-checked on her girl's night out – she had too much to do. But, if she was being completely honest with herself, she hadn't wanted to go in the first place. Now, after her meeting with Grace and Erin Doran, she really wasn't feeling like it anymore.

She opened up her laptop and typed in her password, quickly finding the document she had filed under the name Grace Doran. She clicked on the file and the notes she had made during her morning's meeting appeared on the screen. She reached into her satchel for a notepad and pen. She liked to take notes from her notes, write everything down and then write it down again. She had picked up the habit in law school when she was studying for her exams. It had served her well then, and so she had kept it up in her professional life.

What had happened to Grace had been shocking. What should have been a normal, fun weekend for a young girl with her friend, had turned into her worst nightmare. Grace Doran was lucky to be alive, though Lana suspected right now the girl might prefer not to be. There was a strong bond between the two sisters. They were all alone in the world it seemed – their mother having passed away a few months earlier in the hospital after suffering a second stroke. There was no mention of a father. Erin was clearly the carer today, but Lana suspected the role might have been going on long before the accident. Grace was heavily dependent on her sister but, judging from the way she looked up to her, they had been playing these parts all their lives. She wondered why.

She began to read through the notes she had taken when she had returned to her office after her meeting with Grace and Erin. She had her pen in hand ready to record moments of importance.

Grace, along with her best friend Sarah, travelled to the small coastal fishing village of Castle Cove one year ago on the Saturday of the May bank holiday weekend. They travelled by bus – it was a two-and-a-half-hour journey from Limerick city. They stayed in a house by the sea, The World's End, beyond the harbour, just up from the village. The house had been offered to Harry Reddan, whom Sarah had been dating for over a month. Harry told Sarah that one of his clients owned the house and had offered it to him for the weekend. On arrival, Grace went for a swim in the sea, while Sarah and Harry went back to the house. She joined them later for a barbeque and some drinks. There were two other men there, Declan and Stephen, both friends of Harry. She did not know their surnames. The following day, the boys hired a boat and they all sailed out to a small island, nearby. Nobody lived on the island and there were no other boats out there on that day. One of the guys, Declan, had a bit too much to drink and went into the cabin of the small boat to sleep it off. She remembered there had been an argument between Stephen and Declan, but she didn't know what it was about. Grace and the others swam and ate for the afternoon. Sarah's new boyfriend had brought a portable barbeque. Declan joined them for food and went for a walk up the beach on his own. When it was time to head back to the mainland, Declan hadn't returned and so Harry went to look for him. Grace, Sarah and Stephen stayed behind to clean up the beach. Someone had vomited in the small toilet downstairs inside the cabin and she had cleaned up the mess. She had thought Sarah and Stephen were still up on deck or on the beach clearing up the barbeque area, but when she went back up to throw the bucket of dirty water over the side of the boat, there was no sign of them. There was no sign of anyone. She remembered pouring herself a glass of wine, she thought red. And that was the last clear memory she had. She had a vague recollection of waking while she was on the beach, but she couldn't be sure. A local fisherman had found her on the beach, and she had no recollection of that or how she got up there.

Lana ran her fingers through her short brown hair and leaned back into her chair. *What had happened to Grace Doran?* The microwave pinged that her dinner was ready.

She pushed her notes to the side, took a sip of her wine and retrieved the hot container with a tea towel. Carefully, she peeled back the plastic cover and, grabbing a fork, she dug in, not bothering to take it out of its microwavable container. It actually didn't taste half-bad, she thought, as she realised she hadn't eaten since breakfast. Erin's fresh currant cake had lost its appeal when Grace had recounted her story.

She scanned through her notes again while she ate. Nothing stood out on the first night – it was just a group of friends, or maybe acquaintances was a better word, enjoying some food and drinks in each other's company. The following day, however, seemed to raise a few more questions.

Who were the other men, Harry's friends. Stephen and Declan? She would need to interview both of them, along with Sarah and Harry. Erin had said the man who had found Grace was a local fisherman by the name of Lukasz but, other than the fact that he had found Grace near dead on the beach of the small island while out fishing the following morning, she didn't know anything else about the man.

As she ate, Lana wondered where everyone had gone that day. Grace had mentioned that Declan had slept in the cabin and then left for a walk on his own after their barbeque. She said they had been on the island for over four hours, that there was nothing there except for sand and rocks and she had no idea where Declan had gone, because there didn't appear to be much of an area to explore. She assumed he had fallen asleep somewhere up the beach. He'd had a few drinks on the boat on the way over, they all had, but Declan had started drinking before they had left the mainland – he was well ahead of everyone else.

Lana scrolled down through the rest of the document.

Grace had been in hospital for eight months, in a coma for the first

*three. She had damaged her right leg so badly that it was held together
with screws, pins and a brace. Doctors were unable to save her left leg.
Grace had emerged from her coma without it. The surgeon who had
amputated her leg had no idea how she had sustained her injuries.
Multiple cuts from something extremely sharp, he had told Erin. She
had also broken her cheekbone, and the doctors said that this might
have happened if she hit a hard surface, like wood or a stone. There
was a rocky area to one side of the strand and the Gardaí had
suggested that the right side of her face took the full impact when the
waves had tossed her about.*

Lana had asked whether Grace had heard from any of the people
on the boat and she had shaken her head and looked away. Erin had
intervened. "She doesn't want to see anyone. Sarah, her friend who was
there that day, dropped into the hospital a few times not long after the
accident. She would come quite often for those first couple of months
when she could get away – she had a small child, and she was attending
college as a full-time student. When Grace eventually came out of
the coma, she refused to see Sarah. She didn't want to see anyone.

Lana had also questioned what Sarah thought had happened.
And Erin's answer didn't make sense.

"When I met Sarah in the hospital, she told me that she had
been cleaning up the beach after the barbeque and the other boys
had come back. They all got on the boat and everyone thought that
Grace was having a nap in the cabin. When they arrived back to
the pier, that's when they realised she wasn't on the boat. They had
told the hire-boat operator but it was getting dark at this point and
the operator said that Grace would be alright on the beach and he
would send a boat out for her first thing in the morning. He had
said it happened a lot. People fell asleep on the island and missed

their trip back. It was a short distance, it wasn't a big deal. However, the currents could be dangerous in the evenings and it would be necessary to wait until morning."

Lana found this hard to believe. Firstly, how was it possible that nobody missed Grace on the boat? It wasn't like there was a lot of them out there that day. Five people in total. Surely someone would have missed Grace. And Sarah had been her best friend. Why hadn't she been looking out for her? *Why hadn't she checked the cabin?*

Erin had read her mind. "Sarah had been seeing this guy Harry. Apparently, she was really into him and she hadn't noticed that Grace was not on board. She felt awful about it."

Erin's mouth had turned down when she had related this last fragment of information. Lana suspected Erin didn't like Sarah very much.

Lana checked the Garda report. Harry and Declan had told the exact same story as Sarah. There hadn't been a statement from Stephen. Why had Stephen not given a statement? She read further down the report but there was definitely nothing from Stephen. The Gardaí had made their enquiries and concluded Grace had simply fallen off the boat. They had interviewed all of the parties involved and had decided there was nothing sinister at play. Boat hire was popular in the small fishing village and, sometimes, when alcohol was involved, there was trouble. Mistakes were made. They had concluded that Grace's horrible injuries were the result of an accident. There was no mention of the Gardaí having checked the safety of the boat hired by the group. Lana studied the signature at the end of the report. Garda Donal Mulcahy. She made a note to contact him and ask why there was no statement from Stephen, and why there were no details regarding the safety of the boat.

When she was leaving the house, Lana had asked Erin if there was anyone else in the family to help with Grace's care, but Erin had shaken her head and said it was just her, that she had been working in the local supermarket in town, and had given up her job to look after Grace. She said that the doctors were hopeful they could save her right leg, and with surgery they would begin to rebuild her face. This would take time, but for the most part Grace would never be able to move on if she didn't find out what had really happened that day. Her head was stuck on the island, cemented in her injuries. *Someone should be prosecuted.* In the interim, looking after Grace was a full-time job. She had held Grace's hand the whole time Lana was there – the sisters were obviously very close.

Lana shut the laptop and refilled her glass. She unlocked the patio door of her small apartment and stepped out onto the balcony. There was a strong smell of tobacco in the air and she wished she had bought some. She sipped her wine as she peered out onto the street below. Lana lived in a small picturesque village approximately eight kilometres from Limerick city. Her apartment was situated two floors above an Indian takeaway. She could hear a live band tuning up in a popular bar across the road beside the church and, on this Friday evening, the village was a hive of activity, especially with the long weekend approaching. Everybody seemed to be going somewhere, the scent of excitement hung in the air and there was a feeling of expectation. Just like Grace Doran had been a year before, heading off to the coast for the weekend – but only barely making it back.

Lana drank some more of her wine as she recalled Grace's face, the hollow cheekbone, the jagged scar, the drooping mouth. She pictured her right leg rigidly held together by metal rods, her left leg stopping below the knee. The girl's dark hair falling over sallow skin, so different to Erin's – it was difficult to believe they were two sisters. They looked nothing alike. She wondered what the story was with the girl's mother. Erin had said she was in a nursing home for over a year before she died. Grace and Erin were both young women so their mother must have been quite young herself, yet, neither of the sisters seemed particularly sad for their loss. There was no mention of a dad, or any other siblings – *just the two of us*, Erin had said.

Lana drummed her fingers along the railing of the balcony. What to do first? Sarah, Grace's friend, would shed light on events, she was sure, but first she needed to find some things out herself before she questioned the friend. When she was leaving earlier, Erin had given her a piece of paper with Sarah's mobile number. Lana had phoned Sarah, the call going straight to voicemail. Lana had left a message introducing herself as Grace Doran's private investigator, suggesting a meeting the following week.

She would have to interview the men too – Harry, Stephen and Declan. Erin didn't have their contact details but had said that Sarah would have a number for Harry and she could go from there. Of course, what she should be doing right now would be to delegate this work to Ella, her assistant. Her mother's warning echoed in her head. She would fire off a quick email to Ella in the morning and ask the girl to follow up with Garda Donal Mulcahy, and request his statement.

Why had nobody missed Grace on the boat? Especially her best friend Sarah? Something was very off about that.

Right, she thought, make a plan. Firstly, she wanted to talk with

Lukasz, the fisherman who found Grace on the island. In order to do this, she would have to travel to Castle Cove. She decided she would leave in the morning – there was no time like the present.

Finishing her wine, she locked the patio door, rinsed her glass and placed it on the dish rack before preparing for bed. She set the alarm on her phone and noticed there was one message from her mother wishing her a great night. Lana would have to come up with a lie. As she closed her eyes, she remembered what Grace had said as she was leaving the house that morning. *"Everyone is lying, Lana. It wasn't an accident that I ended up in the water that night. I was pushed. Someone pushed me. But I don't know who."*

26

Stephen was digging in his pocket for the key to his apartment when he heard footsteps behind him in the corridor.

"Stephen. Hey, wait up."

It was Mike from across the hall. *Shit*, he thought. He didn't want to talk to Mike, not now. He was still reeling from what Harry had told him about Grace and the private investigator. Just exchange a few pleasantries and get rid of him, he told himself. He held in the sigh and turned towards his neighbour, painting a false smile on his face.

"Mike, how are you?"

"Grand sure, just out for a walk." Mike leaned his shoulder against the doorframe of his apartment. "How about you?"

"Good, good, everything is good." Stephen fiddled with the keys in his hand.

Mike nodded. "Hey, sorry to hear about your cat. Miko, was it?"

"Milo. Well, what can you do?"

"Just wandered off, did he?" Mike asked.

Stephen turned towards his apartment. "Seems so. I don't know how. He was in the apartment the whole time." He shoved his hands in his pockets. "A right mystery."

Mike nodded. "Didn't think he was the type to wander off?"

"Oh, well, you know cats." Stephen shrugged. "Somehow, he got out."

"Still, that weekend I looked after him, he didn't even get up from your bed when I went in to feed him."

Stephen nodded slowly. He was glad Andy was on the other side of the apartment door and out of earshot. Had Mike gone into their bedroom that weekend?

Mike gestured towards his apartment. "Do you want to have a beer and catch up? Haven't seen you in a while, whatever you have been up to?" Mike raised an eyebrow.

Stephen flashed him a look. He sensed that there was something menacing in Mike's tone.

A few months after that weekend in Castle Cove, he had bumped into Mike in the hall, and Mike had invited him in for a drink. A couple of cans in, they had run out, prompting Mike to produce a bottle of whiskey. Andy had been working late at the art gallery and Stephen had thought what the hell, it was a Friday night, he was off the next day and he was just across the hall if Andy arrived home early. He ended up getting completely hammered and, foolishly, he had confided in Mike about where he had been that weekend Mike had looked after Milo. He had explained that he had been going through a bad patch with Andy at the time, and that they had needed some space from each other. He told Mike that Andy had gone to visit her sister and that she'd thought Stephen had spent the weekend in the apartment working on a presentation. He did reassure Mike that since he got back they were getting on really well and there was no point in telling her where he had been. Mike assured Stephen he would never mention it if he bumped into Andy. Stephen wasn't sure whether they had discussed anything else – he couldn't remember. Stephen had stumbled across the hall, let himself into his own apartment, and thought no more of it.

He hadn't bumped into Mike since, until now, and the stupid idiot brought up minding Milo that weekend? Right outside Stephen's apartment? What was he playing at? Stephen didn't want to engage with Mike. He needed to get home.

He shook his head. "Not tonight. I have some work to do. Another time, yeah?"

Mike nodded, slowly. He didn't unlock his apartment.

Stephen shifted uncomfortably. "Look, I have to get in home. Nice seeing you." He turned the key in the lock. He sensed Mike watching him from behind. He looked back. "Is there something else, Mike?"

"No, another time, yeah? Night, Stephen." Mike unlocked the door to his apartment and disappeared inside.

Stephen stared at the closed door, narrowing his eyes – Mike could be very odd sometimes. He pictured the guy standing on the other side of his door, listening to his movements. The thought creeped him out a bit. He wondered how he knew about Milo going missing. After a moment, he let himself into his apartment.

"Stephen?"

He could hear Andy in the small kitchen, preparing dinner. He welcomed the warm familiarity of her voice.

"Hey." He dropped his laptop on the coffee table and approached the counter, kissing his wife on the cheek. He grabbed a beer from the fridge. Taking a sip, he noticed a half-empty glass of water on the countertop. "Want me to pour you some wine?"

She shook her head. "I'm good, thanks."

Sitting on a stool, he watched Andy as she sliced peppers and chillies, her long blonde hair piled high on her head in a messy bun. She wore a pair of faded blue jeans and a white T-shirt with some art design on the front, her feet were bare, and she had a cardigan tied around her waist. She smiled slowly. "What?"

"It's nice, the way you do that," he observed.

She scrunched up her face. "The way I slice vegetables?"

"Yeah." He came up behind her, wrapping his arms around her waist. He buried his face into the curve of her neck. Her skin was warm and smelt of jasmine.

She picked up a tea towel. "Stop, my hands are all messy."

"I love you." He whispered the words into her soft skin and he meant what he said. They had been through a very difficult time, the worst any couple should ever have to deal with, but they had come out the other side and they were happy again. An image of a young girl with dark hair lying on the beach smiling up at him came to mind. He quickly pushed it away. Andy turned towards him.

"What's wrong?" She searched his eyes.

He held her face in his hands, placing a gentle kiss on her mouth. "Can't I tell my wife I love her?"

Her smile widened. "Sure you can." She returned to preparing dinner. "I just need to finish this while everything is cut fresh."

Stephen let go of his wife and rounded the kitchen counter. He straightened a portrait of himself and Andy framed in the alcove. The photo had been taken on their wedding day in a wooded area outside their hotel, a running stream in the background. The setting was stunning, yet neither of them looked particularly happy to be there and Stephen often wondered why they didn't replace it with another image. Clutching his laptop, he sat on a high stool, keyed in his password and scanned through his emails.

"What's for dinner?" he asked.

"Stir fry. Should be ready soon." He watched as she drizzled oil onto a large pan and added seasoning before tossing in the chopped vegetables. No meat. Again. He pushed aside his disappointment – they only ever seemed to eat some form of a vegetable dish. Andy had turned vegetarian in her teens and she was always trying to make him give up meat.

"Hey, have you seen my pearl earrings? The pair you gave me for my birthday. I left them on my bedside locker."

Stephen shook his head, no.

"Doesn't matter. I'm sure they'll turn up. How was your game of golf?"

Stephen shrugged. "Pretty boring."

"I don't know why you go if you don't like it."

Stephen remained impassive. "Harry called. I told you."

Andy used a spatula to toss the vegetables, while simultaneously dripping soya sauce into the pan. "How was he?"

"Oh, you know Harry."

Andy smiled slowly. "Actually, I can't say I do know Harry. He never really had much time for me. I don't think we have ever even had a proper conversation, without you present."

Stephen looked at Andy. "That's not true?"

"Yes, it is. When we would go out, as a couple, he barely spoke to me." She sprinkled black pepper over the vegetables. "It's fine, it never bothered me then and it doesn't bother me now. He's your friend, not mine." She placed the lid on the pan. "You haven't seen him in a while though, right?"

Stephen turned back towards his laptop and opened his emails. "Both been busy at work, I guess."

She came around to where he sat and leaned against the counter, propping her foot on the bar of his stool, resting her leg against his. She played with a loose thread on the sleeve of her cardigan.

"What is it?" he asked.

"I've been thinking …"

"No, no, we are not getting another cat." He turned his attention back to his emails.

She laughed. "No, not a cat, but … Stephen, look at me?" She pulled the thread free and rolled it between her fingers.

"What is it?" A warning bell went off in his head. Andy was doing great, back to her old self, almost, and he didn't think he could bear it if she slipped again. She clearly wanted to talk about something important – he braced himself for what was to come, pushing aside his resentment. Why did he always feel like he was walking on eggshells around her?

She smiled slowly. "I'm ready."

It took him a moment to figure out what she meant. His heart sank. Swallowing hard, he pushed his laptop away and took a breath. "Andy …" he started when she gently pressed her finger against his lips.

"No, hear me out. It's been three years and I am doing really well, and being around Izzy has made me realise how precious life is." She held his hand. "This is not something that has just popped into my head tonight, Stephen. I've been thinking about it for months. And I know neither of us wanted to start again after we lost …" She stopped. She squeezed his hand. "After we lost Luke." She looked at him now, her eyes searching his.

This was the first time she had said their son's name since he died. He swallowed the lump in his throat.

"It wasn't the right time then. But it is now," she said softly. "We should just go for it. I have been through so much pain and suffering, I have grieved enough. We both have. I'm ready, Stephen."

He tried to hide the fear that was crushing his chest. "Are you sure?"

She leaned in and kissed him gently. "I'm sure." She smiled against his lips. He pulled her towards him and held her close. Things had been so good between them the past few months, better than they had been in years. But, a child? They were still fragile after losing their son. Having a baby right now might put stress and strain on their relationship – he wasn't sure either of them was ready. And, there was the other problem.

The moment was interrupted by the sound of the timer on the hob. She pulled back, wiping a tear from her cheek. "I'm such a soppy idiot." She laughed and went to continue preparing dinner.

Stephen gave a false smile and closed his laptop. His concentration was gone.

27

The only light in the room filtered through the faded pink drapes hanging loosely from the curtain pole, the sun trying to peek through the narrow gap at its centre. Grace had been awake all night, waiting for the first sign of daylight. Her eyelids felt heavy now and she longed for sleep – just a couple of hours would do it, to make the day more bearable. But every time she tried, she felt herself free-falling to the bottom of the ocean, without the security of a downline to guide her, and then she would jolt up in the bed, wide awake and terrified, her lungs burning, her heart pounding in her chest. The nightmare was always the same. She was sinking, deeper and deeper, the pool of light above her head disappearing as she descended, the shape of the boat wavering in the distance, an unknown source pushing her further down. And then, she would wake in terror, gasping for air.

In recent months she had been sleeping better, the nightmares had pretty much stopped, along with the hot flushes and the nausea. She might get about four or five hours straight without waking and she felt calmer, more rested. But, last night the terrors came back, and of course she knew why – the visit from the private investigator must have triggered her memory of the night on the boat, transporting her back to the island, a memory of floating in the water, hanging on to something for dear life. If only she could remember what had actually happened to her. Not knowing how long she was in the sea, or how she got there, was what upset her the most. Dissociative amnesia, the doctors called it. She had blocked out what had happened to her, in order to cope. Ironically, it was the not knowing that crippled her the most.

In her mind, she went through what she remembered from that day once again. She had woken with a very bad hangover, and Sarah had come into her room to encourage her to get out of bed. There was some confusion about what time they were going home, Sarah needing to get back to collect her son from his gran's. They had settled on getting the evening bus. Grace often wondered if Sarah got the bus without her. This she didn't know. She remembered swimming in the pool and when she climbed out, he was standing at the edge, watching her. Stephen, the guy she had liked from the night before, and he had made it clear that he liked her too. On the boat out to the island, one of Harry's friends, Declan, had flirted with her, made unwanted advances, and again, Stephen was there right beside her, coming to her rescue. She remembered a fight between Declan and Stephen, though she didn't know what it was about. She had gone for a walk with Stephen – they had found a quiet spot on the beach. They had spent some time there together, alone. She remembered Stephens's hands on her, touching, exploring … she squeezed her eyes shut, blocking out the memory.

There had been a barbeque – Harry had cooked. Afterwards she had fallen asleep in the sun. When she had woken, the others were getting ready to leave, but Declan hadn't returned from his walk. Harry had gone to look for him and Grace had helped Sarah and

Stephen tidy up the beach after their barbeque. Was there another boat, somewhere? Someone had been sick in the toilet and she had offered to clean it up. She remembered climbing the stairs from the cabin to throw the dirty water over the side of the boat and there had been nobody there. She remembered washing her hands and drinking red wine and then ... *someone had come back* ... Grace opened her eyes. Something snagged at her memory. Someone had come back to the boat and they had a drink together, she was sure of it, but who was it? She searched her memory for a face, but there was nothing there. Had they stayed on the boat or sat on the beach? She felt sure it was the boat, but with who? Was it Sarah or one of the guys? But no matter how hard she tried, no matter how far she reached into the far corners of her mind, she just could not remember.

Her memory of her time in the water was cloudy too. Sometimes, she thought that was a good thing. She had some flashbacks, moments of fluidity, of holding onto something, she didn't know what, and being really cold and not being able to feel her legs, that was about it and she was grateful for that particular memory loss.

She knew it was a miracle that she was alive, that somehow she had been washed ashore and found lying on the beach by a local fisherman. Maybe she had managed to get herself out of the sea and crawled along the sand. Erin had said she was lucky the fisherman had been out that morning. She said that no other fishermen were out on the water, because they had been trawling for most of the weekend and had caught plenty for the local restaurants. If he hadn't been out at sea, she might not have been found for a few days, and then who knows what might have happened. Her pulse was already weak when he found her, she was lucky. That is what Erin kept telling her. *She was lucky.*

She sighed in frustration as she watched the light change outside her bedroom window, the only sound she could hear, the clock ticking in the kitchen, even with her bedroom door closed. There was no point in telling the investigator, Lana Bowen, about this new memory if she couldn't remember who it was that she had a drink with. And, it may not have been important anyway, even though Lana had said every detail could mean something, no matter how minor. Again, she tried to search her memory – she had felt awkward with the person, whoever it was, she wasn't comfortable in his or her presence, she was sure of that. Then it can't have been Sarah, right? Although Sarah had been annoyed with her for being cautious about the trip to the island. Or, was it Stephen – a discomfort developing between them following their intimacy? Maybe Declan? He had made it clear that he was into her. Or was it Harry? But she had barely spoken to Harry. Grace shook the conflicting thoughts out of her head – she just couldn't remember.

Sarah would have answers. Sarah was her best friend. *Was.* Grace had loved her, but she couldn't bring herself to forgive her for the choices she had made that weekend. Even though she knew it was probably breaking Sarah's heart, she just couldn't understand why her friend hadn't bothered to make sure that she was OK.

When she had been found on the island and brought back to the mainland by the fisherman, an ambulance had been called and she was taken to the small hospital in the nearest town. The emergency department quickly realised they didn't have the skills or equipment to deal with her injuries and so she had been air lifted to the university hospital in Limerick city where she was immediately taken into surgery.

She hadn't woken up for a long time, three months in total, and when she had eventually come around and seen the extent of her injuries, she had wanted to fall back into unconsciousness. Erin had brought her home after another five months of surgeries and physio. The occupational therapist paid a visit to her old apartment and quickly decided that there was no way she could go back to live there, not on her own. Erin had removed the furniture in the downstairs living room of their family home, and set up a bed with a locker and a small wardrobe. On the day Grace had been released from hospital, Erin had put fresh flowers in a vase on the bedside locker and she had dressed the bed with new bright-coloured linen, in a vain attempt to make the room appear cheerful, but nothing could mask the dark-blue wallpaper and jaded pink curtains. The room looked as depressed as Grace felt. She didn't know what Erin had done with the old furniture that had been in the living room that was now her bedroom, and she didn't care.

She couldn't believe she was back here, in the house she grew up in. A few months after the accident, their mother had died. She had a massive bleed in the brain and collapsed in the care home before ending up in the stroke unit at the same general hospital as Grace. Erin said she never regained consciousness and just slipped away peacefully, probably the most peaceful Rosie Doran had been her entire life. Erin had organised for their mother to have a cremation, and she related that the service had been short, with only herself and Peggy from the care home in attendance. A short service for a short life. And now, it was just the two of them, Erin and Grace. Their mother's secrets, whatever they were, had been laid to rest with her. Grace wasn't particularly upset about her mother's death, and neither was Erin. They had both grieved for the woman while she was alive.

Slowly but surely, she could hear the familiar sounds of early morning as children's voices drifted, car doors opened and closed on the street outside her window – the neighbours preparing for the long weekend. It must be after eight by now, she thought. Not that it mattered to Grace, she wasn't going anywhere. Not today, not any day.

She closed her eyes and tried to block the echoes of normal life from outside her window, and waited for sleep to take hold. Memories floated around inside her head as she drifted … *red wine, clinking glasses, laughter, lots of laughter, warm sand beneath her as his body moved against hers, a small boat, watching the sea, looking anxiously over her shoulder, holding on to something, freezing cold water.* Something was niggling at her, but she didn't know what it was. And then she was falling, falling, into the water, tumbling, sinking, reaching her hands up towards the pool of light … there was a loud knock on the front door and her eyes shot open. Then she could hear Erin's footsteps on the stairs and the sound of the front door opening. A muffled conversation followed and then the door closed again. She heard a light tap and Erin peeked into her room. Her red hair had been tied in haste, curly red tendrils dancing around her pale skin. She looked like she hadn't slept much either. "Are you awake?" she asked softly, her tone barely a whisper.

"Yeah." Grace's voice didn't sound like her own.

"Did you sleep?"

"A bit," Grace lied.

"Are you up for a visitor?"

Grace froze. Nobody came to the house to see her anymore, at least nobody attempted to come and visit. She refused to see anyone, Sarah, her old boss at the coffee house, work colleagues, she wouldn't let anyone in.

"Who is it, Erin? I don't think I …" She pulled the duvet around her shoulders.

Erin opened the bedroom door wider. A woman with long grey hair stepped into the doorframe, her bright-red coat hanging loosely over her slender frame.

"Hello, Grace," the woman said. She gave a small smile.

She hadn't changed much over the years. Even though Grace had only seen her a few times when she was a young girl, she looked exactly the same now as she did then.

"Can I come in?" she asked gently. It was the old lady who lived next door.

Grace looked at Erin. Her sister smiled and nodded her encouragement. Grace wasn't sure what to do. Nobody had entered her bedroom since she arrived home except for Erin. She glanced back at the old woman whose expression was hopeful. "Come in." She pulled her body up in the bed and gestured towards a chair by the window. Erin removed Grace's clothes so the woman could sit.

"Let me introduce myself." She sat on the edge of the chair. "I'm Maureen Doran. You may have seen me a few times over the years."

Grace frowned. "Doran?"

"I'm your grandmother."

28

Lana drove her small car into the pretty village of Castle Cove. She was surprised she had made it without having to stop at a garage. The car was old and there were quite a few things wrong with it and it wasn't hugely reliable for long journeys any more, but it was still driving and, as far as Lana was concerned, that was the purpose of a car, wasn't it? To get you from one place to the other.

Traffic was heavy this lunchtime with the long weekend well and truly started. She slowed her pace as she drove past the freshly painted coastal cottages overlooking the sea. Earlier that morning, she had phoned the Castle Cove boutique hotel on the main street and she'd been lucky to secure the last room.

"We are flat out for the long weekend, but I have a single room overlooking the sea," the receptionist had told her. "You can see Mutton Island from your balcony. The island has been a real tourist attraction ever since the girl was found on the beach there last summer. People are weird if you ask me – I mean, why would you want to visit an island where a girl was found half-dead?"

The receptionist had rabbited on. Habitually, Lana would interrupt, but, in this instance the girl was talking about Grace Doran.

"What happened to her?" she had asked.

"Well, she went out on a boat with some people she was staying with up in The World's End. And they left her there, can you imagine? Although, nobody really knows what actually happened, but they definitely returned to the mainland without her. If you ask me that World's End is trouble."

"The World's End?" Lana had asked.

"The summerhouse, where the girl and her friends were staying. It attracts townies, if you know what I mean. There are parties until all hours. The locals don't like it, but we put up with it because they spend a lot of money in the village during the season, but they are not like us. I mean, Castle Cove is a small quiet little place really. I don't know why those kinds of people would want to spend a weekend here. The villa is more suitable for families, you know? Will you require breakfast?"

Now Lana wondered about the World's End summerhouse and why the group chose to stay there. Once she checked in, she would take a walk around the village and try to find the house. And she also needed to track down Lukasz Nowak, the local fisherman who had found Grace on the beach.

Lana parked her car on the main street of the village and grabbed her overnight bag from the boot, briefly stopping to take in her surroundings. There wasn't much to see really, on the main street at least. Just a supermarket, a couple of restaurants, a pub and the small boutique hotel she had booked into. She suspected if she drove further along the coast she would find more amenities – it often happened with an advanced coastline like this one – why keep everything in one place when you have miles and miles of shoreline to take advantage of? She wondered what had brought Grace and her friends to this place. What had been the attraction? Grace was only twenty-six years old at the time. According to Erin, Grace's friend Sarah was a year older. Lana assumed Sarah's boyfriend and his friends were around the same age or maybe a little older. She glanced up and down the quiet coastal road. It was definitely not Ibiza.

Lana pushed through the hotel swivel doors and made her way to reception. There was nobody behind the counter, so she pressed the bell. While waiting for someone to attend to her she turned and rested her back against the desk. The lobby was more like a big sitting room, furnished with pale cream sofas and large potted exotic plants. Her eyes were drawn to the swivel doors. She could clearly see the ocean. The scene in front of her was captivating – she couldn't take her eyes off it. The foamy white waves folding over each other, framed by a clear blue sky. If it wasn't for the moving breakers, you would mistake it for a beautiful painting. Not a bad office view, she thought.

"Stunning, isn't it?"

Lana turned to see a young girl standing behind the desk, dressed in dark pants and a short-sleeved white blouse. Her shoulder-length blonde hair was parted at the side, the longer length framing her youthful face. She looked no more than eighteen years old and Lana reckoned she was still in school, probably working in the hotel for the summer. She had a badge on the front of her shirt with the name *Gina* written on it. Lana recognised the voice as the girl who took her booking.

"It really is," she agreed. "I called earlier – Lana Bowen?"

"Ah yes – the single room." She tapped away on a keyboard. "It may be a little bit small but, if you ask me, you have the best view in the whole village. And there is a small balcony where you can sit out and watch the world go by." She beamed as she pushed some paperwork towards Lana. "If you can sign here, please?"

Lana scribbled her signature and Gina handed her an actual key. It was years since she had been given a key for a hotel room.

"First floor, second door on the right. No lift, I'm afraid. If you want anything, just dial O for reception. Enjoy the view," Gina rattled on with a smile.

"Thank you, I will."

Lana climbed the stairs and followed the corridor until she found her room. She inserted the key in the lock and the door opened into a small area with an ensuite bathroom. The french doors leading out onto the balcony were open wide, framed by a set of faded turquoise curtains billowing inwards. She dropped her bag and walked out onto the balcony and her breath caught. The view was even more magnificent from up here – it was all too much to take in at one time. A small white sandy beach was right in front of the hotel – she could see the start of a path leading down to it. Over to the left, she could see the harbour with a row of boats ranging in size. At the far end of the harbour, past the pier, she noticed a big white house overlooking the sea. Lana wondered if it was the same house that Grace had stayed in with her friends. The boats towards the end of the harbour looked like fishing trawlers and Lana guessed she might find Lukasz Nowak there. She checked her watch and realised that it was midday. If he had been out on the water earlier in the morning, he would probably be back by now – if she hurried, she might catch him.

She changed into a pair of white jeans and a black vest top and, grabbing her laptop bag, she left the room and took the stairs to the lobby. Gina was checking in an elderly couple, saying: "The room is small but, if you ask me, you have the best view in the whole village." Lana smiled to herself as she left the hotel. She was beginning to think all the rooms facing the sea must be small, but she felt sure that nobody complained, because Gina was right, the view was just so incredible.

She took a left, passing the supermarket and strolled down the hill towards the harbour. The village was busier down here, with families and dog-walkers enjoying the warm day. The first weekend of the season always seemed to have nice weather. Irish summers tended to go downhill after that.

When she reached the harbour, she noticed that some of the boats were much fancier than the fishing trawlers. There was a hire sign on a placard in front of a small kiosk, and a man wearing a baseball cap, the brim pulled down low, covering his face, was chatting on a phone, while sitting on a deck chair beside the sign. Grace had said that her friends had hired a boat that day and she wondered if it was from this guy. She needed to talk to him – maybe he had worked here the previous summer and been on duty that day when the boat returned to the mainland. But first, she decided, she would try and find Lukasz, in case he was planning on heading home for the day.

She walked further up the harbour, noticing that there was no sign of life on any of the fishing boats. There were several large nets lying around on storage lockers. She was just about to turn back when she saw a young man on one of the boats bent over at the waist, untangling nets. He worked methodically as he pushed the net through with both hands. He must have sensed that someone was watching him because he turned towards her, squinting into the sun.

"Can I help you?" he asked.

His accent wasn't local.

"Hi, yes," Lana replied. "I'm looking for Lukasz? Lukasz Nowak?"

The man didn't reply. He glanced up and down the harbour as if searching for someone. Dropping the net, he stepped down from the boat, and walked over to where Lana was standing, but he still didn't say anything. Up close, he looked older than she initially thought, the skin on his face weathered by the sea. She extended her hand.

"My name is Lana Bowen."

The man, whoever he was, still didn't respond. He continued to stare, a look of wariness in his eyes and Lana wondered why he was so guarded.

"I'm representing Grace, Grace Doran?" The wariness changed to confusion. "The girl found on the island last year?"

Recognition dawned and the man breathed a sigh of relief, or something – Lana wasn't sure. "I'm sorry, yes, my name is Lukasz. I did not know who you were. Why are you representing Grace?"

"I'll get to that." She wondered why he was being so cautious, but she let it go, for now. "Do you have time to grab a quick coffee? I have some questions about the morning you found Grace?"

The man smiled. "Sure. I never refuse coffee." He pointed to his boat. "I'm just finishing up here, preparing for the morning. But I could do with a break." He beamed. "The long weekend, it is busy. Just give me a minute?"

He pulled hard on the rope, to make sure it was secured to the dock cleat.

Satisfied, he turned to Lana. "The kiosk for the hire boats, it has coffee. It is good."

She nodded. "Show me the way!"

They walked in silence through the harbour. Lana watched a family climbing onto a hire boat, preparing to go out for the day. Lukasz followed her gaze.

"They are very busy this year. Every year, there is interest, but this year it is more." They reached the kiosk. "Coffee with milk or without?"

"Oh, no, let me get this …"

"I buy." He lowered his tone. "I get discount."

"Without milk, please."

He smiled. "The only way to drink coffee is without milk. Irish people are obsessed with milk." He grinned. "Milk and potatoes."

A teenage lad with floppy blonde hair had replaced the man with the baseball cap on the deck chair. He was concentrating hard on his phone, and Lana reasoned that he couldn't be more than eighteen or nineteen. His hair was shaved at the nape of his neck, and a long blonde fringe hung over his eyes.

"Two small coffees, Danny, no milk," Lukasz said.

Danny sighed, clearly annoyed at the interruption. He shoved his phone into his pocket and climbed into the kiosk.

Lukasz turned to Lana and grinned. "Not much to do here for his age. He is bored, but at least he is making some money." He counted some coins out onto the counter and they carried their coffees to a wooden bench overlooking the sea.

Lana sat beside Lukasz and they drank in the view as they sipped the steaming hot drink.

Lana stole a quick glance at Lukasz. He was staring at the rolling waves, his expression dark.

"How is she?" he asked.

Lana ignored the question. "Can you tell me what happened that morning, Lukasz?"

"I told the Garda everything that I know."

"I read your statement."

He turned to look at her, alarm in his eyes. "Why did you come here to see me? There is nothing else I can tell you."

Lana smiled. "You can relax, Lukasz. I like to interview witnesses myself, get the full picture. And, besides, I wanted to see the village where it happened."

Lukasz pointed out to sea. "I found her over there. On Mutton Island."

"Can you remember anything else unusual about that weekend? Before that morning?"

Lukasz took a sip of his coffee and Lana felt that he was thinking carefully about his answer. "No, the day was normal. I went out early to fish. The start of the season is always one of the busiest weekends of the summer and it is good opportunity to make money. So, I get up early, I fish, I bring it back here for Tommy." Lukasz looked at Lana. "Tommy is the distributor – he brings the fish to the hotels and restaurants. The next day, I do the same thing."

"Did you see the boat?" she asked. "The day before?"

"Not me, but my friend Peter did. That morning. He said they would be lucky to make it to the island, because they had already started drinking." He shrugged. "That happens all the time, the tourists, they hire the boats, and they have a few drinks. Most of the time, there is no problem."

"Most of the time?"

"Well, occasionally there are problems. Like that weekend, obviously. Something must have happened."

She regarded him for a moment. "Tell me about that morning?"

Lukasz took a breath. There was that cautious look again.

"It was my fourth morning out on the water. I was tired. I was passing over there." He nodded towards the island.

He filled her in on how he had found Grace on the beach, her pulse weak. When he finished, they were both quiet. Lana could see that the memory upset him.

Lana glanced around the harbour. "When you went out on the boat that morning, what direction did you take first?"

Lukasz gestured towards the sea. "I follow the buoys – that is a rule here in the harbour. It is like a clock that goes the other way?"

"Anti-clockwise?"

He nodded. "Yes. You go out one way and you come back in the other, so we won't crash into each other. It is like that in most harbours."

"So, you have to go up past the World's End before you go out to sea?"

Lukasz nodded as he looked towards the big house at the other side of the pier. "Well, yes, there is no other way."

"So, you went out on the morning after the girl went missing, Did you notice anything, when you were passing the house?"

Lukasz shifted his weight on the bench. "Like what?"

Lana shrugged. "I don't know, anything unusual. You said you went out early – what time was it?"

Lukasz shook his head. "About five? No – later than five – it was the last morning and I was tired – it must have been six in the morning."

"But it was quiet around the village?"

"Yes." Lukasz narrowed his eyes.

Lana was sure he wasn't telling her everything.

"What is it?" she encouraged him. "Look, Lukasz, anything you might have seen could help Grace, no matter how insignificant you may think it is?"

"Why are you asking these questions?"

"Grace is confused about what happened, Lukasz. She just wants clarification on a few things."

Lukasz frowned. "It was that time of the morning when the sun is not yet up, but you can see a little?"

"Dawn?"

"Yes, dawn. It was still dark but it was beginning to get brighter, even though I still had my spotlight on, and I could see a little in the distance. There is a pool at the side of the World's End …" He pointed towards the building. "You can see it from the water."

"Go on?"

"There was somebody out by the pool."

"At that time of the morning?"

"I thought it was someone, alone, but when I got closer, I noticed another person. Even though I could not hear anything from where I was on the water, they looked like they were having a fight."

"Why do you say that?"

Lukasz smiled. "Because, you Irish, when you argue, you use your hands. One of the people was throwing their hands in the air." He demonstrated.

"Can you remember anything else? Were they both men? Women? A man and a woman?"

Lukasz shook his head, uncertain. "I don't know. One was definitely a man – the one that was moving the hands. I don't know about the other person."

Lana observed the World's End from the bench.

"I still have bad nightmares," Lukasz continued. "About what I saw that morning." He turned to look at Lana. "They just left her there. Her friends. How could they do that to her? She was a young woman, a girl really."

Lana shook her head and glanced over at the island. "I don't know."

"I heard about the accident on the news at the time. But after a while people stopped talking about it. How is she now?"

Lana thought about her answer. She wanted to be truthful. "She is damaged. Hurt. Inside as well as out. And, she is angry. Very angry. She wants justice."

Lukasz looked at Lana, confused. "Justice?"

Lana watched as one of the hire boats began to move away from the harbour. A young girl held the steering wheel while some one older, maybe the father, covered her hands with his own. "Grace is convinced that she was pushed, Lukasz. She wasn't just left behind on the island, she wasn't just a drunken mistake. Someone pushed her off that boat, and left her in the water to die."

29

Lukasz watched Lana Bowen walk up the harbour until she disappeared from view. He knew she was heading for the World's End summerhouse. He had told her the house had been boarded up the previous summer and it was unlikely she would find anyone to show her around, but she wanted to see it anyway. She also wanted to travel to the island in the afternoon and she asked if he would be willing to take her out there. *"Shit,"* he muttered under his breath. He fired the empty paper coffee cups into the bin beside the kiosk and returned to his boat to tidy up the remainder of the loose nets. Piling the knotted ropes into the storage box, he slammed the lid shut, catching his finger. A sharp pain shot up his arm and he bit on his lip to stop himself from roaring. He felt lightheaded, and for a moment, he thought he might faint.

Take a breath, Lukasz, think.

Holding his injured finger upright, he found some loose ice cubes on the deck and with his free hand, he wrapped the fabric of his T-shirt around the ice before pressing it hard against his finger. Eventually, the pain subsided, fading to a weak throb. He sat on the edge of the storage box and stared out at the island, his thoughts turning to the investigator and what she had just told him.

Lukasz had thought the young girl had been left behind by her friends that evening, that they had got drunk and forgotten about her, and yes, it was a horrible thing to do, but that is what he thought had happened. There were many rumours that other things had gone on, but Lukasz didn't like rumours. Sometimes, the Irish had loose lips and they said things about people that they shouldn't say, altering information for dramatic effect, but he never, not for one moment, imagined that she had been deliberately pushed from the boat – that someone had intentionally shoved her into the water and left her there. Now there would be a court case, and he would have to give evidence. The investigator didn't say as much, but he knew that is what would happen. Lukasz Nowak would have to stand in front of a judge and explain what he was doing that morning, and he would have to explain why he had left Poland. He cursed himself for telling Lana what he had seen – the two people arguing outside the World's End. It most likely meant nothing, a drunken argument. Luckily, he had kept his mouth shut about the other thing.

He heard a van pull up and a door close behind him.

"Hey, Lukasz, how goes it?"

Pete climbed onto his boat moored right next to Lukasz's, and started searching through the empty nets on the deck left there from earlier that morning. "Can't find my bloody phone, must have dropped it here somewhere."

Lukasz continued to stare at the island.

Pete looked up as he rummaged through the nets. "Everything alright, Lukasz?"

"Yes, everything is fine." Lukasz remained solemn. *Everything was not fine.*

Pete's phone fell out of the nets onto the deck with a clatter. "There it is." He turned it over in his hand. "Still working too, a bloody miracle." He grinned.

Lukasz continued to observe the sea in front of him. Pete dropped the nets onto the deck and propped himself against the stern of his boat. He took some tobacco and papers from his pocket and rolled a cigarette. Leaning over the brim of his boat, he offered it to Lukasz who accepted. He then rolled one for himself. Neither of them said anything as they sat and smoked.

The sun was still high in the sky, but there wasn't the same heat as the previous year. Groups of families strolled along the harbour, a few brave souls dared to swim in the sea, and the two fishermen smoked their cigarettes, watching it all.

Lukasz finally spoke. "I have to go away for a while." He had to tell someone – his boat would need looking after.

Pete simply nodded.

"Can you find someone to take care of my boat?"

Pete pulled on his cigarette. "I will look after it myself, sure."

Someone laughed behind them on the pier.

"I remember the first day I arrived in the village. I did not know anyone. I came down here to this harbour, and I saw you, fighting with the nets. You were mad because of the knots." Lukasz smiled at the memory. "I offered to untangle the nets for you, and you offered me a job."

Pete nodded, smiling. "You arrived just at the right time. I was about to throw the whole bloody lot overboard."

"I was so happy. And four years later I was able to buy my own boat." There was a hint of pride in his tone.

"Well, you work hard for it. You deserve it."

Lukasz's smile faded. "Sometimes, no matter how hard you work, it makes no difference." He felt Pete watching him.

"Something to do with home, is it?" Peter asked.

Lukasz nodded slowly. "Yes, something to do with home." He took the keys of his boat out of his pocket. "The girl from the island, the girl I found last year, she says she was pushed off one of Gary's boats." He glanced at Pete. "A woman was here, a private investigator, asking questions. She asked me to take her to the island this afternoon. Can you explain I had some work to do? Her name is Lana Bowen." He handed the keys to Pete.

Pete accepted the keys. "Are you leaving because of the girl?"

"Thank you, Pete, for everything." He turned towards his van. "I will call you."

He climbed into his van and drove out of the harbour. Turning at the corner he spotted the World's End. Lana Bowen was standing outside the building, her hands framing her face as she tried to peer inside one of the windows. Lukasz knew the house was empty and the investigator would be back at the harbour soon. He drove on until he came to a small row of cottages. Unlocking his front door, he started packing his things into a bag. He had no idea where he was going, but he knew he had to keep moving. He tossed his sparse belongings into the back of his van and climbed into the driver's seat, adjusting the sun visor. A photo fell onto his lap, a faded polaroid of a man with his arm around a woman's shoulder, a small child held close to her chest, all three smiling for the camera. Sadness crept over him as he tucked the photo back into the visor, before shoving it closed. He drove down the main street of the village until he came to the junction at the main road. Indicating, he took a left, the sign for Castle Cove in his rear-view mirror.

30

Lana stood outside the World's End drinking in the view in front of her. It was spellbinding. The young girl, Gina, working in the hotel's reception had informed her that her room had the best view in the whole village, and Lana couldn't deny it was very good, but it had nothing on this. The scene in front of her was breathtaking, the expanse of the ocean, the smell of the salt water, the sounds and the spray hypnotic as the white foamy breakers crashed into each other, capturing all her senses. Lana could while away an afternoon here quite easily.

Dragging her gaze away, she turned back to the house. The blinds were pulled down low in most of the windows, making it almost impossible to see inside the building. What little she could see hadn't revealed much. The furniture was covered with white sheeting, hinting that nobody had stayed in the house for a while, and clearly it wasn't occupied this weekend either, the first big holiday weekend of the year. Lana wondered why that was, and who actually owned the property. She thought Grace had said it was a client of one of the guys, Sarah's boyfriend Harry, and that the client had offered it to him for the weekend. It was quite a generous offer. A house like this could easily fetch a couple of grand for a long weekend rental – she would have to check her notes. Whoever did own the house wasn't relying on a rental income, that was evident.

Looking up, she noticed two balconies on the second floor. Long, transparent voile curtains lined the full-length windows on the inside. One of the balconies extended around the corner of the building, providing a view of the front and rear. There was a barbeque area to the side of the pool. Grace had said that they had eaten outside on the first night they had arrived and she had quite a lot to drink, along with a couple of the guys. There was a large corner seating area with a fire pit in the centre, and Lana could picture Grace sitting there, drinking and eating with her friends, enjoying this beautiful sight, in this stunning house. A gorgeous young girl with her whole life ahead of her. Little did she know that twenty-four hours later, that would change forever.

The pool appeared clean, the tiles spotless, with no sediment around the edges, debris or leaves floating on the surface, hinting that someone was coming in regularly to maintain its upkeep. She would ask Gina in the hotel if she knew anything about it. Perhaps there was a maintenance company nearby – maybe she would be able to track the owner through them. She glanced around the pool area once more. It must have been out here that Lukasz had seen two people arguing.

There was nothing to see here, Lana decided. Apart from the incredible view, she felt sure that she wouldn't learn anything new. She decided to head back to the harbour to see if Lukasz was ready to sail over to the island. She smiled when she thought of the fisherman she had met earlier. She could tell that he was a sensitive soul. He was very touched by Grace and what had happened to her.

Lana could visualise the painful memory etched on his face, when he talked about finding her that morning, and the look of shock when she told him that Grace had been deliberately pushed. She had felt sure he was hiding something, though she had not wanted to pursue it earlier. Hopefully, he would be more forthcoming on their trip to the island during the afternoon.

She rounded the corner of the property and strolled down the road towards the harbour. There were several boats out on the water now, some making their way over to the island, some not moving at all. It was early in the afternoon and the sun was a little warmer. Passing the small kiosk, she noted there was still no sign of the man with the baseball cap and she wondered if he was gone for the day. His replacement, the young lad with the floppy blonde hair, was counting cash on top of the counter. Lana approached and the young lad jumped.

"Jesus, you frightened the shit out of me!" His eyes darted around the harbour as he realised what he had just said, probably searching for his boss.

"Sorry, I didn't mean to startle you."

"It's OK – sorry, I didn't mean to sound rude, miss." He nodded towards the cash. "My boss, Gary, he's always telling me not to count the cash on the counter. But the kiosk is too dark inside and I make mistakes." He slipped the money into an envelope and tucked it into the bag wrapped around his waist.

Lana looked around the harbour. There were a lot of people milling around now, much more than earlier. She understood his unease.

"Can I have a word about your boat rentals?" she said.

The boy started shaking his head. "Sorry, miss, all the boats are booked up for the weekend – actually I just rented the last one. If you come back tomorrow, there might be a cancellation, but come early to avoid disappointment, yeah?" He rattled off his answer as if he had delivered this line many times before.

"Thank you, but I'm not here to hire a boat. I just want to ask you a few questions, if that's OK? Danny, isn't it?"

The boy's eyes narrowed. "How do you know my name?"

"I was with Lukasz earlier – we bought coffee," Lana said.

The boy shrugged, as if to say *lots of people buy coffee.*

"Were you working here last year, Danny?"

The boy looked uncertain. "*Em*, yeah, last summer. Why do you want to know that?"

"Just curious. There must be plenty of summer jobs around for your age."

"Yeah. I had just finished with my final exams at school, and my uncle, Gary Duke, asked me to help him run this place for the summer. It gets very busy during the season, you know, with the boats. He was here earlier – he's just gone to meet someone or something, I don't know." He rolled his eyes. "Gary is always meeting someone."

"That man with the baseball hat is your Uncle Gary?"

"Yep. He's my mom's younger brother."

"Your uncle owns the boats?"

"I think so." He shrugged. "It's hard to know with Uncle Gary, to be fair. He moors them here at the harbour during the summer, for hire, so he can make some money out of them. He manages the rentals and looks after their maintenance."

"I get it. So, this is your second summer working here?"

"Like I said, I started just after I finished school last year. I worked the whole summer." He glanced up and down the harbour, a small smile spreading across his face. "I go to college now. Up in Limerick."

Lana nodded. "What are you studying?"

His smile widened. "Jeez, you ask a lot of questions!" He straightened his shoulders. "I study Law Plus. There's a lot of reading, but I like it, so far anyway. The college has its own mock courtroom in the library."

"Impressive." Lana grinned. "I worked as a prosecutor."

The boy's eyes widened. "Really? Oh my God, that's so cool. Criminal or family law?"

"Criminal. And you are right, there is a lot of reading, but most of it is really interesting, and useful." She fiddled with the brochure on the counter. She was confident now that they had found common ground. "So, you were here last summer when the group from the World's End hired the boat? The one where the girl was left on the beach?"

His face darkened. "Oh yeah, that was pretty bad. She almost died out there on the island, didn't she? If it wasn't for Lukasz – she mightn't have been found for days." His eyes narrowed. "Wait, are you here because of her? I mean, there were rumours, but …"

"What kind of rumours?" Lana asked.

"Ah, it's just people talk shit sometimes … sorry." He grimaced. "I thought it was an accident?"

Lana evaded the question. "Can you remember anything about the group that hired the boat?"

The boy looked towards the harbour. "Ah, I think so. It was just one guy and he came on his own. I remember him because …" Danny glanced back at Lana and lowered his voice, "he was a bit pissed."

"Can you remember his name?"

"Well, it's probably in the logbook." He appeared unsure about what to do next. "But I'm not supposed to give out the personal information about our customers." He shrugged. "Client confidentiality, you know?"

Lana smiled slowly. "I think I know who it is. I just want to be sure?"

He peered over Lana's shoulder and, after a moment, he seemed to make a decision. He pulled a large leather-bound book that had seen better days from under the counter. "It was this weekend last year, right?"

Lana nodded and he flicked through the tags at the bottom of the book before finding the month he was looking for. He scanned the list of names with his finger, stopping halfway down the page. He turned the book towards Lana and pointed at the signature. *Declan Slattery.*

Lana nodded. "What time was the boat signed back in?"

He turned the book around and ran his finger across the page. "It should be here." He stopped. "Yeah, see this?" He pointed towards the *Time in* column. "Mr. Slattery collected the boat, the *Karina*, just after midday and he brought it back ..." He moved his finger further across the page. "Six?" He frowned. "Man, that didn't happen."

"What didn't happen?"

"I was here and that boat wasn't back by six. I would have remembered. Because there was a tidal change that evening, see here?" He pointed at another column on the book, listing low tides and high tides. "If the tide is high, we always advise our clients to get back early, to avoid getting caught in a rip, like six or seven at the latest, before dark so they can see what they are doing. That boat definitely wasn't back by the time I left – I remember Uncle Gary was doing his nut." Danny frowned as he scanned the book. Unless …"

Lana leaned forward. "Unless what?"

"Well, sometimes they can keep the boat out longer." He shifted his weight from one foot to another. He looked uncomfortable. "The hire rate is until six, that's when the insurance runs out. Sometimes, my uncle allows people to hold onto the boats if they pay him extra."

"So they're not covered with insurance?"

The lad pushed his blonde hair back from his forehead. "Look, it has nothing to do with me. I come every day, do my shift and usually leave about six. If the boats aren't back on time, my uncle signs them in. It's not my problem. Mum says Gary's business is his own and to stay out of it." He shook his head. "But, that day, I don't think the clients had asked for extra time."

"Why do you say that?"

"Cos Uncle Gary was not happy."

Lana nodded. "Will he be back soon? Your uncle?"

Danny looked nervous now and Lana was quick to reassure him.

"I just want to talk to him about the people who rented the boat last year. Don't worry, I won't mention what you told me."

He nodded, relieved. "Uncle Gary was here earlier, then he had to go off on business somewhere, he didn't say anything else. Like I said, he's always in a meeting with someone, but my shift finishes at six so he should be back by then, to take the cash and lock up." He glanced back at the logbook, a frown on his face.

"Is there something else, Danny?" Lana asked.

The boy shook his head. "I don't know. It's probably nothing."

Lana smiled slowly. "The devil is in the detail, Danny. You'll learn that at law school."

"I had forgotten, but ..." He hesitated. "It's just that, the next morning, when I arrived for work, the boat wasn't here. The boat Declan Slattery signed for."

Lana frowned. "Where was it?"

"I don't know. Gary said something about a repair."

"What kind of repair?"

"I don't know, sorry."

"Does that happen often? That boats need repairing?"

Danny shook his head. "Not often with the cuddy boats. But Gary is responsible for health and safety and all that stuff."

"When did he get the boat back?"

Danny flipped a page and scanned the content. "*Em*, that boat wasn't signed out again for another week."

Lana nodded slowly. "Thank you for chatting with me, Danny. You've been a great help." She walked away, calling over her shoulder. "Good luck with college! I might see you in court someday."

Lana continued down the harbour. There was no sign of Lukasz on his boat. She glanced around the harbour, but she couldn't see him anywhere. She felt her stomach rumble and she realised that she hadn't eaten since she had left home that morning. She decided she would leave a message for Lukasz and get something to eat at the hotel. And she needed to check in with her mother. She took a notebook from her bag and scribbled her name and number on a piece of paper. She ripped it out and folded it over, writing Lukasz in capital letters on the other side. She climbed onto the boat and tucked the note under the door of the small cabin. She stepped off the boat. As she was walking away from the harbour, she felt like someone was watching her, but when she turned around there was nobody there.

31

"So, what you have to do is make the presentation about your audience. Instead of focusing on what you want to sell, focus on *who* you want to sell to, what type of buyer is out there. Their age group, gender, background, and probably the most important thing, their disposable income." Stephen scanned the room, his eyes resting on the pretty young blonde girl sitting at the front right-hand side of the oval table. "Therefore, yes, all these factors must be taken into consideration when you are marketing a product. Use the word *you*, make the product about the buyer – make them think they already own it." He observed their eager faces, hanging on his every word. Fucking idiots, he thought. "We never want the customer to just like the product – we want them to *care* about the product. When they care, they will buy."

Stephen clicked on his final link. The word **YOU** appeared on the screen in bold capital letters.

"Right, that's it for now. Ciara in reception has allocated your departments – she has my direct line if any of you have any questions." Stephen glanced at the small group of people sitting around the table in the boardroom, bursting with nervous enthusiasm. He tried to hide his irritation. "Thank you for giving up your time on a Saturday morning for this induction but, as you can appreciate, we can get straight into work on Monday. Time is precious in the marketing world. Welcome to Jennings Studio 61. Have a nice weekend." Several muttered responses greeted him and his impatience grew. Just one day out of their safe college environment – give them a couple of weeks in a marketing department and they would be running back to university to rethink their career choice. "You have two weeks to prove yourselves. Don't waste it."

Stephen shut his laptop, tucked it under his arm and left the room. His team leader had asked him to give an induction to the new summer recruits who had applied for work experience in the marketing department and set them up with tasks to separate *the weak from the strong*, his words. There were ten young graduates sitting round that table, having been carefully selected from the hundreds of CVs the company received at the beginning of each summer. Only one would end up actually working for the company, maybe two if they impressed. Hopefully, the pretty blonde would make the cut.

He arrived at his desk and quickly checked his emails. He found one from the company CEO, Luke Jennings – Andy's dad. His father-in-law was inviting them both for dinner at his country residence the following weekend. The man spent most of his time in his villa in the South of France with his second wife, Ruby – Andy's stepmom. Andy's birth mother had died from alcoholism when she was a teenager. Luke's invite finished with an interesting statement. **I think it's time I handed over the reins, Stephen.** What the fuck? Was Luke planning on making him the new CEO? He had hinted as much a few times, particularly during the time when

Stephen had his transgression with the young intern. "We all make mistakes, Stephen. I have plans for you. Don't fuck up." He erased the pretty blonde sitting at the induction table from his memory. He skimmed through the remaining unopened emails in his inbox and decided there was nothing that couldn't wait until after the weekend.

Slipping his laptop into its sleeve, he left the office, his thoughts preoccupied by the email he had just received. This would change everything, for him and for Andy. "*Don't fuck up.*" His father-in-law's words echoed in his mind. He had fucked up already, hadn't he? The lift was occupied so he took the stairs to the ground floor.

He rounded the corner of his office building and advanced up the busy street. It was coming up to lunchtime and there were a lot of people milling around, grabbing coffees or a bite of lunch. He crossed the street at the lights and reached his destination. The pub was quiet inside, the lunchtime trade not having arrived yet, and he walked straight through to the back, finding a table in the small beer garden. A young man dressed in a black shirt and pants, a small pink apron wrapped around his waist, approached and offered him a menu. Stephen held up his hand. "Just a coffee, mate, milk, no sugar." The waiter nodded and retreated into the pub. Stephen glanced around the small beer garden – he was completely alone.

He took out his laptop and keyed in his password. Noting the WIFI code written in chalk on the blackboard hanging from the stone wall, Stephen carefully typed in each digit. He opened Google and keyed the words **Castle Cove** and **Grace Doran** into the search engine. A picture of a small coastal town appeared on the screen beside Grace's photo, her head tilted to the side, the hint of a smile on her beautiful young face. The story underneath hadn't changed since the last time he read the article:

A young woman was found on the beach of Mutton Island, a small island off the coastal village of Castle Cove, during the May bank holiday weekend by a local fisherman. He had been out on his boat early that morning when he saw her apparently lifeless body lying on the sand. He brought her back to the mainland and alerted the emergency services. Her condition remains critical in hospital. Gardaí are appealing for witnesses who were in Castle Cove during the long weekend to come forward, particularly anyone who visited the harbour area or was in the vicinity of the island, either the previous evening or early the following morning. They are not treating the incident as suspicious.

Stephen turned his attention back to the image of Grace, her pretty eyes smiling out at him as he remembered their afternoon on the beach. They had found a secluded spot further up the strand, away from the others and the conversation had been easy between them. Grace had been teasing him about something and suddenly he was on top of her and she was responding, the sun, the sand, her warm body moving against his. It had been the most perfect afternoon and, then, everything had gone to hell.

Stephen scrolled down the screen for any more articles or updates. There was nothing new. If Grace had gone about hiring legal representation, she hadn't made it public yet.

He enlarged the image on his screen.

He sighed and leaned back on his chair, clasping his hands behind his neck. Since his game of golf with Harry the other day, he hadn't been able to get her out of his head. The waiter approached and placed the steaming mug of coffee in front of him, discreetly tucking the paper bill under the saucer. Stephen thanked him and sipped the hot drink without taking his eyes off Grace's face. He leaned forward to take a closer look at the photo. She was wearing a white string vest top and her long dark hair was hanging loosely over her shoulder. The sky was clear blue behind her and you could just about make out the corner of a white building framing the edge of a swimming pool. He frowned. The image might have been taken that weekend at the World's End. He wondered who had given it to the gardaí. Maybe it was Sarah. He deliberated how many more images might be out there from that weekend. He definitely hadn't taken any photos and he was careful that there wouldn't be any taken of him … at least he hoped he had been. If Sarah had any pictures of him, he was not aware of it. He trusted this was the only one she handed over. Harry had said she would be discreet – that he had made sure of it, whatever that meant. Stephen hoped he was right about that.

He closed out of the screen and erased the viewing history. Andy never used his laptop, but he still had to be careful. *Just in case.* In case she reverted to the paranoid phase she had gone through before. She would get up in the middle of the night to check his messages, his emails, websites he had visited. There was nothing out of bounds.

He thought about the previous night and the bombshell she had delivered. It had taken every bit of strength he had in him to hide what he was feeling from her. The truth was, he didn't want another child. He did at the start. After Luke died, he thought it might solve all their problems, but not anymore. He would never get over it if they lost a second child. And as the years went by, he thought Andy felt the same. After all the stages of grief they had been through, he thought they were happy again, maybe happier than they ever had been, but the look on her face last night told him something entirely different. Andy appeared cheerful for a different reason. He couldn't tell her how he felt, he couldn't ruin the moment for her – she didn't deserve it. He would have to tell her – but not yet.

"If we lie to the people we love, we lose their trust, and when we lose their trust they know who we really are." His mother's words whenever she mentioned Stephen's father. The man had died of a brain tumour when Stephen was just two years old, so long ago that he had no memory of him. It turned out that he had re-mortgaged the family home to pay off a gambling debt, and so his mother worked two jobs to help pay off the balance, and to keep Stephen in school. By the time he got to college, his mother's health was failing and Stephen took over the role of earning money to keep a roof over both their heads. His mother died the week after he graduated – it was as if her work was done. But not for Stephen – he was completely alone in the world. Andy often teased him, said that he was an avoider, because of his challenging childhood. Maybe she was right – he found it easier to bury his head in the sand. Was that what he was doing now?

The back door leading out to the beer garden swung open and Harry approached and took a seat opposite him, grinning. "Didn't know you worked Saturdays?"

"Had to give a presentation to a bunch of interns."

The waiter arrived with a menu once again and Harry ordered a glass of tap water. The pub was not going to make the big bucks from either of them today. The waiter didn't react either way. When he left, Stephen didn't waste any time.

"What did you find out?"

Harry let out a breath. "Not much, I'm afraid. Well, not much more than what I told you on the golf course." He leaned in close and rested his arms on the glass table. "The investigator's office has been in touch and she wants to interview all of us."

Stephen shook his head, alarmed. "I can't be interviewed, Harry. Andy doesn't know I was there. Nobody does. If her father finds out, that's me finished. "*I have plans for you, Stephen, don't fuck up.*"

Harry held up his hand. "Relax, Stephen. It's cool."

When Grace was in the hospital, she was still in a coma so she couldn't have spoken to anyone about who she was with that weekend, and Harry had warned Sarah not to mention Stephen. He had explained about Andy. Sarah was mad at Harry for lying to her, but she forgot about it quick enough. For whatever reason, the girl had stayed quiet and the longer Grace remained in a coma, the less important it seemed. Then Grace had recovered consciousness and Harry had texted Stephen, Just two words: **No memory**.

Neither of them spoke. The waiter returned with a jug of iced water and a tumbler. Harry poured the cold drink into his glass and drained it in one gulp before refilling it.

Stephen noticed Harry's hand was trembling slightly. He regarded him for a moment. "Harry, you're telling me to relax, that everything is cool – but you're all wound up yourself."

"Ah, just busy with work, you know how it is. I have a big deal ongoing at the moment, made the final pitch this morning." He glanced at his phone. "I'm waiting on a call about it actually." He drummed his fingers on the table. "You know me." He grinned. "The adrenaline keeps building until I have the contract airtight."

Stephen nodded slowly and looked away.

"I've always been like this when it comes to closing a deal, you know that." Harry seemed earnest.

Stephen smiled, despite himself. "I know. You were the same in college. Whether it was an exam, a match, or some girl, the chase was always the most exciting part for you."

"That's right." Harry picked up his glass and took a long drink of water. His eyes skirted around the empty garden.

He was definitely nervous, jumpy, thought Stephen. "Have you spoken to Sarah?" he asked.

Harry shook his head. "Nah, not since last year. It was just a casual thing in the end and, besides, when that shit happened with her friend, Grace, she kind of zoned out." He held up his hand. "Don't worry, she won't say anything about you being there. As I said, I made sure of that."

"Maybe Grace told the investigator I was there?"

Harry hesitated. "Look, you were gone when the Gardaí arrived. Nobody took a statement from you. So, if Grace does remember, it's her word against yours, if it comes to it."

Stephen observed his friend. *If it comes to it.* So, it could 'come to it'. "Why didn't you contact me, Harry? A whole year went by and I didn't hear a word from you."

"I thought it best to keep our distance. You wanted to be left out of the Garda enquiry – it was easier to take a break from each other for a while, until everything calmed down. And, the other stuff ..." He glanced around the small garden. "But the thing is ... it's Declan."

"What about Declan?"

"Well, he called round last night, after I got back from our game of golf. I couldn't believe it when he showed up, it was like he was waiting for me, or something. I mean, I haven't seen him since that weekend last year." His eyes were wide. "Honestly, Stephen, I haven't seen or spoken to him."

"What did he want?" Stephen asked.

Harry hesitated. "I had texted him and asked to meet up, that I needed to talk to him about something. He wanted to know what about. I didn't want to write anything in a text – I wanted to see him in person, you know? Like I did with you? Next thing I know, he's beating the door down. I told him about the investigator and he starts going mental, asking all these questions, you know what he's like."

"What kind of questions?"

Harry looked at Stephen, his hand firmly holding the glass, the shake more prominent now. "About you. He said the investigator, Lana Bowen is her name, had called him and left a message asking for a meeting to discuss the events of that weekend. She wants everyone to come to her office next week and … she had all our names, including yours." He kept twisting his glass between his fingers. "Grace told her about you."

"*Grace!* But she had no memory of what happened."

"Well, she remembers now, it seems. Lana Bowen wanted to know why there was no statement from you. Declan went crazy, said we shouldn't have lied about you being there, it makes us look guilty, he went on and on and on …"

"Guilty about what, Harry?"

"About what happened to Grace, obviously. But then he kept talking about you and Andy and how your relationship wasn't a good enough reason to lie –"

"Me and Andy?" Stephen stiffened.

"Look, I can fix it. I can handle Declan. Just leave it with me … but, if the investigator does contact you, stick to the story, and … don't mention the other stuff …" He seemed to hesitate.

"There is something else, isn't there?"

"Yeah. He said he was going to tell Andy about you and Grace."

And there it was. *If we lie to the people we love, we lose their trust, and when we lose their trust, they know who we really are.*

194

32

Lana pushed away her half-empty plate and reached for her glass of water. Leaning back in her chair, she sipped the cold drink as she took in the view from her balcony. When she had returned to her hotel, the dining area appeared busy with guests so she had decided to have her lunch in her room and enjoy the scenery. She had ordered a chicken salad and lain on her bed to rest while she waited, only to wake a short time later with someone from room service knocking on her door.

She checked her phone on the bedside locker, noticing a text from her mum asking where she was. *Damn.* She had meant to call her. She had only booked into the hotel for one night. She had a few more people she wanted to meet and if she managed to do that, she would be back on the road by the following afternoon. She texted her mum back that she would drop over with a takeaway the following evening and stay over. She suggested they could watch a movie together.

Lana was very close to her mam – it was just the two of them after her father had died of cancer ten years earlier. He had been an active and vibrant man all his life. Her mother used to say that he never walked anywhere, he ran. So, when he was caught by the horrible disease, it took hold of him quite quickly. Whether he had just admitted defeat and let the cancer take control, Lana would never know – he hadn't been prepared to fight it anyhow, and he had died within seven months of his diagnosis. Lana had only just graduated from college the previous year, and so she threw herself into her work at the office of the Director of Public Prosecutions, allowing her time to spend her evenings and weekends with her mother. This worked out fine for a while – they were both grieving and they needed each other – but, at her mother's insistence, Lana eventually moved out. "You need to live your own life, Lana, it is time," her mother had told her, and she was trying to do just that. They still talked every day on the phone several times, and they always saw each other at weekends, whether it was for coffee, lunch or a takeout. Truth be known, Lana missed her mother a lot during the week – she sometimes wondered whether she needed her mother more than her mother needed her. Of course, her mum had pulled her through a very difficult time after a tragic incident occurred during a case Lana had been working on. It was hard to let go of her mother's strength and stand on her own.

There was still nothing from Lukasz.

She had brought her lunch out on to the balcony, disappointed that the chicken was a little dry and tasteless. But the salad was crisp and fresh, laced with a delicious vinaigrette dressing, so she ate enough to abate her hunger. Now, she sipped her water and watched the scene in front of her. It really was like a moving picture. Boats bobbed in the water and people swam in the sea or strolled along the pier, or picnicked on the beach, and yet, despite all this activity, the village appeared peaceful and quiet. The scene in front of her was postcard perfect. In fact, no matter where you stood in this town, the feeling was idyllic, presenting an unspoiled location to get away and enjoy the natural beauty of the Irish coastline, without having to deal with noisy children or partying twenty somethings. She wondered why she had never visited before. She made a mental note to come back sometime and bring her mother. She would love it here, the walks, the tranquillity, the view. Though she would probably suggest Lana take a friend her own age.

She checked her phone again – there were still no missed calls or messages. Where was Lukasz? She'd been sure she would have heard from him by now.

She went inside to use the bathroom and brush her teeth. She rinsed her mouth and spat into the sink and watched the toothpaste swirling around the bowl. She thought about Grace cleaning up the vomit in the cabin toilet that weekend and pitied the poor girl – there really was nothing worse than cleaning up someone else's spew. She tried to remember how Grace had got rid of the vomit. Hadn't she said she had cleaned it up with a mop and bucket? And, when she came back up to throw it over the side of the boat, there was nobody around. Where had everyone gone? She had mentioned that Declan had taken a stroll up the beach, but had not returned and that Harry had gone to look for him. She had helped Sarah and another guy clean up. She checked her memory for the notes she had taken. Stephen. There was no mention of Stephen in the police report, but Grace said he was there. Sarah, Harry, Declan and Stephen. So, Stephen must have been cleaning up the beach with Sarah while Grace was inside the boat.

She walked back out to the balcony, resting her gaze on the small island directly in front of her. It was nothing much to look at from where she was standing, just a piece of land, a small shape, breaking the linear contour of the ocean. She wondered why nobody lived over there or had set up business there – maybe the unpredictable currents had prevented that. It was close enough to the mainland to receive supplies and there seemed to be plenty of boats going over and back. And even though it might not attract customers during the winter months, surely the summer would be a different story? She also wondered if the island was privately owned. It wouldn't be unheard of. She remembered attending a party years before, held by her old boss where one of his guests boasted about buying an island off the coast of Clare. He had smelled of whiskey and body odour. She had wanted to suggest he invest in a bottle of deodorant instead. She made a mental note to ask Gina in reception – if anyone had that information, Gina would.

Her phone vibrated in her pocket, and when she checked the screen she noticed the caller ID was withheld. Lana rarely answered the phone if she didn't know who was calling her, but maybe it was Lukasz. She pressed answer. "Hello?" There was static and then …" Hi … hel … can …" The line went dead. Lana frowned at the screen before deciding that whoever it was would ring back if it was important. She turned her gaze towards the harbour where Lukasz's boat was moored and wondered if the message she had left him had somehow blown away. And that maybe he was actually waiting for her to contact him.

She took another sip of her water and grabbed her sweater – she might need it later. Her phone rang again as she was leaving the room. This time, her mother's name flashed across the screen. She hesitated before answering. She needed to get down to the harbour, so they could have plenty of time to sail out to the island for a look around before the tide turned but, if she didn't answer, her mother would just keep ringing. She hit the green button.

"Hi, Mum."

"Lana? Where are you, love? I called around to your apartment."

"You did?" Lana heard her mother sigh.

"Lunch? Remember? You invited me over for lunch. And what's this about a takeaway?"

Lana frowned. She was sure she hadn't planned to meet her mum for lunch today. Or had she? Her mum was getting a bit confused lately, about small little things. She would be telling Lana a story and, mid-sentence, she would stop and lose her train of thought. She decided to play it the other way. Informing her mother that she was wrong about their plans would only upset her.

"Oh, Mum, I'm so sorry, I completely forgot. I took on this new case and I had to travel down to the south coast to make some enquiries. I forgot all about our lunch date."

"Don't worry, Lana love, it's fine. Sure, I read my book and watered your plants. God only knows when they last got a cup of water – they were dying with the thirst."

Lana smiled – it was her mother who had bought the plants. "I don't water them because I know you do it."

"Mind your cheek!" Her mother chuckled. "How did you enjoy your night out?"

Lana hesitated – she wasn't sure whether to lie or fess up. She decided on the latter, her mother could always see through her white lies. "I didn't go, Mum. Look, it's a long story and I know I should take a break from work but, if you knew the details, you would understand."

Her mum sighed again. "You need to get out, Lana love."

"I know, Mum."

"You have been through a great deal …"

"I know, Mum."

"It wasn't your fault, love …"

"I know."

* * *

A few years ago Lana had been working on a case while employed with the Department of Public Prosecution. A young woman, Chloe Long and her daughter, Zara, were under witness protection while waiting to give evidence in the trial of her abusive husband. Lana was assigned to the case to gather evidence. Chloe's husband was behind bars, awaiting trial for stabbing his wife and child in an unprovoked attack. Chloe had enraged his family by reporting their precious son to the authorities. The fact that he had left them both for dead didn't matter. Chloe had betrayed the *family*.

Chloe's little girl, Zara, was seven years old when Lana first called to the safe house. Lana and the young girl had hit it off from that first meeting – they had formed a strong bond from the moment they met. Chloe used to laugh at how enamoured Zara was with her. *"She's really taken with you, Lana – she keeps asking me when you are next coming to visit!"* Chloe would say whenever they met. *"Well, the feeling is mutual,"* Lana would reply. *"She is adorable. And super smart."*

One afternoon, a few weeks before the trial, when Lana went to visit the Longs safe house, there appeared to be nobody at home. Lana was confused. They had arranged to meet at their usual time to review the case and it was unlike Chloe not to call if something had come up. Lana had knocked on the door a few times but nobody had answered. She had called Chloe's mobile, and that was when she had heard the faint tone of the phone ringing on the other side of the door. She had knocked again, more persistently, and eventually Zara answered, peeking her little blonde head out the side of the door, holding the handle in place to hide her tiny frame. She told Lana she was completely alone in the house and she couldn't let a stranger in. Lana had laughed and said her mum wouldn't mind – she wasn't a stranger, surely? So Zara should just let her in and she would talk to her mum later and explain.

Lana should have seen it sooner – the fear in Zara's eyes, the slight shake of her head, the whiteness of her knuckles as she held on to the side of the door, the mouth quietly mouthing, *Don't come in, Lana*. Before she could react, Zara was pulled back abruptly and the door was banged shut. Lana heard a scream and then another and then another door slammed somewhere in the house, and then … nothing. She had started hammering on the door and shouting for Chloe and Zara but nobody came. She had called the emergency services and given the address of the safe house, but she knew it was too late. The deafening silence from the other side of that door told her it was too late. Bill Long's brother had found out where Chloe and Zara were hiding, somehow, and he had got into the house and terrorised them both. When Lana knocked on the front door, he warned Zara to keep quiet, and the little girl had obeyed. But Lana kept knocking. She heard Chloe's phone ring and she kept knocking, and she had got the little girl killed.

The fear in Zara's eyes had stayed with her: *Don't come in, Lana*. Why hadn't she said something like, *I'll talk to your mam tomorrow, OK, Zara? I must have got the day wrong*. Instead, she had continued with her knocking and laughed when the little girl called her a stranger. They had talked about the use of the word *stranger* in the past – it was their code name for Zara's dad's family. For danger. It was Lana's idea that they use a code if they were worried or frightened about something. *Stranger* was the code. *Zara* had given the code directly to Lana, and she hadn't picked up on it. Chloe Long had been strangled at some point that morning. She was already dead when Lana got to the house. But Zara was alive when Lana arrived. Bill Long's brother killed her after Lana knocked on that door.

Lana had left her job with the Department of Public Prosecutions. She couldn't continue with the case.

The panic attacks had started soon after, crippling her whenever she found herself alone, or in an environment where she felt out of control. At her mother's insistence, she had gone to counselling, which helped her to put structures in place in order to deal with the attacks. Sometimes they worked. Sometimes they didn't.

* * *

"Life is not all about work, you know?" her mother said.

"I know, Mum."

"Look at what happened to your father."

"I know, Mum." Her father had worked day and night his entire life. He died within seven months of his retirement.

"Where are you anyway?" her mother asked.

"A small coastal town, by the name of Castle Cove." She was glad the subject had changed. "Ever heard of it?"

"Castle Cove? It does ring a bell but I don't know why. Did something happen there?" Her mother started tut-tutting on the other end of the line. "Was there a drowning? A young man – it happened years ago, I think?"

There it was again, the confusion. "Not exactly – there's an island close by and a girl was found on the beach there, this same weekend last summer. She almost died. A fisherman found her, barely alive."

"Is it far from Limerick?"

"It's about a two-hour drive down south."

"And how did you get down there?" Her mother tutted. "Oh, Lana, you didn't take that little car of yours, did you?"

"Yes, Mum, I drove my little car and there were no problems. I got here in one piece."

"Still, that thing is only good for going to the local shops, definitely not for long journeys."

Lana decided to change the subject. "I'll be back tomorrow, we can do something then. I'll bring takeout? Chinese, your favourite?"

"That sounds nice, but you shouldn't be spending your free time with your old mother."

Lana smiled. "I love spending my free time with my old mother."

"Ah, excuse me, I can call myself old, but you can't!"

Lana thought of something. "Mum, did you call me just before –"

"Oh, I know why I remember Castle Cove," her mother interrupted. "Your father and I spent a weekend there, not long before he passed away. I remember there was a small island near the mainland. We wanted to sail over, but we didn't book the boat on time. We always promised each other we would go back, but then …" Her voice trailed off.

"Oh, and now I'm here … I'm sure Dad is pleased."

"Yes, he must be. I'll see you tomorrow evening around six," her mum said. "Now, make sure to layer up – it's not as warm as it looks. There is a sharp bite in that wind, and it looks like it's going to rain here in Limerick. *If March doesn't kill you, April will try and –*"

"*May will tell whether you live or die!*" Lana finished. "It's really warm down here, Mum, but I will wrap up, I promise."

"See you tomorrow, bye, love."

Lana ended the call and took the stairs to the ground floor. The restaurant was much quieter now she noticed and, as she passed through reception, there was no sign of Gina or anyone else covering the desk. She would have to ask her questions later.

She strolled down the road towards the harbour and turned onto the pier, passing the kiosk. The man with the baseball hat was back in position, talking into his phone – she decided she would come back to him. She kept going until she found Lukasz's boat. There was no sign of the fisherman. She could see the note she had written sticking out from under the door, exactly where she had left it.

Lana was confused. Where was he? And what should she do now? He had assured her he would be free. She heard someone cough nearby and noticed a man untangling nets on the trawler beside Lukasz's. She hadn't realised there was anyone there at all.

He looked up and nodded, a cigarette dangling from his mouth. "How're ya?"

Lana longingly inhaled the smell of tobacco wafting in her direction.

Lana gave a small smile. "Fine, thank you." She nodded at Lukasz's boat. "Excuse me, do you know Lukasz? I met him here earlier, I think this is his boat."

The man nodded yes. "Ah, yeah, that's his boat alright."

"Do you know where he is?" Lana enquired.

"He had to go away for a while."

Lana frowned. "He did? But I only met him this morning and he promised he would be here."

He laughed. "Ah sure, you know how it is!" He grabbed the mooring rope and stepped off the boat. "Think he had to head home, something to do with his family." He tightened the rope and started twisting it around one of the hooks at the back of the trawler.

"Oh." She glanced at Lukasz's boat. She wasn't sure what to do. "Where is home for Lukasz?"

He stopped winding the rope. "Poland."

"Right."

"He arrived here five years ago."

"OK."

"Four years and he sounds less Irish than he did when he got here!" He laughed. He was standing in front of Lana now, his brown eyes peering intently into her own. His black hair curled around the tanned skin of his face. He was wearing a white T-shirt and blue jeans. He was ruggedly handsome and Lana reckoned he knew it.

"If Lukasz gets in touch, can you ask him to call me?"

"Sure."

"Thanks."

She started to walk away.

"Hey, wait up! Is this about the trip to the island?" he called after her.

Lana stopped. "He told you about that?"

"He did, yeah." He took a tobacco pouch and papers from his pocket, grinning. "He asked me to take you over there." He tipped tobacco onto paper and rolled the skin back and forth, the woody scent drifting towards her. "Lana Bowen, that your name?"

Lana weighed up what to do. She had met Lukasz earlier and she had liked him, she had trusted him. She didn't know this man at all, but she didn't really know Lukasz either, did she? She watched the man light his cigarette, a complete stranger, offering to take her out to the island on his boat. He was watching her too, waiting for her to make a decision.

She smiled. "I am free to go now, if you are?"

33

Sarah chewed on her bottom lip, a habit she had picked up when she was a small child whenever she felt nervous. The voice on the answer service rattled off its usual instruction, informing her to leave a message. She hung up before the beep and fired off an angry text instead – **Get back to me for fuck sake, some investigator just left me a message**. Throwing the phone into her bag, she rummaged around for her vape. Cupping it in the palm of her hand, she pulled on it hard as she stepped to the front of the bus shelter and peered up the street for any sign of her bus. She had been standing at the stop for over ten minutes now. The weather had turned and the rain had been pouring steadily and the cold was beginning to set in. Stepping back into the shelter, she pulled the top of her light jumper up around her neck, wondering what to do. *He* wouldn't answer her calls, nor would he return them. Sarah was at a loss and getting more and more frustrated.

Sighing, she looked at her watch. If a bus arrived in the next few minutes, she would still be in plenty time to get across town to collect Zack from his gran's. She needn't worry just yet, she would make it on time. Provided she didn't perish from the cold first. It was at times like these that she wished she had learned to drive when she was younger. Her father would take her older brother out for lessons, but Sarah waved him off whenever he made the same offer to her. They had lived close to the city and she didn't think that she would ever need a car, with a bus stop right outside her front door. She hadn't thought ahead – to a time that she might want to move out of her parents' house. But she hadn't missed it at all, until she had Zack. Now she longed to be able to drive her child to and from school, or take him away for a long weekend to the beach, or drive to the supermarket, instead of hauling heavy bags of groceries and relying on public transport to get around. Even going to college was a pain. The building was located on the other side of town from Zack's school and her classes had been timetabled sporadically across the week, so she always had to arrive early, because of the scheduled bus times, and hang around in between lectures. Once she finished her course, she vowed to herself that she would make learning to drive a priority. Besides, she had the money to buy a car now, didn't she?

Sarah had done everything the hard way, unintentionally. She had stuck her head into the books at school to get the results she needed to go on to third level, sacrificing nights out with the girls and relationships with boys in order to concentrate on her studies. So, when she finished school and got accepted into the course she had applied for, she settled into university life, making up for lost time, going out and socialising with her peers, getting to know people and forming friendships. Unfortunately, she got to know one of them a little bit too well, and by Christmas that first semester, she was pregnant. She couldn't believe it and, what was worse, her pregnancy was nearly five months along when she had it confirmed. She hadn't even noticed that her periods had stopped, until one of the girls had a complete meltdown one night at a party and blamed it on pre-menstrual tension. As Sarah tried to calm the girl down, she realised that she couldn't remember when she had last had a period herself. She decided to keep an eye on things but as the weeks rolled on and there was still no sign of a bleed, she started to wonder if there was another reason for their absence. She had been casually seeing a boy, Alex, a postgraduate studying medicine. They had met at one of the student parties and got along well, and slept together a few times, but there was nothing in it really, for either of them, just physical attraction. Sarah was studying Business and she wanted to major in Economics and hoped to spend at least one semester in Europe, and Alex wanted to be a doctor. So, the casual fling or whatever it was, had suited them both. And they had been careful. Sarah knew he had used a condom, she saw him put the bloody thing on. She had convinced herself that she couldn't possibly be pregnant and, besides, she had no symptoms. No morning sickness, no tiredness, no weird food cravings. There had to be another reason for her absent periods.

As the weeks moved on, and with still no sign, she decided to take a test, just to rule it out. She vomited for the first time when she saw the two clear blue lines appear on the pregnancy test. When her head cleared, she decided to tell Alex, and once he got over the shock they both agreed that they were too young to raise a child and the best thing would be for Sarah to have a termination. Together, they went to see the campus doctor and when Sarah couldn't calculate when she last had a period, the doctor decided to send her for an ultrasound to determine the age of the foetus. She vomited for the second time when the nurse told her she was approximately four months along.

So, Sarah had left college and travelled home that Christmas and told her parents about her pregnancy. Just under five months later, Zack was born. She decided she would defer her studies for a year and, once the child arrived, Alex would help with his care, but, things hadn't worked out that way. Alex was training to be a doctor, and he regularly went out on placement in the hospitals and worked fifteen-hour shifts. He was exhausted most of the time and his family were no help to her at all. So, the following September arrived and Sarah didn't return to college, nor did she return the subsequent September. Instead, she settled into life as a single parent. When Zack was barely a year old, they moved out of her parents' house as things had got a bit over crowded. Her parents gave her a small sum of money to cover a deposit and a month's rent for a flat in town, and she found a crèche for Zack nearby. She picked up a part-time job to help cover the bills. Money was always a problem, the bills piled up, bills she often ignored, and it wasn't until Zack started pre-school that she was able to resume her studies. Up until last year, Sarah's life was beginning to take shape again. Zack's dad's family were finally taking a more active role in his care, and Sarah had more time for herself. She had met a new guy and things were going well. Until that weekend at the coast.

She took another pull of her vape and adjusted her rucksack on her shoulders. She had borrowed two heavy hardbacks from the library and the edges were digging into her back. She had assignments due – there was no such thing as a long weekend when it came to college. She glanced across the street as a van pulled out into traffic, noticing a girl with long dark hair sitting inside the window of a coffee shop staring at her phone. *Lucky for you,* she thought, *nice and warm.* It was after lunchtime and the café appeared quiet. The girl's hair was pulled to one side over her shoulder and even from this side of the street Sarah could see the dark colour of her eyes. There was something familiar about her, wasn't there? The girl lifted her head slightly and stared directly at Sarah. Sarah's heart climbed into her chest. The girl in the window was Grace Doran. *What the hell?* Grace's sister Erin had told Sarah that Grace wouldn't leave the house, that she was depressed and spent most of her time in her bedroom. What was she doing in a café, drinking coffee? What had changed? Was she able to walk again? Sarah threw the vape into her bag and checked the traffic on both sides before quickly crossing the street towards the café. When she reached the footpath on the other side, the girl had disappeared from the window. Sarah peered in through the glass, and she could see the girl at the cash register paying for her coffee. Sarah couldn't believe what she was seeing – Grace Doran was standing on both of her legs. Had Erin been lying to her all this time?

Sarah watched as the cashier handed over change and the girl disappeared around the corner towards the back of the café. Sarah glanced up the street. There was still no sign of her bus. Before she could stop herself, she pushed open the door of the café and followed the direction the girl had taken. There were two doors at the back of the café – one for staff only and one for the toilets. Sarah entered the bathroom, noticing that one of the two cubicle doors was closed. Grace Doran was behind that door. Sarah took a breath. *Calm down, Sarah,* she warned herself. She hadn't seen Grace in a year. Her friend had refused to let her visit at the hospital when she had emerged from her coma, nor would she see her when Sarah called to her home, though Sarah thought Erin might have had something to do with that. Grace wouldn't take her phone calls, and her texts had gone unanswered. Now here she was, in a public place and Sarah would have a chance to speak with her, without Erin's presence. She took a deep breath to stop her heart from beating wildly in her chest.

She checked her appearance in the mirror and noticed how flushed her cheeks were. Turning on the tap, she lightly splashed cool water onto her face before patting it dry with a paper towel. The cubicle door opened and the girl stepped out. Sarah turned towards Grace, a smile spreading across her face. She caught sight of the girl's refection in the mirror. The nose was too long, the cheeks were too round and there was a faded birthmark on her forehead. It wasn't Grace. The girl smiled at Sarah, and then her expression changed to concern.

Sarah's breath caught and she turned and pressed her hands onto the cold marble sink.

"Are you alright?"

Sarah looked up to see the girl's worried face reflected in the mirror. She turned on the tap again, wet the hand paper towel, and dabbed at the skin on her neck and face.

"Can I get you some water?" the girl asked.

She was closer now and Sarah wondered why she thought it might have been Grace. The girl was much taller and probably a good five years older.

Sarah gave a small smile and shook her head. "Thank you, I'm alright, I just felt a bit dizzy. I'll be fine."

The girl smiled back warmly. "Well, if you're sure."

Sarah nodded and the girl left. Sarah leaned over, grabbed the edge of the sink and let the nausea pass. She so desperately wanted the girl to be Grace, she couldn't bear the disappointment. When she thought about that night one year earlier, she dropped her head in shame. Grabbing the hand paper, she wiped the sweat from her forehead. Hurrying out of the café, she saw her bus pulling away from her stop. *Shit.* She glanced up the hill, but there was no sign of another one. It could be ten or fifteen minutes before one arrived, and sometimes they wouldn't show at all. She would never make it across town to collect Zack. Sighing, she crossed the street and hailed a taxi. It wasn't like she couldn't afford it. She sat into the back of the cab, her heart heavy.

34

Lana leaned against the rail of Peter's boat as the breeze whipped loose strands of her short hair around her face. She tied the arms of her sweater around her neck to keep out the chill air. It was times like these that she regretted cutting her long hair. She was glad she had taken her mother's advice – it was much cooler out on the water. She heard her mother's warning echo in her ears: *If March doesn't kill, April will try and May will tell whether you live or die.* Lana smiled – her mother was forever the pessimist!

"Cracking view, isn't it?" Peter said.

"It is quite the picture, yeah," Lana agreed.

She watched as he turned the boat's wheel in the direction of the island and the vessel began to shift. They had just left the harbour, taking the route that Grace's boat must have taken one year ago today, following the buoys out along the water and turning just before reaching the World's End house.

"Sometimes, you get lost in it and forget the job in hand – catching fish," Peter said with a grin. "Most of us fishermen like to come out early and get the work done so we can enjoy the rest of the day, but the view is a sight to behold and on a slow day, say when the fish are scarce, it is hard to drag your eyes away."

"You're lucky to live here." She nodded appreciatively.

"Ah, it's magic alright, most of the time." His face clouded. "But when the winter kicks in, it can be a bit bleak for the locals. There isn't a lot of money circulating off season, with no tourists here spending their earnings, and we do get down about that. We have to stick together, and support each other. There is a real sense of community during the winter months, but summers are different. Everyone is out for themselves." Peter's fingers gripped the steering wheel firmly as the boat kept up a slow and steady pace towards the island.

Lana watched the landscape of Mutton Island begin to take shape. "What is the story with the island? Why has nobody built property there? I mean, I understand it is cut off from the mainland, without supplies during the winter and all that, but the summer months must bring a great deal of tourism to the area?"

"Ah, the currents have a lot to do with it to be fair." Peter was quiet for a moment. "Someone died on the island – it happened years ago, a young lad."

So her mother had been right! Lana smiled inwardly, annoyed with herself for doubting her.

"He swam over and … maybe he got caught in the rips, well, that's what the Gardaí said. It was sort of a drunken challenge. Nobody knows if he made it to the island or got into trouble halfway across the water, but his body was found on the beach, over by the rocks." He turned his head towards her. "Just like your friend. What was her name?"

"My client," she corrected him. "Grace Doran."

"Yeah, Grace Doran."

Lana wondered about the young man who had died. She was just about to ask when Peter spoke.

"So, what is it you do?" His tone was lighter. "When you're not playing Nancy Drew?"

"I'm not playing Nancy Drew."

Peter grinned at her reply.

"I'm investigating a case. It's my job."

He nodded, a playful expression on his face.

"And I spend time with my mother."

He raised an eyebrow and smiled at her. "Just like me? I catch fish and I spend time with *my* mother." He winked at her. "I guess we both need to get out more."

She looked away, blushing. Was he flirting with her?

"What is it you are hoping to achieve?" he asked. "When you get to the island?"

"That remains to be seen."

The island was much closer now – the rocks to the side and the sandy beach ahead with the turn on the bend.

"Like, I'm not sure what you are expecting to find," he went on. "The girl, Grace, at some point she ended up in the water. And then she was found on the beach by Lukasz."

Lana nodded slowly, not sure what he was getting at. She didn't mention that Grace was pushed – possibly Lukasz had already told him the fact.

"So, she had a few drinks and fell off the boat," he continued. "And the others didn't notice until they got back to the World's End. Not the nicest thing to do, but there's no law against being a shit friend!"

"True."

"So, what will a visit to the island achieve for you? It's not going to change what happened, it's just the location of where it happened."

Lana shrugged. "I don't really know. I probably won't learn anything, but I like to visit the location – it gives me a sense of where the victim's head was at, you know? So, I can sort of retrace their steps. It gives me a clearer picture of the events of that day, what happened in the hours prior to her ending up on the beach. Do you see what I mean?"

Peter was watching her carefully. He shrugged. "I suppose."

They were near the island now, and Peter slowed his pace. There were a few other boats moored along the jetty and Lana wasn't sure why, but she felt comfort in knowing that she was in the company of strangers. She remembered Grace had said theirs was the only boat on the island the day they had visited – with no one to witness events, other than her friends.

"Tell me about the young man who drowned?" she said.

Peter steered the boat close to the jetty, before jumping off to tie the thick rope around a bollard. He extended his hand to Lana.

"Here, there is a bit of a gap, you don't want to miss the jetty and fall in."

Lana noticed the space between the boat and the quay – you would want to have your wits about you climbing down. She wondered if her mother would be able for it. She accepted his hand and carefully stepped down from the boat onto the pier, the movement causing her sweater to rise up, exposing her bare midriff. She straightened her sweater and was once again glad that there were other people on the island. The discomfort was all hers though – Peter had turned his attention elsewhere. He was pointing to a site further up the beach.

"Up there." He started walking along the pier towards the rocky side of the beach, beckoning for Lana to follow him. "Mikey

217

Clancy, he was only nineteen years old when he died."

They passed a family setting up a barbeque. A young woman with long blonde hair tied up in a high pony tail, dressed in a pink gingham sun dress, was fighting the breeze as she tried to light the coals on a disposable barbeque container, one hand holding the tray as she flicked a lighter with the other. She stoked a firelighter and dropped it onto the coals. A small flame immediately ignited, spreading rapidly around the tray. Everyone cheered. Lana remembered Grace saying they had barbequed on the beach. She could see another group of four, strolling further up the strand. It really was a beautiful beach and she wondered again why the island had not been developed for commercial use.

"This island, it's beautiful. Must attract a lot of tourists for Castle Cove during the summer."

"Yeah. And if the weather is good we are always in for a bumper season."

"I imagine everyone is relieved when it's over."

"Relieved and exhausted. Over the years the locals started a sort of festival in Castle Cove at the end of the summer, to celebrate the close of the season," Peter said. "It was never about making a profit really – people work hard here during the summer months, sometimes not getting a day off for weeks on end, and by the time we get to late August, well, everyone is exhausted. We have money in our pockets, but we are tired – so, we celebrate. The local musicians play everywhere for the weekend, from six on a Friday evening to midnight on the Sunday. In the bars, hotels, coffee shops, out on the street, down at the harbour, you can't turn a corner in Castle Cove but you hear music on festival weekend. Everyone comes out, people barbeque on the beach, we all share food and drinks. As I said, it's not about making a profit, it's a celebration."

"Sounds like a nice way to end the summer."

"It is. Everyone loves it, especially the young ones. And a lot of them worked throughout the season, summer jobs, watching the tourists enjoying themselves all summer long. So, it's their opportunity to have a bit of craic before the winter sets in."

He stopped beside the rocks.

"Here." He gestured towards the largest boulder. "He was tucked in behind this rock, hidden from view from the sea – that's why he wasn't found for a few days – nobody could see him from the water. It happened on the Friday night, the first evening of the festival. I remember that the wind had picked up a bit."

Lana watched as Peter regarded the sea. The water was calm today, gentle waves rolling over each other.

"What happened?" she asked.

"He had quite a bit to drink." Peter sighed. "We all had."

"You were there?"

Peter nodded. "I was with him on the beach over in Castle Cove, yeah." He hesitated. "We started chatting about the island. The summer had been particularly good that year, the weather was amazing and tourists had flocked to Castle Cove to get away from the city, and so all the locals had been flat out all summer. There was a fair amount of money around. A rumour started circulating that the local council were making plans to invest in the island, you know, develop it as a tourist attraction in its own right. Maybe a theme park with holiday rentals, a restaurant or two, a sort of extension of Castle Cove. There was even talk about a bridge, I mean, it's not that far from the mainland so it would have worked,

I suppose." He returned his gaze to the rocks. "Someone, I can't remember who, said it would be cool to swim across. Mikey said he could do it. Everyone had laughed. I mean, don't get me wrong, Mikey was a strong swimmer. When you grow up on the coast you swim every day of the summer, but there are currents out there, and at certain times of the day or night it is not safe. A few people tried to dissuade him, but there were a few who were egging him on too." Peter's face darkened and Lana guessed he was part of the latter group. "None of us thought he would actually do it, though – I mean, it was all a bit of a joke. The party continued." Peter took a breath. "It was a while before we noticed that Mikey was missing. The next time anyone saw him was right here at this spot, four days later, his head battered in. The Gardaí suspected he became exhausted halfway or three-quarters way across, and he had quite a lot to drink, so ..." His voice trailed off. "They think his head injuries came after he died, when he was washed up on the rocks, but I ..."

"What?"

Peter cleared his throat. "I found him. Everybody was out looking for him and by day four people were losing hope and the Coast Guard wanted to scale down the search. You see, if you get past a certain point, the sea could take you out further and you might never be found. That was what people were beginning to think had happened to Mikey, but I kept searching. And on that day, when folks were beginning to lose faith, I found him and he ... it's hard to explain." Peter hesitated. He glanced towards Lana, his expression pained. She didn't interrupt. "He looked like he was carefully positioned behind this rock."

Lana frowned. "What do you mean?"

"I think someone put him there. I don't think he was washed up – I don't see how it could have been possible."

Lana waited for him to elaborate. When he didn't, she asked. "He was in the ocean, wasn't he? Even the strongest swimmers can't be too careful. The sea is unpredictable."

"The Gardaí arrived from the next town – they ruled it as an accidental drowning but they don't know the route to the island like I do. I grew up here, my dad was a fisherman before me. I was out on his boat before I could tie my shoelaces, and, yeah, maybe Mikey did get caught in a rip, I don't know, but if you saw him, the way he was lying there, his position. It was like someone had put him there." He was staring down at the rocks now, lost in the memory.

"It must have been very traumatic for you, finding him like that?" Lana said gently. "How old were you?"

"Eighteen." There was real sadness in his eyes now.

"You were good friends?" she asked quietly.

He looked up at her then, his expression torn. "Brothers. Mikey Clancy was my brother. My name is Peter Clancy." He glanced up the beach then. "So, your client, Grace, is the second young person to end up on the beach in Mutton Island. In suspicious circumstances." He turned to Lana. "It wasn't an accident, was it? The girl, Grace Doran, she didn't just fall off the boat that night, did she?"

35

Lana slipped out of her trainers and stretched out on the large double bed in her hotel room. The day had been long and she was physically and mentally drained. She was waiting for the dinner she had ordered from the bar to be delivered to her room along with a glass of white wine. She had ordered two and carried one upstairs. She took a long drink and the sweet fruity flavour was both welcome and essential. After Peter told her the story about his brother's death, he had gone back to wait on the boat to give her time to explore the island on her own. The rocks made one section of the island inaccessible, and so, she had taken off up the beach in the opposite direction – the same route that Declan, one of Grace's friends, had taken that day. He had not returned when they were due to leave the island, she had said. The further Lana advanced up the beach, the more she felt like she was stepping off the face of the earth – all she could see was sand and sky.

She took another sip of her wine and her thoughts drifted to Peter. He had been very quiet on their return to the harbour and Lana hadn't pushed for conversation. When they arrived back at the pier, she asked how much she owed him for the afternoon trip and he had waved his hand dismissively, refusing to take any money.

He scribbled his number on a piece of paper and asked if she would keep him informed of any further developments about Grace. The sadness in his eyes wasn't lost on Lana as she took the note, carefully folding it into her purse. Deep down, he must realise that the death of his brother over twenty years earlier and Grace's accident couldn't possibly be connected. No doubt old memories and intense sorrow clouded his judgement.

She wondered how someone could get over that kind of loss, to have been with his brother the night he died, partying together with their friends on the beach, and then to be the one to find his battered and bruised body four days later. Then, to spend the next twenty-odd years, every single day, travelling the same route his brother had, sailing the waters where he had taken his last breath. Perhaps Peter felt he had to stay in Castle Cove, to keep the memory of his brother alive, to find out what really had happened to him. The fisherman confided that he had broken down after his brother's death – "left society for a while," he had said. Unfortunately for Peter, he would probably never know the full truth. When she was leaving the harbour, she had remembered to ask him if he had seen the party of five at any stage during that weekend the previous year, and he said, yes, he had seen them heading out on the boat. He mentioned they had already started drinking, but that there was nothing unusual about that – tourists taking the boats out would often take a picnic and maybe a few bottles of beer or wine with them. It was up to the hire company to warn them about the currents, and he assumed they had. He also added that the hire company wasn't too strict on safety. She had questioned him about that and he had informed her that, in his opinion, there should be an experienced helmsman taking tourists to the island – that the sea is uncertain.

She slipped off the bed and took her glass out to the balcony. The sun was well and truly set now and darkness had fallen over Mutton Island, making it lose its definition. Circular white lights dotted the harbour as tourists strolled up and down the pier, as they stepped out for an evening meal or a drink in one of the bars, their distant chatter lingering in the air. Lana had only seen one pub on the main street, but Peter had informed her that there were two more further up the road if you continued past the entrance to the beach. She had planned to take a walk the following morning, before heading to the harbour to try and catch the elusive boat hire guy with the baseball hat, Gary Duke. When she had arrived back with Peter, there was no sign of him at the kiosk, just his nephew Danny with the bleached-blonde hair. She would talk to Gary in the morning before Danny arrived and, in the afternoon, she would check out, head home and have dinner with her mother.

Her thoughts were interrupted by a knock on her door. *Finally,* she thought, as she set her glass down on the side table. She was ravenous after being out in the sea breeze all afternoon. But when she opened the door, it wasn't room service on the other side.

Instead, Lukasz Novak the fisherman was standing in front of her.

"Can I come in?" he asked, tentatively.

He looked tired as his eyes darted up and down the corridor outside the hotel room. Lana thought that it would be a bad idea to let him in and she was about to suggest that she would meet him down in the bar when he took a step closer, his tone urgent.

"Look, I don't have long. I need to leave village again. I was nearly thirty miles away when I decided to come back, to talk to you. I did try to call you, but there was a poor signal."

Lana didn't move. Her heart started to pump in her chest. *No,* she pleaded, *not again. Breathe, Lana,* she told herself, in through the nose and hold for three seconds, out through the mouth. Repeat. She was annoyed that she had opened the door without checking through the peephole. *Why the fuck had she done that?* She was acutely conscious that the hallway appeared empty. She felt the familiar sensation as her legs turned to jelly and she tightened her grip on the door handle to steady her balance. She repeated the instructions she had learned in counselling. Don't let him see that you are scared. Take control before the terror controls you. Somehow, she found her voice. "Why did you come back, Lukasz? Why did you leave for that matter?" She was aware of how hoarse she sounded.

"Please, I will only stay for ten minutes – we can leave the door open if you are scared. Please, let me speak with you before I change my mind? It is important. For Grace. Please?"

Lana sighed. This man wasn't a threat to her, he looked more frightened himself. She slowly nodded, and stepped aside. Her heart rate began to return to normal. Lukasz walked quickly past her. She pressed the door against the magnetic door-catch to keep it from closing, and followed him into the room. He sat on the edge of the chair by the small coffee table. Lana stood by the bathroom entrance, watching, as he rubbed the palms of his hands together, over and over. She continued her breathing technique as she waited for him to speak.

"I cannot give evidence. At the girl's trial. If her case goes to court, I cannot be there."

He looked up but Lana remained close-lipped – she had learned a long time ago that the best way to get information from someone is not to interrupt, just let them talk, and Lukasz clearly wanted to talk.

"I got involved in something that I should not have, when I live in Poland," he continued. "I had to leave overnight because of

Policja. It was not my fault but I cannot go back there." He glanced around the room. "It was not my fault," he repeated.

"Go on?" Lana encouraged.

Lukasz rubbed his hands up and down the side of his thighs, his body rocking gently back and forward, his focus on the cream carpet. "I never liked school, all that learning, rules, books, it was not for me, and so I left when I was teenager and got job on a fishing boat with a man – he said he was a friend of my father. I did not know much about fishing, but I learned quickly from him. He gave me start and I was grateful to him. And I liked it, out on the water for hours on my own – you need to have discipline for that, and I did. I do. My father died when I was young boy, I do not have any brothers or sisters, it was just my mother and me, and she worked every day to pay the bills, and I was on my own, most of the time."

"The man, my boss, he started to give me more and more responsibility, and there were many mornings he would let me take the boat out on my own." He looked out towards the balcony at the sea beyond and his expression darkened. "It was not long before I realised he had other business, not just catching fish. One morning he asked me to meet someone out on the water, a customer he said. There was a box in the cabin and all I had to do was hand it over. He told me the name of the boat I had to meet and that it would find me out on the water. It seemed easy enough, so I went out on my usual route and, sure enough, a short time later, there was another boat. Two men lifted the box onto their boat and thanked me and that was that. Then it became more regular thing, a couple of times a week. I would meet this boat, out on the water, and the same two men would carry the box onto their boat. I did not know where they were from – they did not speak much – but their accent, it was not Polish. Then my boss started putting a few extra *złoty* in my wage packet. I began to get suspicious about the contents of the boxes, and so, one morning, I opened one." He looked up at Lana. "I found drugs, cocaine, lots of it. I did not know what to do – if I told the *Policja*, I would betray this man who had given me a chance and taught me a new skill, but if I continued to sail the boat, I was committing a crime, knowingly playing a part in smuggling drugs. An accomplice. I just did not know what to do." He glanced towards the hallway and then back at Lana. "That night I went out to sea, the night after I opened the box, but I took a different route. I threw the boxes of cocaine overboard. I do not know how much it was worth, a lot I think, but I did not care. I got rid of it. And then I left Poland. I did not even tell my mother. I had to protect her. I had saved some money and so I bought a ticket for the ferry to England, and another one to Ireland. Then I took a train and bus and then other bus. I did not know where I was going, I just keep moving, until I come here. I met Peter at the harbour, and he gave me a job, and I worked hard and I saved enough money to buy my own boat. It is small but it is mine, but I can never go back to Poland. The man, my old boss, he called to my mother's house asking for me. My mother said she did not know where I was, that I had disappeared. He threatened her, but she did not tell him anything, because she did not know where I was, she still doesn't know. I have a friend, who lives on the road where I grew up, and my mother told him about the man. I call him sometimes to see how she is. I had to leave her to protect her, it is the sacrifice I had to make. And even though I miss my mother and my home, every day, I have made a new life here. Until today, when you told me about Grace, that someone pushed her off the boat. You will need me as a witness, yes?"

Lana was confused. She didn't think she needed to call Lukasz as a witness – he hadn't told her anything new about the weekend Grace had spent in Castle Cove with her friends. She came to sit on the chair opposite him and leaned forward.

"Lukasz, I didn't say anything about you possibly being called as a witness? You didn't have to leave Castle Cove today."

His eyebrows shot up. "What? But I thought …"

"You didn't have anything new to tell me, only that you saw two people outside the summerhouse, possibly arguing – well, that doesn't prove that Grace was pushed off the hire boat."

Lukasz looked at the soft carpet and neither of them moved. She knew there was more, her hunch had been right, the fisherman was holding something back. He slowly met her eyes. "Actually, I do. I saw something." His eyes flickered towards the open door of the hotel room and then back to Lana. "The boat Grace was on, it left the harbour again that night, after dark. And I lied about it being there the next morning."

"The *Karina*?"

"Yes."

The silence hung between them. Lana crossed the room and closed the door. She returned to her seat. "Tell me what you saw, Lukasz?" She sat back in her chair.

"The night before I found Grace on the beach, I was tidying up my boat. The weekend had been busy and I wanted to clean the storage boxes and deck before heading out to sea the next morning. I waited until late in the evening to avoid the tourists."

"What time was this?"

"About eight, I think. Or just after. The harbour was quiet when I got there. There was no sign of Peter or the other fishermen. I thought they were probably in the pub. I got busy with my work and when I was finishing up I heard people talking, further up the harbour. They were arguing."

"How do you know they were?"

He shook his head. "One of them was shouting 'You fucking idiots!'."

"Who were they? Could you see them?"

"Yes." He nodded. "Three people, standing beside the *Karina*."

"Men? Women?"

"I'm sure they were men."

"Then what?"

"Two of the men climbed onto the boat while the other untied the rope from the bollard. The engine started, the third man jumped on and the boat moved off."

"Did you recognise any of the men?"

"Gary Duke was one of them. The guy who hires out the boats."

"Did you tell anyone?"

"No." He shrugged. "The sea was calm that night, and Gary was with the two men, and the boats are his responsibility, so I didn't think that the men were doing anything dangerous. Or illegal."

"What did you do then?"

"I finished up my work and I went home."

"And the next morning you saw two people arguing outside the World's End?"

"Yes. And ..." He hesitated.

"Go on?" Lana encouraged.

"They were the same two men I saw with Gary the night before."

"Are you sure?"

"I am sure."

36

Stephen sipped his coffee as he scanned the note written on the calendar pinned to the kitchen wall – *App next Tuesday with gynaecologist, 4.45pm.* He sighed as he loosened his tie. Andy hadn't wasted any time, had she? The previous evening, she tells him she wants to try for a baby, and already she has arranged to see a consultant. He vaguely wondered if she had made the appointment before their chat. He finished the rest of his coffee and placed his cup in the dishwasher. The machine was full so he found a tablet in the cupboard under the sink and put it into the bottom of the machine. Closing the door, he pushed the power button and a moment later he heard the gentle swish of water rinsing dishes as the machine began its cycle. He pressed the palms of his hands onto the counter, and closed his eyes. *Shit*, he thought, everything was going to *shit*. He checked his watch, Andy would be at work still. There was an exhibition at the art gallery this evening. The artist was well known nationally and Andy had worked hard on securing the presentation at her boss's gallery, and, having invited a lot of important figures in the art world, she really wanted to impress. Especially after all the time she had taken off. She wouldn't get back until late, he was sure, at least another couple of hours. If he left now he could be back before she arrived home.

He grabbed his phone and car keys. Stephen didn't know much about Declan's lifestyle, but what he did know was that the man had an obsession with the gym, and, he would bet on it that hadn't changed. Declan had talked about it during the weekend at the World's End last year, even mentioning the name of the gym he visited every evening straight after work, trying to impress Grace, though she didn't bite. He said he never changed his routine, even on the weekend. It was located on the north side of the city. Traffic would be heavy at this time of the evening, but if he took the motorway and entered town from the other side, he should make it just as Declan was heading for the showers. He didn't trust Harry. He felt his friend was keeping something from him. He had to talk to Declan – sooner rather than later.

As he was about to leave the apartment he heard a noise, a sort of shuffling sound, scraping or scratching at something. He froze. *What the hell was that?* He listened, but the house was completely quiet again, and for a brief moment he wondered if he had heard anything at all? He didn't move for a second, remaining perfectly still, and just when he thought he had imagined it, he heard the sound again. He couldn't be sure but he thought it might be coming from the bedroom. His heart hammering in his chest, he told himself to get a grip as he quietly made his way over to the kitchen and grabbed a bread knife. Just in case. The sound was more prominent now, definitely more like a scraping sound. He wondered if it was a mouse and, briefly, felt a bit ridiculous holding the bread knife in his hand. He moved into the hall and approached the bedroom, noticing the door was slightly ajar as he crept along the corridor. He could see something moving on the bed, something furry. *Jesus Christ! What the fuck?* His heart pounded in his chest as he slowly pushed the bedroom door open. Stunned, he saw what was making the sound – Milo, their missing cat, was sitting on the bed, his paws playing with the silky fabric of the duvet. He looked up when Stephen approached, his green eyes sheathed in his black coat. Milo had been missing for over a week. Where had he been all this time and how did he get back into the apartment? Had he been here all along? Surely that wasn't possible. Stephen had just come in from his meeting with Harry and made coffee, and so he hadn't been home that long. Maybe Andy found the cat during the afternoon before she left for the art gallery, and forgot to mention it. He would talk to her when she got home. He checked his watch – he'd better hurry if he wanted to catch Declan.

As he was passing the kitchen, he noticed the picture frame of his wedding day lying flat on the kitchen counter. Andy must have removed it from its place on the alcove wall – possibly with the intention of replacing it with another image. She probably felt the same as he did about the portrait. Turning his key to lock the apartment, he heard a door open across the corridor behind him. He closed his eyes and uttered a silent curse. Mike. It was as if the man was listening on the other side of his door, waiting for him to leave his apartment.

"Hey, Stephen, do you want to catch that beer?"

Stephen turned towards Mike, preparing his excuse. "Sorry, mate, I'm in a rush. Meeting a client."

Mike nodded but Stephen could tell by the look on his face that he didn't believe him.

"You work too hard. Mate. It's Saturday," Mike observed, his tone full of sarcasm. "You should relax in the evening, have a beer with your neighbour."

Stephen smiled awkwardly. "I know, you're right, but sometimes clients can't meet during business hours and so I do have to make allowances." He wondered why he was making excuses to his neighbour – he didn't owe him an explanation for how he led his life. Though something about the way Mike was watching him was making him feel nervous.

"Tell you what, I should get finished in about an hour. I can fit you in then?"

Mike laughed, a little too loud. "Fit me in? That's very generous of you, Stephen!"

Stephen quickly shook his head, embarrassed. "I didn't mean it to come out like that ..."

"It's OK, Stephen, I know you didn't."

"Right, well ..." Stephen made to leave.

"How's Andy?"

Stephen felt his blood run cold. What the hell was Mike playing at? He never asked after Andy. He swallowed what he wanted to say. "She's fine." He glanced at his watch. "Look, I'll be back in a while, OK? We can have that beer?"

"Yeah, I should be here. Hopefully you can fit me in." Mike winked. "Only kidding."

Stephen started to back down the corridor. "I'll bring a six-pack." He turned and strode off, acutely aware that Mike hadn't gone back into his apartment. He turned the corner and took the stairs down to the carpark, feeling uneasy. It was only when he opened the door leading into the cold basement that he realised he had been holding his breath. What the hell was wrong with Mike? He had been acting strangely around Stephen recently, every time they met. OK, they hadn't had drinks together since that one time and the man must be pissed off about that, but they were hardly mates, were they? He didn't owe him anything, they were just neighbours who had a casual drink together occasionally, at least, that's how he saw it. Again, he was annoyed with himself that he had confided in Mike about his weekend away, without Andy. Note to self: *Stop getting pissed with the creepy neighbour guy.*

He unlocked his car and started the engine. A moment later he was driving out of the carpark. He took the route that would lead him to the exit for the motorway. Drumming his fingers on the steering wheel, he tried not to think about what he would say to Declan, deciding he would play it casual, act surprised, that they had bumped into each other. *A coincidence.* He switched on the radio and flicked through the channels, hoping to find something to listen to, to distract him. But the action was making him more nervous. He flicked the switch off again and told himself to *calm the fuck down.* It was at times like these that he felt like a cigarette. It had been years since he smoked tobacco and every now and then he was surprised that he still got cravings.

The truth was that Stephen had been on edge ever since Harry had dropped his bombshell about Declan, and he was equally confused that Declan wanted to talk now. Why did he want to tell the investigator that he had been with them that weekend? Stephen had kept quiet about events. He had left that same evening they arrived back from the island, the second everyone realised that Grace Doran wasn't on the boat, when the panic had set in. So he was gone when the Gardaí arrived, and nobody had mentioned him, Harry made sure of that. Anyway, the Gardaí believed that Grace had too much to drink and had fallen off the boat. It was an accident, they said, an unfortunate accident. Stephen, Harry,

Declan and Sarah had all got on with their lives. In any case, Declan was merely an acquaintance, a guy he met for the odd pint when in Harry's company. The man came from a wealthy family, and while in college he ran in different circles to Stephen who was always working a couple of jobs, trying to make ends meet. So, it wasn't unusual that he hadn't heard from Declan – they were never close. The only noticeable absence this past year had been Harry.

He took the exit for the motorway. Traffic was less busy now and he picked up speed, and ten minutes later he took the route that would bring him back to the north side of the city. The gym was on his right, just off the end of the slip road. He pulled into the carpark and found an empty space at the rear. He sat for a moment, trying to decide how he was going to approach Declan. The two of them had never really had much time for each other, and that weekend last year hadn't exactly cemented their friendship. Declan had fancied Grace. Grace liked Stephen. *The sound of the waves breaking, warm sand, his hand moving up her thigh, a smile playing on her soft lips … terrified eyes, blood, a torn dress …* he shook the memory aside, he needed to focus. He climbed out of his car and locked the door. The gym was lit up for all the world to see – bright florescent bulbs illuminated the glass panelled building highlighting Lycra-clad men and women as they ran on treadmills, pumped iron, or engaged in aerobic classes. He could hear the pulsating music from the carpark, the loud beat inspiring its members to keep moving. Stephen could never understand people's obsession with gyms. To him, they were sweaty buildings, generally with poor ventilation. He preferred to exercise outdoors, in the fresh air. A group of girls emerged through the swivel door, laughing. They were discussing where they were going to eat, one of them suggesting curry chips, the others eagerly agreed. He smiled to himself at the irony, but who was he to judge – he guessed one justified the other, right?

He contemplated going into the gym and confronting Declan inside the building, but now that he was here, he was having second thoughts about that. Declan was unpredictable at the best of times and he was likely to make a scene if he felt backed into a corner, and Stephen wanted to avoid that. He decided to stay out in the car park and wait for him. He would act surprised, as if he had just happened to be in the area. Then, he would bring up the weekend in Castle Cove and ask him, no, *tell him,* not to mention his presence at the summerhouse. Tell him again about the situation with Andy – and that, after the email he received from Luke Jennings that afternoon, the stakes were much higher. If Declan showed resistance, he would have no problem reminding him that he had kept quiet about the other issue.

A van pulled out of a spot near the front door of the gym and Stephen quickly ran back to his car so he could drive into the space. He would have a better view of the entrance from there. Luckily, it was still available when he drove up through the park. He switched off the ignition and checked his watch. It was exactly seven. If Declan wasn't lying about his gym routine, he should be out soon enough. Stephen hoped so – he wanted to get back before Andy returned. Even if he was having a beer with Mike across the hall, he could text that he was in the building, and had been there all evening. Andy was doing much better, but there was no point giving her cause for suspicion.

The swivel doors opened and, sure enough, Declan appeared in a T-shirt and shorts, his hair wet, a gear bag slung over his shoulder.

Stephen opened his car door and was just about to get out when he noticed Declan turning to say something to the person behind him. As he moved away from the door, Stephen could see who he was talking to. *Harry.* Declan was laughing at something Harry was saying. *What the hell?* What was Harry doing here? He said he had only seen Declan once since that weekend a year earlier. A couple of nights ago. He *told* Stephen this in the afternoon. Judging by their body language, they didn't look like they hadn't been in touch for a while. They appeared very pally as they strolled across the carpark, climbing into the same car. Something was very off about this.

He watched as Declan started the car while Harry sat into the passenger seat. Stephen took his phone out of his pocket and quickly scrolled through his contacts until he found Harry's name. He tapped the call button. He watched as Harry reached into his jacket pocket, pulled out his phone, glanced at the screen before putting his phone away. Unanswered.

Stephen stopped the call and sat back in the driver's seat. He didn't know what to make of what he had just seen. What was Harry playing at? Declan drove past his car and out of the carpark. Stephen contemplated following the two but he didn't know what that would achieve. He gripped the wheel and decided to send Harry an email and suggest they meet. He would get the truth out of him, they were old friends. So whatever his relationship was with Declan, surely his loyalty was to Stephen? Unless that other business was still going on, but Harry had sworn that weekend had been their first and last time.

Another image resurfaced: *dark hair, twisted limbs, dead eyes,, blood* ... he felt the nausea rise up in his chest. Opening his door, he leaned out and threw up on the pavement. *Jesus, get a grip.*

He wiped his mouth with the back of his hand and closed the door. Grabbing a packet of gum from the glove compartment, he popped one into his mouth. A moment later, he pulled out of the park. He decided to drive across town instead of taking the motorway home – traffic would be lighter now with the rush hour over. He would stop into the off licence on his street and pick up a six-pack of beer. He needed it.

Twenty minutes later, he parked his car in the same underground parking spot and climbed the stairs to his floor two at a time. He took a moment to steady his breathing before knocking on Mike's door. When there was no answer, he knocked again. There was still no reply, no sound of movement behind the door. He pressed his ear to the wooden frame. He was sure he could hear voices, muffled. Maybe Mike had fallen asleep watching the TV. He checked his watch, confused – it was just before eight. Mike was hardly asleep this early, was he? Stephen hadn't been gone that long. Perhaps his neighbour had got the hump with Stephen's earlier rebuttal. Stephen was relieved – he wasn't exactly keen on the idea of listening to Mike droning on about whatever bullshit documentary he was obsessing about.

He crossed the hall and unlocked the door of his apartment. The room was in darkness, which meant that Andy was still not home. He flicked the switch on the wall. The quietness unnerved him. In the kitchen, he found a bottle opener and uncapped one of the beers. He took a long drink and ran over what he had witnessed that evening. Harry and Declan were still in regular contact – that was clear. But why had he lied? Stephen remembered the fight he had with Declan on the island. Had Harry been lying because of that? Were the two men still embroiled in whatever had gone on last year?

He put the rest of the beers in the fridge and placed his half-empty bottle on the marble counter. Glancing around the apartment, he had the same feeling that he had earlier – something was off, but what? Milo suddenly appeared and twisted his body around Stephen's legs, crying and growling in protest. *Stupid fucking cat.* There was no way he was letting him out of the apartment at this time of night. His laptop sat open on the coffee table where he had left it earlier. Had he not closed it? His jacket was draped over the back of the sofa. He scanned the kitchen until his eyes landed on the cup he had been drinking coffee from before he had left the apartment, now hanging from a hook on the wall. *What the hell?*

Stephen opened the dishwasher. It was empty. He felt the hair rise on the back of his neck as he peered inside the machine. Someone had been in the apartment and emptied the dishwasher.

37

Grace woke with a start – she was drenched in sweat. She had been dreaming that she was steering a boat and the wheel kept pulling to one side and no matter how hard she twisted and turned the wheel, she couldn't straighten the vessel. She was screaming over her shoulder for help, but she couldn't get the words out. There had been someone in the water, right in front of her, arms flailing in the air. The *someone* had no face, and the boat seemed to speed up the closer she got. She was heading straight for the person. Desperately, she tried to turn the wheel, twisting it harder and harder, but nothing would work. She shielded her eyes from the inevitable impact, while at the same time she shot up in bed, her lungs ready to explode. It took her a few moments to realise that it was just a dream. She had the same dream before, always the same. But she could never see the face of the person, and she always woke up just before they collided.

The bedroom was dark. Checking the time on her phone, she saw that it was just after three in the morning. She reached for the glass of water on her bedside locker and emptied it in one gulp, but when she finished she was still thirsty. She decided she needed to use the bathroom and get something to drink, but she didn't want to wake Erin. Tears prickled the backs of her eyes at how helpless she had become. She was twenty-seven years old and she was an invalid, completely dependent on her older sister for everything. It just wasn't fair. *Why her?* Why did this have to happen to her? She had endured a shit childhood with little or no love from her mother. She didn't know much about her father, that is, until their neighbour's surprise visit the day before. College hadn't worked out, but, she had been gaining confidence, she had started to build a life for herself, she had her own job, her own money and she had a couple of friends, a social life, she had plans for her future, and now, it was all gone and she didn't know how or why it had happened.

She felt like the dream was trying to tell her something, but every time she pushed for an answer, the distorted images spun around in her head, and her memory would fail her.

She leaned back against the bedframe and closed her eyes. Her left leg ached. The doctors had told her that the pins and metal rods were holding it in place and helping it heal, and if she could just be patient with it for a couple of more months, she would hopefully not lose a second limb. They rattled this off as if it was something to look forward to, but Grace wondered if it was worth the pain. Maybe she should get rid of it now and be done with it. How quickly we adapt to our environment, she thought, as if no other world existed before but the one she lived in now.

Her mind drifted back to the visit they had earlier from their neighbour next door. What she had to say was a shock to say the least, but the more she thought about it, the more it made sense. Grace had always wondered what had happened to her father, as had Erin. And now they knew. They had not dared ask their mother – she had made it clear when they were still very young that their father was never to be mentioned in the house. Erin had been quiet after the old lady left – she clearly didn't want to talk about what they had learned. Erin could be like that, she needed time to process things. She had helped Grace get ready for bed and they had said their goodnights and, no doubt, tomorrow Erin would want to talk.

Grace's mouth was dry with the thirst and she felt as if her bladder was about to burst – she couldn't ignore it any longer. She found the light on her phone and saw that her wheelchair was nearby. If she could just pull it closer to her bed, she could slip off the edge and onto the chair. She carefully positioned the phone against her empty glass on the bedside locker so that the light was facing the chair. It wasn't that far, she reasoned, she could reach it if she pushed her body forward, just enough to grab the chair. She leaned over the side of the bed, the handle was in reach, if she just pressed a little further, just a little. There, she grabbed the armrest of the wheelchair, but when she touched the support, the chair moved, bringing her with it. The brakes had been disabled. She tumbled forward and collapsed in a heap on the floor beside her bed, a sharp pain darting up her left leg as the pins shifted. *Oh God no*, she thought. Feeling around her knee in the dark, she felt that she might have moved one of the pins out of place. In fact, she was sure of it – not a good outcome for the bone attached. Warm liquid pooled around the front of her nightdress.

Tears slipped down her cheeks and onto the hard floor. She let the pain and humiliation take over. She would not call her sister. She would lie here all night if she had to. She didn't care anymore. What was the point? She had lost everything anyway, hadn't she? What was the point in fighting anymore?

She couldn't even bring herself to look in the mirror after that one time in the hospital when she had begged Erin to bring in a hand mirror and, after much persuasion, her sister had finally conceded. Grace never asked again. She was ruined and she was ugly, with half of her face replaced by an angry scar. She couldn't dress herself on her own, prepare food, or do her own washing, all the things she had taken for granted. She couldn't even get a glass of water on her own without falling out of her bed.

She noticed a light come on in the hall, a shaft of brightness streaming under her door, and then, the sound of footsteps and the shadow of a figure, a nightdress wavering in the pool of light. Erin gently pushed the door fully open and entered the room. Grace pressed her face further into the floor, squeezing her eyes shut as light flooded the room.

"Grace! My God, what happened to you?"

Grace didn't answer, she let the tears fall freely – she couldn't stop them.

Erin crouched down and assessed the damage. She placed her hand over Grace's, covering her leg. "Does it hurt?"

Grace simply nodded.

"Where?" Erin asked.

Grace moved her hand up her left leg, stopping just above her knee. She felt the dampness on the fabric of her nightdress, the smell of urine filling the room. She was more embarrassed than she had ever been in her whole life. For something like this to happen in the hospital, when she was being cared for by a complete stranger, didn't bother her so much, but for it to happen in front of her sister was unbearable.

However, Erin didn't react. "OK, let's get you cleaned up and then we can see if we need to call an ambulance."

Grace looked on as Erin set to work, her movements fluid, her expression kind. Erin had always been meticulous in everything she did. She remembered a time when Erin had given up sweets for the whole of Lent, and every time someone gave her a jelly or a square of chocolate, she made a space in her drawer in their bedroom, carefully placing the sweets in rows, lining them up beside each other. When their mother did her shopping, the sisters would always get a bar of milk chocolate to share – it was their weekly treat. During Lent, that year, Erin would put her half of the bar away. If a teacher gave her a jelly sweet for her writing skills, it went straight into that drawer. By the time Easter Sunday arrived, she had gathered up quite a few treats for herself, even though the jellies had started to soften and stick to the plywood lining the drawer and some of the chocolate had melted. After dinner, she had taken Grace by the hand and they both climbed the stairs, closed their bedroom door, and together they ate every treat, savouring each bite, their fingers sticky from the chewy sweets. Erin had shared everything with Grace, after weeks of sacrifice. Grace was reminded of that now, and how Erin had always looked out for her. In a way, it was as if their path was set out for them both, even when they were small.

Sometime later, Erin had removed the soiled nightdress and replaced it with a fresh one, she had lifted Grace onto the wheelchair and cleaned the floor, she had given Grace some pain relief and a cup of tea, and she was carefully examining the pins in her leg, particularly the one just above her knee. Her red hair had come free and hung loosely around her shoulders.

"I don't think they have moved, but the skin around this one?" Her finger rested on the metal bar below Grace's knee. "It's a little bit red. I'll ring the doctor in the morning and see what he says – we may need to keep an eye on the insertion area, for infection."

The concern on Erin's face made Grace want to cry again. She reached out and tucked a loose strand of hair behind Erin's ear. Erin looked up, the concern in her eyes drawing fresh tears. "What is it, Grace?"

"I'm sorry, Erin. For everything."

Erin started to protest. "Don't be daft, Grace, there's no need to apologise."

Grace stopped her sister. "No, there is. You have always looked after me, from when we were kids, and you sacrificed your own chance of college so I could have one. You looked after Mam and I know that wasn't easy, and now, here you are, stuck with me. I didn't tell you I was going away that weekend." She couldn't stop the crying now, the tears fell easily. "If only I hadn't gone down there. If only ... I was so stupid."

Erin held Grace and let her cry, smoothing her hair back from her face. She cried and cried and when she was finished, Erin handed her some tissues.

"I knew. About dad." Erin's spoke softly in the quiet room.

Grace looked up, confused. "What?"

"Mam told me about Dad, not long after she had the first stroke. It was the reason she moved into the care home. I wouldn't look after her any more. She had lied to us, for so many years. Lying about our father, that was the final straw for me."

Grace narrowed her eyes. "But you never said anything."

"No. Mam asked me not to tell you, she said I could never tell you, she was so ashamed. I didn't know what to do. I wanted to tell you ... but then the truth was so terrible ... our uncle was

245

responsible for the death of his own brother. Mam was always afraid he would come back. Remember, she used to look down the hall all the time, at the front door, smoking her cigarettes, pretending to do her crosswords, and we were never allowed to play with other kids? And Mam told me the woman next door, Maureen Doran, was her mother-in-law."

All these years, living next door to each other, separated by a wall, Grace had no idea. But Erin already knew, for some time at least.

Now Maureen had heard about Grace's accident and she wanted to help, financially. She wanted to pay for any surgeries Grace might need.

Grace remembered something. "Erin, someone was visiting Mam."

Erin looked up, a question on her face. "What?" She shook her head. "No, nobody ever went to visit Mam in the care home, except you and me."

Grace sniffed. "No, last year, when I went to see her – the evening before I travelled to Castle Cove – I checked the visitor's logbook and someone had been to see her the day before. I couldn't make out the signature, and then Peggy came along and I forgot about it, but, when I entered her room that night, she just freaked out. I mean, she often freaked out when she saw me, but that night she was really terrified of something. Maybe it had something to do with her visitor?" Grace took a breath. "Who could it have been? Do you think it was him? Our uncle?"

Erin looked momentarily startled, then she composed herself. She gave Grace a strange look. "No, it couldn't have been him. Mam said he moved to the other side of the world, that he just disappeared. You were only two at the time and I was five. I don't remember him at all."

They were both quiet for a moment, absorbed in their own thoughts.

"What do you think they were arguing about that night?" Grace asked then. "The two brothers."

Erin's expression softened. "Mam told me something. Not long after she had the first stroke. That's why she moved into a care home. I refused to look after her. I couldn't handle any more of her lies."

"What did she tell you?"

"I thought Maureen might mention it …"

"What did she tell you, Erin?"

Erin reached up and gently ran her finger along the scar on Grace's cheek. "My uncle is your father."

38

Lana switched off the shower and blindly reached for a towel from the rack. Wrapping the soft cloth around her body, she stepped onto the cool tiles. The mirror in the small bathroom had fogged up while she showered and she wiped the condensation clear with the edge of a facecloth. Her cheeks were flushed inside the small space. She turned on the tap and splashed some cold water onto her face to cool down. She could hear the Sunday morning news on the TV in the other room. The anchor was reporting about a raid at a private residence. The criminal assets bureau had taken possession of a house, as part of a five-year investigation into the activities of an organised crime gang. Her interest was piqued when she heard the broadcaster mention Limerick. She entered the bedroom and grabbed her make-up bag. The inquiry began when the lavish lifestyle by the known suspect caused suspicion in the area. Assets including a luxury car, laptops and other items had been seized. The probe focused on bogus investment opportunities, among other criminal activities. Gardaí were continuing with their investigations. Lana folded her arms and watched the screen as footage showed the property in question. She wondered about the exact location of the investigation – city or county? It looked familiar but she couldn't be sure having missed the beginning of the broadcast.

She returned to the bathroom and squeezed some body moisturizer onto the palm of her hand and began to lather the cream onto her skin. She wiped the excess from her hands on the towel and shook her short hair loose. She was still not used to the length, having chosen the new style on a whim. Her mother had been livid. But Lana had her reasons. Her long blonde hair was a constant reminder of the person she was, the mistakes she had made. Moving back into the bedroom, she dressed quickly in black jeans and a grey T-shirt. Running a comb through her damp hair, her eyes rested on a piece of paper on the table with Lukasz's mobile number. She sipped some coffee from the cup she had made earlier from the hotel room machine, grimacing at its bitter taste.

She hadn't slept well – she had tossed and turned all night thinking about the Polish fisherman and what he had told her. Eventually, she had given up on sleep, taken out her laptop and updated her notes on the Grace Doran case.

He had been so frightened when he first arrived. And she had been quite scared herself, initially, but the more he talked about his story from home, explaining why he had left so suddenly, the more she realised he was more fearful for his family back in Poland and dragging her into something that might endanger her life. Clearly, he was petrified of his old boss and it must have taken a lot for him to travel back to Castle Cove to talk to her. She felt sorry for the young man that had taken so easily to his role as a fisherman, only to be exploited to the point where he felt he had no choice but to leave his home and family, for their own safety, as well as his own. She had promised him that she would try to help him when she got back to the city. Lana had a friend who worked in the drugs importation unit. She would contact him and relate Lukasz's story. Circumstances might have changed – a great deal can happen in five years. Because now, Lana knew that Lukasz would definitely be required to testify in court. If Grace wanted to pursue a criminal case, the fisherman would be her strongest witness so far. From what he had seen, it was obvious something more sinister was at play. Lukasz had scribbled his mobile number on a piece of paper and left just after eleven. He hadn't told her where he was going and she hadn't asked. Her cold, uneaten dinner rested on the bedside locker.

Walking back into the bathroom, she smoothed moisturiser onto her face and neck, applied a pale pink pencil to her lips, a dark brown liner and mascara to her lashes and she was good to go. She gathered her toiletries into her wash bag and placed it on top of her overnight carrier. The news anchor was still harping on about the organised crime gang in the background, now adding people-smuggling to the list of offences.

"*The man under investigation is linked to the disappearance of a young woman, an Eastern European national, Eva Mroz. No arrests have been made at this stage ...*"

The guy was in the shit, Lana thought. She placed the bag along with her laptop on the bed, to retrieve later when she was checking out. Glancing at her watch, she realised it was just before eight in the morning. Danny had said that his uncle, Gary Duke, usually arrived at about nine – she didn't want to hang around the harbour waiting, so she decided she would take a stroll in the opposite direction of the harbour and call her mother. She would then head towards the harbour and find the mysterious Gary. Peter, Lukasz and the nephew had presented a few question marks around Gary's business dealings and she needed to talk to him.

She grabbed her phone, some loose change and her key and left the room, taking the stairs to the lobby. Gina was behind the reception desk.

"Morning, Ms. Bowen, you're up early." She smiled sweetly. "Would you like some breakfast?"

Lana shook her head. "Not at the moment, thanks, Gina. What time do you finish serving? I'm just heading out for a walk."

"Oh, you have plenty of time. The chef keeps serving until ten. We won't see you hungry." The young girl beamed.

Lana remembered something. "Actually, Gina, maybe you can tell me something I'm wondering about?"

Gina nodded. "Go ahead, Ms. Bowen, that's what we're here for."

"Do you know who owns the World's End, the summerhouse, at the other side of the harbour? I passed it when I was walking along the pier yesterday. It would be a nice house to take for a summer rental."

"Some big noise from the city owns it, well, that's what the locals say. He hires a maintenance company to clean the house. Some of the staff live locally. They look after most of the holiday homes in Castle Cove." She hesitated. "Look, between you and me, that house has changed owners so many times it's hard to know anymore."

"So, could the owner be someone from Castle Cove?" Lana asked.

Gina shrugged. "I doubt it. People around here, we all know each-other's business, so, if someone local had bought that house, we would know about it. Anyway, nobody has stayed there for ages.

Maybe the banks own it now. NAMA or one of those vulture funds?"

"Thanks, Gina."

"You're welcome, Ms. Bowen. Enjoy your walk." Her bright smile lit up the desk.

Lana tried to smile back, barely making it. She was tired and she was hungry, but she needed to touch base with her mother, and she wanted to chat with Gary Duke before considering food. Besides, it was too early for Gina's enthusiasm. She nodded and left the hotel.

The road was quiet for this time of morning, there was nobody out. Lana stopped into the newsagent's and picked up a bottle of water before heading downhill, away from the small village. She passed the path leading down to the beach and noticed how steep it was. Going down would be easy enough, she surmised, but climbing back up after a swim would require youth and fitness. Grace Doran had both, before the incident. She continued on as the coastline cleared. She could see all the way over to Mutton Island from this stretch of road. One boat bobbed in the water, close to the island, and Lana wondered if it was Peter out for his morning's catch. He would be busier now, with Lukasz gone. Lana blushed when she thought about the fisherman and the way he had looked at her, his hand resting on her waist as she climbed down from his boat.

Reaching into her pocket, she pulled out her phone and dialled her mother's mobile number – there was no answer. Lana frowned at the phone as the number rang out. Her mother was always up early, even on long weekends – the woman was a creature of habit. She would go for a walk before eight, every single morning, and she would be back home in her kitchen, preparing her breakfast in time for the nine o'clock news. Maybe she was in the shower or out in the garden. Lana decided she would give her a few minutes and try again. She took a sip of her water and continued on down the road, passing a small pub on her left. Lana noticed a wide decking area, looking out onto the beach below. The view must be remarkable of an evening, she thought, for anyone enjoying a meal or a cold drink. If you had the weather, there would be no need for Spain or Portugal with this sight in front of you. Lana could see another pub, a little further along. Peter was right, there were plenty of watering holes for Castle Cove's tourists to enjoy.

She decided to try her mother once more as she turned back towards the harbour. She wanted to tell her about this place, describe it in real time, but when she dialled the number there was still no answer. She called the landline, but again there was no response. She fired off a quick text: **Where are you?** She really wanted to show her mother this view, and bring her here when they both had time. She would make a booking with Gina for a twin room when she checked out – it would be a nice surprise for her mam, and they would go out to the island together. A trip that her mother had wanted to take with her dad.

Her return journey was a bit of a climb. It was a warm day, much milder than the day before. The sea barely moved, seagulls swooped down low over the small swells. It was just coming up to eight thirty when she arrived at the harbour. Lukasz's boat was tied up at the pier and there was a gap where Peter's had been. The kiosk shutter was closed. She checked her watch again – it was just after eight thirty. On a bank holiday weekend, she would have thought the kiosk would be open early for business. She spotted a cabin at the end of the harbour and made her way over. The door was wide open and a woman with short red hair sat at a desk, tapping away on an adding machine with one hand, while writing into what looked like a ledger with the other.

Lana smiled as she took in the small cabin – *people still used adding-machines and ledgers*? She knocked lightly on the door. "Excuse me?"

The woman didn't look up, just held her left hand flat in the air, a look of concentration on her face as she counted. Lana leaned against the doorframe and waited. She gazed around the small cabin, her eyes resting on a framed picture hanging on the wood panelled wall, behind a grey filing cabinet. Three men stood proudly, grinning for the camera, a large fish cradled in the arms of the one in the middle – Peter and Lukasz and a third man she hadn't met. The front of the cabin featured glass from the ceiling to the floor, with a wide view of the whole harbour. Lana could see the World's End from where she stood. Not a bad spot to spend your working days, she thought.

"Now, sorry about that, love, but if I lose my concentration, I'm done for." The woman with the short red hair closed the ledger and pushed away the adding machine. "How can I help you?"

Lana pointed up the pier. "The kiosk, do you know what time it opens?"

The woman followed her gaze. "Gary's boat hire?" She checked her watch. "Usually opened by now, but on a Sunday he doesn't show up until around nine." The woman tutted. "Well for him I say, the rest of us have to keep to our normal hours." She went back to her books. When Lana didn't move she glanced up again. "Anything else?"

"Yes, actually. My name is Lana Bowen." She extended her hand. "I'm representing Grace Doran."

The woman narrowed her eyes, confused. She didn't take Lana's hand.

"And who might that be?" she asked.

Lana pushed her hands into her pockets and leaned against the doorframe. "Grace Doran? She was found on the island this same weekend last year, by one of the fishermen here in Castle Cove. Lukasz Nowak? Do you know him?"

"What's all this about? Why are you representing Grace? Are you a solicitor?"

"I'm a private investigator. Grace has very little memory about what happened to her on Mutton Island last year. She knows that Lukasz Nowak saved her life. But she knows nothing about him. I am trying to help her piece it all together."

The woman's expression softened now and she put down her pen. She leaned back in her chair and peered out at the harbour. "I do know Lukasz, and I was here the morning he brought that poor girl back from the island." The woman pointed towards a wooden crate. "Have a seat, it's the only one I have. Would you like a cup of coffee? I just made of pot. Sorry, it's a bit rough and ready in here, but I'm not used to having visitors." She smiled. "My coffee is the good stuff though. You can ask Lukasz, wherever the bloody hell he is."

Lana said she would love some.

"He was a right mess when he got back to the harbour that morning," the woman continued. "He was drenched in sweat and he had that poor girl's blood on his clothes. He kept talking about her legs. He was still in shock at the sight of them. I can't say I blame him. She was in a terrible state." She poured coffee into an

255

enamel cup and handed it to Lana. "I hope you like it black. The supermarket was shut on my way in this morning so I didn't get a chance to buy any milk." She laughed. "Everyone has a lie-in on a Sunday around here, except for me, it seems."

Lana smiled and sipped her coffee. The woman was right, it was good, far better than what she had in her hotel room.

"Sorry, excuse me, my name is Nora, Nora Bourke. I manage the port. I make sure the boats book their spots and pay up on time, and they do, more often than not. The fishermen are great, very reliable, but some of the leisure boats, now that's a different story." She rolled her eyes. "You have to keep an eye on them."

Lana smiled, but didn't interrupt.

Nora tutted as she shook her head. "That poor girl, she is lucky to be alive, the condition she was in. I was a nurse for years before I took on this job. I have seen my fair share of cuts and bruises, but she was in an awful way. Lukasz took good care of her. He saved her life that morning, I mean, if it hadn't been for him, well ..." She left the thought hang in the air.

Lana nodded in agreement. "Who hires out the boats?" she asked, even though she knew it was Gary.

Nora grimaced. "Gary Duke, the lad you're looking for. He has four boats that he hires out to the tourists. He leaves them here all summer. Makes a killing when we are in season. He takes them away then, come the end of August, don't ask me where, I have no clue. Then he's back again the following May and that poor nephew of his sits in that kiosk all day long, taking bookings."

Lana nodded. Although she knew the answer, she asked anyway. "How long do the boats stay out?" She didn't miss the look on Nora's face.

"They go out any time after nine in the morning, but they have to be back by six. The currents, they can be dangerous, and, particularly when it starts to get dark of an evening, you need to be able to see what you're doing." She gestured towards the sea. "That water is full of rip tides – it's very changeable, so you have to be very careful." She shrugged. "But, sometimes people break the rules."

"What happens if they don't come back by six?"

Nora shrugged. "I don't know, to be honest, that's Gary's business, but I suspect he charges them extra, a fine maybe. The harbour closes at six and I try to be out of here by that time. Summer can be bedlam though, so that's not always possible." She sighed. "Look, if you want my honest opinion, people shouldn't be allowed to take the boats out on their own. It's a risk, if you ask me." She pointed towards the ocean. "That sea is unpredictable." She threw her hands in the air. "But, that's just my opinion."

Peter had said the same thing.

Lana leaned forward on the wooden box and rested her elbows on her knees. "Were you here that evening, Nora? When the boat came back in? The boat Grace Doran had been on?"

Nora laughed. "Sure I'm always here, I never take a day off during the season. Most of the locals work seven days a week during the summer months, make hay while the sun shines and all that." Her laugh faded. "Look, if you're asking me if I saw the girl get off that boat, or any of her friends, then the answer is no. Mornings and evenings are the busiest times here at the harbour. The fishermen go out early and the boat hire parties arrive in dribs and drabs throughout the morning. They make the most of their hire time and then they all tend to come back in at the same time. It is possible that I did see her, but, if I did, I don't remember. As far as I'm concerned, the first time I laid eyes on that girl was when Lukasz brought her back early that bank holiday Monday morning." Nora's attention was drawn to movement out on the platform. "Ah, speak of the devil ..."

Lana followed her gaze, to see a man approaching. He appeared to be in his thirties, wearing grey jeans and a dark hoodie, a baseball cap pulled down low over his eyes. She recognised him from the day before, outside the kiosk, Gary Duke, the boat hire guy.

"What does he want now?"

Lana was sure that's what Nora had muttered under her breath, but by the time Gary arrived at the door of the cabin, she was all smiles. "What can I do for you, Gary?"

"Morning, Nora, do you know what's going on up at the ..." He stopped when he stepped inside the cabin and noticed Lana, clearly not expecting Nora to have company at this time of the morning. "Oh, sorry, I didn't see you there."

"This is Lana Bowen. She is here about Grace Doran."

Gary nodded, his expression blank.

"The girl Lukasz found on the island, remember?"

If Gary was surprised about this, he hid it well. He continued to nod his head. "Oh yeah, terrible tragedy, terrible. She died, didn't she?"

Lana shook her head. She didn't like this guy. "No, Grace didn't die. She has had a very rough time of it, but she didn't die. She is recovering, slowly. And she is remembering."

His eyes narrowed slightly, but he continued to nod his head, up and down, up and down. "Yeah, she was unlucky." Then, as if realising something, he said: "Wait, this isn't about one of my boats, is it? Because my boats are safe. I get them checked every year, right before the season starts. I have the full safety certificate to prove it. You can check if you want."

"No, this is not about the safety of your boats, Gary, even though those documents will most likely be needed. For the trial."

Both Nora and Gary looked at Lana then, a question on their faces.

Lana took a deep breath. "Grace Doran claims she was pushed off one of your boats, Gary. Deliberately."

39

Grace wheeled her chair into the small garden, her eyes fixed firmly on the neighbour's back door, willing her to open it and come outside. She was angry. It was bad enough to find out that the woman living next door all these years was her grandmother but, on top of that, to learn that both of her sons were the respective fathers to Erin and her, and that one had killed the other. *Jesus*, she thought, *you could not write this*. Maureen Doran had omitted that little piece of information. A spasm shot up her leg and she shifted in her chair to release the tension. She squeezed her eyes shut, counting the seconds until it eased.

A memory came to her about a time she had asked her mother about her father, something innocent like "*What did he look like?*"

* * *

Father's Day had been approaching and the schoolteacher she had that year, Sister Margaret, was a real *make and doer*. She loved blue tack, glue, paints, coloured paper, sparkles and stickers. The class had spent that year making cards for every event on the calendar, from Halloween, Christmas, Valentine's, Mother's Day to St.

Patricks day, Easter and then, finally, the last event of the year, Father's Day, which was looming. Sister Margaret had set her students the task of making a card for their dads. She had given them a challenge – the person with the most creative card would win a whole bar of milk chocolate, not just a square, but a whole bar. Sister Margaret, thinking she was being helpful, made suggestions on the blackboard about the card: **Find out something personal about your dad – or make the message about your dad – draw a picture of your dad in his favourite jumper or jacket – draw him doing what he liked best – what is his shoe size?** Her list went on and on and on. Sister Margaret was very excited – the possibilities were endless, she said, and, they were. The only problem for Grace was that she didn't know one thing about her dad, definitely not his shoe size or what clothes he liked to wear. She fretted for days about what she should do. If she asked her mother about him, she risked being shouted at, or told to mind her own business. On the other hand, if she told Sister Margaret that she didn't have a father, she was afraid the nun would call the whole thing off, and then everyone might guess it was because of her. She felt sure she was the only kid in the class with no dad. Grace had herself tied up in knots about what to do. In the end, she decided to ask her mother – what harm could it do? A daughter asking a question about her father, so she could make him a card for Father's Day? It was perfectly normal, wasn't it?

A few nights before the cards were due for inspection, after she and Erin had completed their nightly routine of teeth-brushing and prayer-saying, she announced that she was thirsty and was going downstairs to get a drink of water. Erin didn't reply. Grace guessed she was already asleep. She crept down the stairs in her bare feet, holding her favourite doll, Becky, under her arm. *Her only doll.* She could see her mother through the crack in the kitchen door, watching the small black-and-white TV, smoking a cigarette, the images from the screen flickering across her face in the dark room. Her expression was blank. Grace reckoned she probably wasn't even paying attention to whatever show was on, just like the crosswords she looked at all day, but never finished. The large old clock ticked on the wall. Grace pushed the kitchen door open slightly and her mother jumped, the expression on her face quickly changing from fear to annoyance.

"Oh, for God's sake, Grace, you frightened me half to death. What are you doing up? It's past your bedtime." Her tone was stern, bordering on hostile.

Grace carefully held Becky under her arm, rubbing her eye with her fist. "I'm thirsty."

Her mother sighed. She placed her cigarette in the ashtray and sauntered to the sink, her worn slippers scraping against the tiled floor. She poured a glass of water and handed it to Grace. The water out of their kitchen sink tap was always lukewarm on first pour, you had to let it run for a few seconds so it cooled a bit. Her mother didn't bother. Grace watched her mother return to her seat and pick up her cigarette over the rim of her glass as she sipped the warm liquid, her stomach turning, the strong metallic taste causing her to gag. She placed the glass back on the draining board.

"Just leave it there and go back to bed!" her mother called over her shoulder. She continued to stare at the small screen as she inhaled deeply, drawing tobacco into her lungs.

Grace didn't know what to do. She was so curious about her father. She would watch the other kids at school being collected by their dads or talking about things they did together on the weekends, she just wanted to know something about him. In the end, she decided that she would just ask her straight out – after all, she was entitled to know who he was, or where he was, at least, wasn't she? The man was her father, she deserved to know. And, she had to make a stupid card about him.

She took a deep breath. "Mam?"

Her mother sighed again, louder this time. "What is it, Grace? Don't ask for another drink of water, you might wet the bed." She regarded Grace now, eyes narrowed. "And we have had enough of that over the years, haven't we?" She waved her hand dismissively. "Now, off with you, up the stairs, you have school in the morning."

Grace felt her face redden. She had wet the bed for as long as she could remember. She didn't know why, but every morning she woke up drenched in her own urine. In fairness to her mother, she rarely mentioned it over the years, she just silently turned the mattress each morning, gathered Grace's wet sheets, and walked out of the bedroom without saying a word. Then, last year, right before Christmas, Grace stopped wetting, out of the blue, at the grand old age of nine. She had been dry for six months, three weeks and four days.

Why was her mother so heartless and cold? She deserved to know who her father was. And right now, she desperately wished she lived with him, instead of the bitter woman sitting in front of her. Suddenly, she felt brave. Taking a step closer to her mother, she cleared her throat.

"Where is my dad? I want to know who he is."

Her mother turned towards her, her mouth slackened, a look of horror on her face. She extinguished her cigarette.

Grace tucked her doll into the pit of her arm, edging further into the kitchen, towards her mother.

"I want to know about my father. I want to know who he is."

The clock ticked on the wall. Her mother clicked her tongue, her stare intense.

After what seemed like a long time, Rosie Doran's chair scraped off the floor as she pushed it back, and stood towering over Grace. She raised her right hand, and, for a moment, Grace thought her mother was going to strike her. This would be a first – the woman was cold and cruel at times, but she had never hit her before. She closed her eyes and braced herself for the slap, but it never came.

Instead, she smelt her mother's cigarette breath as the woman leaned forward and hissed in her ear.

"*Don't you ever ask me that question again – do you hear me? Never again.*" She whipped Becky out from under her arm and pointed her towards the stairs. "*Now if you want this stupid doll back in the morning, you better go to bed, right now.*"

Grace looked at her beloved doll, the silky blonde hair twisted around her mother's tobacco-stained fingers. She felt the tears sting her eyes, but, determined not to cry in front of her mother, she turned and ran down the hall, up the stairs to her bedroom. She pulled the cold, scratchy blanket up over her head, so Erin wouldn't hear her crying. She sobbed quietly into the rough fabric at the injustice of it all. A while later, she felt the blanket shift, and Erin's warm body slipped in next to her own, wrapping her long slender arm around Grace's waist.

Two days later, the day she was due to present her card in class, Grace feigned sickness.

* * *

Grace remembered that night now, as she watched her neighbour's back door remain stubbornly shut. Why hadn't Maureen told her that she had a different father to Erin? Why not come clean and tell her everything? What was with the Dorans and their bloody secrets? She sighed in frustration at the wrongness of her life – her father killed, a different father to her sister, the same mother who had decided to keep this information from them, and yet treated them, Grace in particular, like an inconvenience, an annoyance, a constant burden. Their mother had tolerated Erin, but she hated Grace, she had made that very clear, and, somehow, Grace had always felt like she was a failure.

She watched Erin prepare lunch through the kitchen window, buttering bread, layering slices of ham and cheese, a tray of tea and sandwiches. Her heart filled with warmth. If it wasn't for her sister, Grace was sure she wouldn't be alive anymore. What would be the point? She wasn't sure there was one.

She closed her eyes as she allowed herself to remember back to that weekend last year. *Him.* Stephen. The way he had looked at her, held her, kissed her. She had really felt something and she thought he had felt it too, the others had said so. They had alluded to as much, many times, over the weekend. What had gone so wrong that she ended up in the water? Did he have something to do with it? Did he know who pushed her, or did he do it himself? No matter how hard she tried, she just couldn't remember what had happened.

Her thoughts were distracted by a sound from nearby, bottles clanking against each other. She turned her attention back to her neighbour's door, but still it didn't open.

"Here we go!" Erin arrived with a tray of sandwiches and tea.

Pulling the table closer to Grace's chair, she placed a plate and cup within her reach.

Grace sipped her tea, aware that Erin was watching her.

"Grace, I'm sorry I didn't tell you, but your best interests were in my heart, I swear that, and I know Mam was harder on you than me, when we were growing up. I wanted for you to get away from here and make a life for yourself. I hoped that you would never need to know the truth about our birth fathers."

Grace flashed her sister a look. "I'm not angry with you, Erin, I could never be angry with you. I'm angry with our mother for making me feel like I had done something wrong, all my life, I kept disappointing her, and then I find out that the woman next door is our grandmother? And why didn't Maureen tell us?" She gestured towards the garden next door. "She should have stood up to Mam. We could have had a relationship with her."

Erin shook her head. "Mam wouldn't let it happen – she was afraid our grandmother would tell us something. You know what she was like." She leaned forward and took Grace's hand, tears brimming over her eyes.

Grace never appreciated how difficult life had been for her sister and she felt a pang of guilt.

"Grace, the past is the past, we can't change it. We have to look to the future, and finding out the truth, about what happened to you. Whoever did this to you. Only then can we concentrate on your recovery."

Grace shook her head. "I'm not going to recover, Erin." She looked down at her only leg held together with metal pins. "This is as good as it gets."

Erin squeezed Grace's hand. "You *will*. The doctor said you just need to give it time for the bones to knit, and with physio and exercise. And I will be here every step of the way. We will do it together."

Grace smiled at Erin, though she didn't feel it inside. Erin was trying so hard.

The neighbouring back door opened and their grandmother stepped outside, holding a large leather-bound book in her hand. She tentatively walked over to the low wall dividing the two houses and offered the book.

"I thought you might want to see these."

Erin stood and accepted the book. She began to slowly flick through the pages. "What is this?"

"A photo album, of when you were little." She hesitated. "With your fathers. I thought you might like to see it." She nodded and turned to go back inside.

Erin looked towards Grace, a question in her eyes. Grace nodded.

"Would you like some tea? I can get another cup?" Erin asked.

Their grandmother turned, glancing from one sister to the other. She appeared uncertain at first, and then she seemed to decide. "That would be lovely, but you'll have to help me over that wall – I'm not as lively as I used to be." She smiled.

Erin helped her over the wall and, when they were seated, poured her a cup of tea.

"Lovely, thanks, Erin."

Maureen opened the album, the first page revealing a photo of two young boys dressed in their school uniforms, grinning for the camera.

"They were such happy children. They rarely argued. They just liked to play football with their friends or ride their bikes, just normal stuff." Her expression changed. "Then your mother moved in next door with her parents."

"What age were the boys then?" Grace asked.

"Michael was sixteen, a year older than James and Rosie. The minute he met your mother, he was smitten. They both were." She turned the page. "The relationship developed quite quickly. They wanted to start a life together, buy a house, but there were no jobs around here at the time. Michael had a friend who had gone to Liverpool to work on the building sites. He said there were loads of opportunities to make money. He decided to head over for a couple of years, save, come home and marry Rosie. That was their plan."

"Why didn't Rosie go with him?" Erin asked.

Maureen shrugged. "When Michael left she would have been about seventeen and still in school. She might have followed him over, eventually, I'm sure. Only, her parents died in a road accident. Rosie was an only child. Suddenly she found herself completely alone in the world. James helped out with the funeral arrangements and they grew close during the months that followed. By the time Michael returned home eighteen months after Rosie's parents died – James and Rosie were dating. They got married and Michael was their best man. They settled into married life. There were no hard feelings." Maureen shrugged. "I thought the relationship between Michael and Rosie had run its course." She sighed. "I was wrong. It wasn't long before Rosie and Michael rekindled their romance. When James found out about the affair, he went crazy. He confronted him." She nodded towards her house. "Next door. They argued and a few punches were thrown. James fell and hit his head off the corner of the kitchen table. We tried to revive him, but it was no use – it was clear he was dead." Maureen sniffed. She took a tissue out of her pocket and blew her nose.

Grace reached out and touched her arm. "It's OK, Maureen, you can stop if you want …"

Maureen shook her head. "No. You deserve to know the truth." She swallowed. "I had some savings. I gave them to Michael and told him to pack his things and get as far away from Ireland as possible. I waited a few hours before calling the Gardaí. I explained that I had been resting and when I came down to the kitchen, James was lying unconscious on the floor. I said he must have had a few pints, stumbled, and hit his head." She shook her head. "They believed my story."

"And Rosie?" Grace asked.

"I think that Rosie knew – that James had found out about the affair. She forbade me from seeing you both. She lived her days in fear that Michael would return. Days that were wasted, because he never did come back." She paused. "I am sorry for the lost years. What happened was an accident but Michael feared that nobody would believe him. They were different times. They were good boys, I swear. Their only mistake in life was falling in love with the same woman."

"Did you ever hear from Michael?" Grace asked.

"Yes. At the beginning, he used to write every so often. Now, he calls me from time to time." She smiled sadly. "I would love to see him some day. But he is still afraid to come back to Ireland." She closed the photo album. "Maybe he will now that Rosie is dead. He was always worried that she would talk to the Gardaí. And that it would look bad for him, because he had apparently run away." She smiled. "The small bit of money I gave him, he spent it wisely. Invested in a derelict, run-down hotel, a building that had been closed for years. He picked up some casual work on construction sites, and in his free time he went about renovating the hotel. He tells me he's doing very well. He was always gifted with his hands." She paused and looked at her granddaughters. "Yes, a tragic story – but I am so happy to be sitting here now with you."

"I used to be so scared of you." Grace smiled. "Mam said you suffered from your nerves."

"The irony of that!" Maureen laughed.

"It's not too late, you know," Grace said. "For us to start again."

She reached out and drew Maureen towards her, the closest she could get from her chair. Maureen shifted her position to make it easier for them both. Grace felt a mix of emotions flood through her as her tears started to flow. A deep sadness for all the time lost, but also, happiness that her family wasn't as small as she had thought.

She glanced over at Erin and realised that her sister was crying too.

40

Lana hauled her small travel bag into the boot of her car and climbed into the front seat. She checked her phone for messages before starting the engine: there was still nothing from her mother. Frowning, she dialled her numbers again, both the landline and mobile – both devices rang out. She turned the key in her little car and, with relief, the engine ticked over. She indicated to move out onto the road, and, a few kilometres later, she took the exit for home, settling into the long drive. The best thing she could do was get back to the city and go straight to her mam's house, she was sure there was a perfectly reasonable explanation for the radio silence.

She stole a quick glance at the heavy traffic coming towards her, heading into Castle Cove, no doubt. It was still only Sunday of the long weekend and even though the temperatures were cooler, it was dry and sunny. A Garda car passed her, lights flashing, sirens on. She hoped there hadn't been another accident in the water, another family upset. She thought about her overnight stay in the small fishing village and what she had learned from her visit. Lukasz's story was definitely the most revealing insight that something was going on down at the harbour.

The lights changed from amber to red and Lana slowed to a stop.

She unlocked her phone and dialled her mother again, but there was still no answer. She scrolled through her list of contacts, and, finding the Dorans' name, she hit the call button before tapping the speaker symbol. The traffic light turned green and she started to move off just as Grace answered the phone.

"Grace? It's Lana. How are you?"

Grace was quiet for a moment and then. "I'm OK, I guess."

"I thought Erin would answer. But it is you I wanted to speak with."

"Erin went out, to do some errands. She left the portable phone beside me." She hesitated. "How was it down …?" She didn't finish her sentence.

"I'm just heading back to Limerick now."

"Did you find out anything?"

"I spoke to Lukasz – the fisherman who found you that morning on the beach."

"Yes, yes, I know who Lukasz is. What did he say?"

"He said he saw three men arguing at the harbour the night before you were found. One of them was the guy who hires out the boats and they were all standing beside the vessel you and your friends hired. The *Karina*. He said the three men got on the boat and left the harbour. Lukasz also said he saw two people who appeared to be arguing, out by the World's End pool when he left to go fishing the following morning – it was early, about six. He said they were the same two men who got on the *Karina* with Gary the night before and that the boat hadn't returned to the harbour by the following morning. I also spoke with the young boy who works at the kiosk where you pay for boat hire, and he let it slip that sometimes his uncle, who is also his boss, hired the boats after hours for extra cash and that he doesn't put it through the books.

He remembered who came to pay for the boat that day you and your friends travelled to the island. He said the guy was a little bit drunk when he arrived at the kiosk – the signature on their log book was a Declan Slattery – but here's the thing, the boat hadn't come back by the time the nephew finished work at six. The uncle told the nephew to head home, that he would wait around for the boat. And when the boy arrived to work the next morning, the boat wasn't moored at the harbour. The uncle told him that the boat had been damaged and taken away for repairs. So, it did come back at some stage that evening, but went out again."

Grace was silent on the other end of the phone. "I'm not sure what all this means though? It doesn't explain how or why I ended up in the water?"

"No, it doesn't, but what we do know is that the boat you were on arrived back later than scheduled, and, that it left the harbour again that night with Gary and possibly two of your friends on board. We know that the boat was sent for repairs, for whatever reason, and we also know that somebody was out by the pool early the morning after you went missing. Gary is definitely hiding something, though that may not relate to you." Lana thought of something else. "You told me you started packing up the beach about five in the evening, and, sometime after that, you ended up in the water, but, what if you were still on the boat when it came back to the harbour, and later that night when whoever it was took it back out on the water, to the island?"

"It's possible, I guess ..." Grace began. "But I don't understand why anyone would take me back out on the boat? It doesn't make sense?"

"You said you had a bit to drink. Is it possible you went down to the cabin to sleep it off?"

"Yeah, it's possible, I guess. I have no memory of doing that, but …"

"But what, Grace?"

"I think someone came back to the boat and we had a drink together, but I don't know who it was. Anyway, if I did fall asleep in the cabin, why didn't one of the others wake me up when we got back? Sarah, my friend, I mean, she would have woken me up. I know she would."

"Did you ask her?"

Grace was quiet again. "No. I haven't spoken to her since that weekend. She has called, to the hospital and stuff. Erin told you that, but I didn't want to see her." She sighed. "I didn't want to see anyone." She hesitated. "And, I keep having this dream."

"About what?"

"Someone is in the water, and I'm controlling the steering wheel of the boat and I'm heading straight for them and I can't change the direction. And I can't see who the person is." She sighed. "It probably means nothing, but the dream is always the same."

"That could be important, Grace. That could very well be a memory but a confused one."

"Yes, I feel it's important too. It really disturbs me."

"But, Grace, I need to talk to Sarah. And it would be best if you were there."

Grace didn't reply.

"Grace? What do you think?"

"OK." Grace's answer was short, but at least she had agreed.

"Great, I will call her and make arrangements. Tomorrow at your house OK? Say mid-morning. I can be there just after ten. I'll ask Sarah to come for ten thirty. We can chat before she arrives."

"Yeah, that should be fine." Grace's tone didn't sound keen.

"Grace, don't worry. I will be there. I just want to ask her a few questions. I feel she will be completely honest with me if you are present, you understand?"

"I do. It's just, I haven't seen her since that weekend, and when she sees me, when she sees my face, my legs ... my leg ..."

"I understand, Grace, but you need to do this."

"Yes, I can do this. I have to do this – I have to face her at some point. I have to face all of them."

"You'll be fine. I'll text you to confirm. Just a minute ..." Lana indicated and overtook a slow-moving campervan. "One more thing, when I called to your house, you mentioned that you went for a walk on the island?"

"Yeah?"

"On your own?" Grace was silent. "With Sarah, was it?"

"No, Sarah was with Harry all afternoon." Lana waited. "I went with Stephen. We were together that afternoon."

Lana's hunch was right. Grace had been intimate with Stephen.

Lana told Grace she would see her in the morning and ended the call. She quickly checked the time on her watch, deducing she would be another hour on the road before she hit home. She pulled into the next garage on her route to top up on fuel. She grabbed a bottle of water and paid at the counter.

Sitting into her car, she called Ella and the girl picked up.

"Bowen Investigations, Ella speaking, how can I help you?" Dear God, *what*? When did the girl decide to use that greeting? Having said that, Lana was grateful that Ella had agreed to work on Sunday.

"Ella, can you check something for me?"

"Oh, hi, Ms. Bowen. How are you?"

"I'm good. Halfway back from Castle Cove."

"How did it go?"

"I'll fill you in when I'm back in the office."

"Is there anything I can do?"

"Yeah, there is. I was watching the news earlier about a property in Limerick under investigation. Will you see if you can find out where it is?"

"Sure. What information do you have?"

"Not much, I'm afraid. But the Criminal Assets Bureau are involved. It was on the news this morning so I'm sure you will find something online about it."

"I'll have a look. Anything else?"

"The news bulletin mentioned a connection with a missing person by the name of Eva Mroz?" She could hear Ella typing in the background.

"Eva Mroz, from Estonia, missing since April 22nd 2018, has been linked to an independent investigation into organised crime. Money laundering, bogus business deals –"

Lana cut her off. "Thanks, Ella." She thought of something else. "Can you find out if there is a boat repair service in Castle Cove or the surrounding area?"

"Sure thing," Ella replied. "Anything else, Ms. Bowen?"

"Did my mother call by any chance?"

"Nope, not today, Ms. Bowen."

"Thanks, Ella." Lana sighed. "Actually, Ella. Can you change your phone greeting? Bowen Investigations sounds … pretentious."

Lana hung up before Ella could reply. She found Sarah's number on her contacts and hit the call button. She would then phone Garda Donal Mulcahy – she had a few questions for him too. As she waited for Sarah to answer, her thoughts turned to her mother.

41

Sarah lifted her son out of the bath and wrapped him in a fluffy white towel.

"*Mum, I'm ffffreezing!*" he squealed at the top of his voice.

She folded him into her arms and planted a kiss on his forehead while carrying him across the hall to his room. He sat on the edge of his bed shivering as she moved around the room gathering pyjamas, slippers and a dressing gown.

"Can I have a story, Mum? Please?"

She smiled. "Can you have a story?" she teased. "*Hmm*, let me see if I have time?"

He made a face and continued to shudder, his little teeth clattering together, clearly not in the mood for joking around. The child had no interest in stories up to a few weeks ago, despite her encouragement, but now he demanded one every night. And it had to be the same story, *The Little Mermaid*. Sarah would snuggle up beside his warm little body and she would read him the same story, using an animated voice, and he would laugh and gasp appropriately. He was the best audience a reader could have.

"Course you can," she reassured him. "Now, get into your jimjams and brush your teeth. I'll fill your hot water bottle and meet you back here in five minutes. Hurry, come on! Five minutes!"

He slipped off the bed and started dressing at speed. She smiled as she picked up the wet towel and headed down the hall towards the kitchen of their small apartment. Sometimes, she thought her heart might explode, she loved him so much. She marvelled at how much he had matured since starting school, wanting to do everything himself. She placed the damp towel into the drum of the washing machine and piled in the rest of the clothes from the laundry basket before setting a wash programme. Filling the kettle from the sink, she waited for it to boil. She checked her watch – it was just coming up on six in the evening. Good, she thought, Zack would be out like a light in the next half hour, allowing her enough time to complete her college assignment. It was due in by the following evening, and she cursed herself for procrastinating with her college work, but at the same time, she surmised that she would probably never be any different.

Her phone rang on the kitchen counter, and at a glance Sarah didn't recognise the number. She wasn't going to answer, but then she thought it might be one of her fellow students. She was working on a project with a few undergraduates from her course and she had passed on her contact details to the group, but didn't get a chance to input and save all of their numbers yet. Maybe there was a suggestion about the project that might save her time. She picked up the phone and answered. "Hi?"

"Hello, am I speaking to Sarah Greene?" The voice on the other end of the phone sounded formal, far too official to be a learner from her college team.

"Yes, who is this?"

"My name is Lana Bowen. I am a private investigator,

representing Grace Doran. I believe my assistant has been in touch with you?"

Sarah's heart started to race. She gripped the kitchen counter and took a breath. *Not again.* She had ignored the messages, hoping the woman would go away.

"Are you still there?"

Somehow, she found her voice. "Yes, I'm here. What's this about? Why are you representing Grace?" She could hear the woman hesitate on the other end of the phone, choosing her words carefully no doubt.

"I have some questions for you, Sarah. About the day you all travelled to Mutton Island last year. How does tomorrow suit you for a meeting?"

Sarah's mind raced through what she had to do the following day. It was the beginning of the week, but a bank holiday Monday and Alex's mother had offered to take Zack so Sarah could complete her assignments. She guessed she could spare an hour in the morning, but what was this about? *Did Grace remember?* "*Em*, yeah, I can do tomorrow morning. For about an hour – I have a college assignment and am pressed for time."

"Fine."

"What time?"

"Say, ten thirty?"

"Where is your office?"

"Not my office. Can you come to Grace's house?"

"Grace's house?" Sarah was stunned. "You want me to come meet with you there? But Grace and I haven't ..."

"Grace knows you're coming. Do you need her address?"

Sarah didn't know what to make of this. She had been trying for the past twelve months to get Grace to talk to her and now she

279

wanted her to come to the house? She swallowed hard. "No, I don't need the address, I know where Grace lives." She idly moved some crumbs around the kitchen counter with her thumb. Something told her this wasn't going to be a happy reunion. "Does she remember?"

"We can talk in the morning, Sarah." The tone was crisp.

"I will be there."

She ended the call and leaned over the kitchen sink. She felt sick. What was going on? Why was Grace suddenly OK with meeting up with her, and why had she hired a private investigator?

"*Mum!*" her son's little voice shouted from his bedroom.

"*I'm ready!*" Sarah called back as she filled the hot water bottle, pressing the top half to release the excess air. She secured the lid and walked down the hall to her son's room, her mind elsewhere.

Zack was already in bed when she arrived, beaming from ear to ear, excited about his story time. She read to him for the next twenty minutes, trying and failing to keep the story upbeat. When she finished, she kissed him good night and dimmed the light on his bedside locker, before quietly padding out of the room, leaving the door partially open.

Back in the kitchen, she abandoned the idea of a cup of tea and rooted around in one of the cupboards until she put her hands on a half-empty bottle of rum. She poured a large shot into a small glass and drank it neat, coughing as the strong liquor burnt her throat. She picked up her phone and scrolled through her contacts until she found his name, her finger hoovering over the number. What was the point, she thought, he won't answer, he hadn't answered the other times. She stood at the sink and tipped another shot of rum into her glass, one question churning around in her head. *What did Grace remember?*

42

"There were just the two lads in the house when I called, no sign of anybody else. It's some house though!"

Lana heard Garda Donal Mulcahy whistle down the phone. She pulled into the gravelled driveway of her family home, noticing her mother's car parked at the side of the house.

"Did they say anything about having guests for the weekend?"

The outside of the house looked remarkable in the early evening sun. Her mother had hired a company to power-wash the old stone grey building a month earlier and, for the first time in years, Lana could see the contour of the brickwork.

"Just one other girl. Sarah Greene, I think her name was. She had left by the time I arrived. I spoke to her on the phone though, and she backed up what the boys had said."

"Do you know anything about the owner of the summerhouse? The World's End?" She heard paper rustling in the background as the Garda checked his notes.

The garden was beautifully designed with different varieties of flowers in full bloom. Lana's mother was a keen gardener all her life and spent a great deal of her time planting and weeding and nurturing. There was no sign of her mother out in her garden today.

"*Em*, the property is owned by a company. Registered to Slattery Holdings."

Something jarred in Lana's memory. She had heard that name mentioned recently, hadn't she?

"Was there anything else, Ms. Bowen?"

Lana was delaying getting out of the car. She had been increasingly nervous during her trip back from Castle Cove, imagining all sorts of misfortunes that could have happened to her mother, and there was nobody she could call to drop in and check on her. She had no contact details for any of her mother's pals.

"Just one more thing. Did anyone mention a guy by the name of Stephen? He was with them on the island that day."

"No. As I said, it was just the two lads in the house when I called to them." He laughed. "They had some heads on them. I'd reckon they were at it all night."

"What makes you say that?"

"Ah, they had that dog-tired look about them. Red eyes, the works. I'd say they hadn't been to bed at all when I called."

She thanked him and hung up the phone. Glancing at the upstairs window of her mother's bedroom, she noticed the curtains were drawn, meaning that her mother must have got up at some stage, providing she had gone to bed in the first place. Lana tried to remember when she had last spoken with her mother – it was the previous afternoon, wasn't it? They had arranged to meet here, and stay in and have a takeaway.

She tried Ella's number again, she would ask her to run a search on Slattery Holdings. The number rang out. Christ's sake, what was the point in having an assistant if she didn't answer the phone?

Though, she shouldn't be so hard on the girl – it was a Sunday evening on a bank holiday weekend.

Her shoes crunched on gravel as she walked across the pebbled driveway. She tried the front door, but it was locked. Moving around the corner of the building, she noticed the side gate was shut, bolted from the other side. She ran back to her car to search for her key, but when she tried to twist it in the lock, the catch moved, but the second lock was secured in place. Lana only had a key for the bottom lock. *Shit*. This wasn't good – her mother only enabled the double locks at night, which meant she hadn't left the house.

She knocked gently on the door. "*Mam? It's me, Lana. Mam?*" There was a glass panel at the side of the front door and Lana cupped her face with her hands to peer inside. The hallway was neat, a pale green floor mat ran the length of the wide hall, and her mother's pink walking jacket hung over the banister. The door to the kitchen was half-open. The glare coming from the kitchen was brighter than in the hall – it appeared as though the overhead light was on, even though it was still sunny outside.

Lana knocked again, louder this time. "Mam?" she called. "Mam?" She moved to the sitting-room window where the blind was up. She could see the television screen was grey and fuzzy – it happened when the set was still on but a channel hadn't been changed for a while. The device would go into standby mode. Lana felt the familiar panic start to build in her chest. She took a breath to steady its pace. Now was not the time to have a panic attack. *Something was very wrong*. Her mother was a woman of routine. She did the same things every day, got up at the same time, went for a walk, had her breakfast, and tended to her garden. She never left the light or the television on, this wasn't like her, at all. Lana was at that crucial moment when she had to decide if she was over reacting, or whether she should break the glass on the side panel of the front door. She felt completely alone in the world. Her mother was right – she had isolated herself, she was wholly absorbed in her work. She wished her dad was here, he would know what to do. Tears stung the backs of her eyes.

"Hello?"

Lana turned to see a man standing at the end of the driveway dressed casually in a pair of cream chinos and a navy-blue sweater, a white collar peeking over the neckline. Lana couldn't put an age on him, but she guessed he was maybe in his early sixties.

"I live across the road. My name is Norman."

Lana hadn't seen him on the road before, he must be a more recent arrival. She gave a quick smile and nodded hello. She turned her attention back towards her mother's house.

"Are you in trouble?" the man asked.

"I'm fine, forgot my key." She sighed in frustration. "Actually, have you seen my mother today?"

"Ah, you must be Julia's daughter? Lana?"

Lana glanced over her shoulder. "You know Mum?"

"As I said, I live across the road, moved in six months ago."

"Have you seen her today?"

"Not today, no." He searched his pocket. "I have a key for your house. I can let you in."

His tone was gentle. Maybe he was wondering the same thing as Lana – *that something was wrong*. Lana nodded and stepped aside.

The man, Norman, reached into his pocket and took out a bunch of keys. "Julia locked herself out last month but, luckily, that day, she had left the back door open. I have a small stepladder so I used it to climb over the side gate and let her in the front. She cut a spare set of keys and gave one to me, in case it happened again."

"And did it?"

He smiled, sadly. That meant yes. *Damn it*. Why hadn't she paid more attention?

He turned the key in the second lock and pushed the door open. Lana stepped inside the front hall. There was a leaflet lying on the floor advertising pizza deals. That same dread crept over her.

"Do you want me to go in with you?" Norman asked.

Lana nodded, yes. She advanced down the hall, aware that Norman was behind her. It felt like one of those moments you longed for time to stand still, where you wanted everything to stay exactly as it was, you didn't want to move forward, because you knew if you kept moving, you would see something you didn't want to see. She got to the edge of the kitchen and noticed that she was right about the kitchen light switch. It was on. There was an island in the centre of the room, a cup sat on top of the counter, a carton of milk alongside it. Lana walked around the island.

Her mother was lying on her side. Lana crouched down beside her and felt for a pulse. "She's still breathing," she whispered. "Call an ambulance." Her eyes filled with tears. She heard Norman talking on the phone in the hallway. "*Oh, Mam.*"

43

Stephen dropped his keys onto the kitchen counter and grabbed a cold bottle of water from the fridge. Taking a long drink, he entered the bedroom and changed out of his running gear. He had run for over an hour, out to the university and back along the canal route and his muscles were burning. After a quick shower, he pulled on a pair of jeans and a T-shirt. Drying his hair with a towel, he scanned the bedroom for a sign that somebody had been there while he was out for his run, but the place seemed to be exactly as he had left it. Milo was fast asleep on the bed, and the second drawer of the dresser was half-open – the door to the walk-in closet firmly shut. He was still unnerved from the previous night, and the fact that there was no explanation for the empty dishwasher. He had decided that Andy must have come home while he was out, to change her clothes for the exhibition, or something, and she must have emptied the machine – that had to be the reason. He didn't get to talk to her the previous night. She had texted to say that the exhibition had been a huge success and she was heading out for a drink with a few of the artists and not to wait up. He was fast asleep by the time she got home and her side of the bed was empty when he woke up, a handwritten note lying on her pillow:

Gone to the art gallery to clean up. Left the place in a mess. Great about Milo! Where did you find him? Can you make dinner? Later xx

He walked back into the living room and noticed his laptop on the coffee table, open. He narrowed his eyes. He had closed it before he left for his run, hadn't he? Slowly, he crossed the room and pulled up the screen, typing in his password. A file began to load from the bottom up, and, a moment later, a photo started to feed onto the monitor. *What the fuck?*

Dark hair draped over lightly tanned shoulders, framing high cheek bones. When the screen revealed the girl's whole image, Stephen staggered back, falling onto the sofa, inhaling sharply. *"Jesus Christ!"* Grace Doran's smiling eyes stared back at him from his laptop. She was wearing a strappy white outfit, similar to the one she had been wearing the day they had travelled to the island on the boat. *Who the fuck had opened this page?* It wasn't him. Yes, he had typed the name Grace Doran into the search engine a few times, but he had always made sure to delete the history. He briefly wondered if it was Andy, but she didn't know about Grace, she couldn't know, he had been so careful.

His thoughts were interrupted by a loud banging on the door. He quickly glanced at the laptop screen as the pounding continued. *Mike.* That guy needed to be put in his place. Stephen had had enough of the man. He darted across the room and pulled the door open. Harry Reddan punched him straight in the mouth. He fell backwards, holding onto his jaw.

"*What the hell?*" he managed.

"Stephen, you fucked it up!"

Stephen looked up at him, dazed. "What are you talking about, Harry?"

"You couldn't keep your stupid mouth shut, could you?" Harry hissed, louder this time.

"Harry, slow down …"

"Did you see the news? The Gardaí arrested Declan at his house. They're at my office now and they're taking everything, laptops, computers, phones, files, everything. Nobody else knew, Stephen. Nobody but you. What did you tell them?"

Stephen felt the heat rise inside his T-shirt. "Harry, I didn't say anything to anybody, I swear. You are the one keeping secrets, you told me you haven't been in regular contact with Declan and I saw you both at the gym yesterday evening."

"Wait? Are you joking? Were you following me?"

"I wanted to talk with Declan about that weekend," Stephen defended himself. "You lied to *me!* I saw the two of you leaving the gym together, looking very friendly …"

"Jesus Christ, are you serious?"

"What happened on the island, Harry? What did you do with …"

"I took care of it."

"What do you mean you took care of it? I saw *three dead bodies!*"

"I said I fucking took care of it." he replied in a harsh whisper. He slammed the door of the apartment. "Look, I haven't time for this shit, Stephen. Stay out of my business, you hear me? And keep your mouth shut, or I might have a conversation with Andy's dad."

Stephen couldn't believe what he was hearing. "Hang on a minute, Harry, I don't think you are in a position to threaten me, not after what I saw on the beach!" He tried to sit up.

Harry was on top of him before he could move any further. *"Listen to me, you stupid fuck!"* he raged. *"That shit is my business, not yours!"*

"You brought me to the World's End, Harry. You *made* it my business." Stephen wiped his mouth with the back of his hand. "You know, the minute I sat into your expensive car, I knew you were up to your old tricks. And you probably got Declan Slattery involved. He's stupid enough and he has his father's money. Only problem with Declan is, the man's a liability."

That's what they had argued about on the island, when Stephen had ended up in the water. Declan got hammered drunk and started throwing his weight around, claiming he owned the summerhouse, The World's End, and Stephen was a lucky bastard to be staying *in his house*, and to *back off* from Grace, that he would have a choice of other girls to avail of that evening, prettier girls, *easier girls*. Stephen had been furious. He was the one to land the first punch on Declan, demanding they go straight back to the mainland or he would call the Gardaí. Harry had intervened, insisting Stephen calm down – that Declan was spoofing.

"What is it with you, Harry? I bailed you out before, remember?"

Not long after they had left college, Harry had dabbled in bogus business deals, offering a service to clients that didn't exist, a Ponzi scheme. Eventually, he got caught out. He arrived at Stephens's flat one night, badly beaten, blood dripping down his face, a few broken ribs. He begged Stephen for money, his life depended on it, he had said. One of Harry's customers had figured out his proposals were a scam. Harry promised Stephen that he would stop. He confessed that he had been sucked in by the idea of making a shit load of money, but it was too risky and he was leaving that life behind. Stephen found out during that long weekend stay at The World's End that Harry had been bullshitting him.

"Why did Declan buy the summerhouse in Castle Cove?" he

asked. "And, why did you have to involve me?"

Harry rolled off Stephen and stood. "The gardaí were watching us. We needed to take the heat off, make the weekend look normal."

Declan had gone up the beach that day but he took too long, and so Harry had gone to look for him. Stephen had helped Grace and Sarah clean up the beach, and then, suspicious himself, he had decided to follow Harry. Nothing could have prepared him for what he discovered. Three girls, Eastern European, handcuffed, thrown on the sand like pieces of rubbish. There was no sign of the small boat he had seen earlier. Declan, the bastard, had been telling the truth about the girls. Stephen had gone crazy. He wanted nothing to do with whatever the boys had got themselves involved in. He demanded they leave the girls on the island and head back to Castle Cove or he would call the Gardaí. Reluctantly, the boys complied. The three men returned to their hire boat. Declan went briefly below deck to use the toilet and when he arrived back on deck, Harry asked him if he had seen Sarah and Grace. He said they were asleep in the cabin. They sailed back to Castle Cove and it was only then that Sarah woke up asking for Grace. Nobody knew where Grace was, not even Sarah – she was just as baffled as everyone else. Declan swore he had seen them both sleeping. Stephen panicked. Everything had gone to shit. He grabbed his bag, jumped in his car and left the World's End immediately. He didn't know what Declan and Harry were going to do with the bodies of the three girls and he didn't care. And he had never talked about it. Harry promised he had taken care of it. Harry paid Sarah not to talk, and Stephen figured she must have changed her mind about that if Harry and Declan were being investigated. Harry had chosen to blame Stephen. Thanks, *mate*.

"Look, just stay out of my business. Keep your mouth shut, yeah?" Harry left the apartment.

"*Fuuuuck!*" Stephen roared. He stood and made his way to the sink, cupping some cold water into his mouth.

He leaned against the counter, his gaze resting on his laptop. He still didn't know who the hell had been in his apartment, had emptied his dishwasher and pulled up an image of Grace Doran. It could not have been Andy, could it? Or how Milo had vanished and suddenly reappeared.

There was a knock on the door. Stephen kept quiet. If he ignored them, whoever it was, they would just go away. The picture of Grace remained on his screen, her warm smile drawing him in. She was such a beautiful girl. The knock came again and he told himself not to respond. Then, it sounded again, louder this time, and more urgent. *Shit.* Maybe Andy had forgotten her key. He crossed the room, smoothing his hair down while passing the mirror by the door. His lip was beginning to swell. He pulled back the latch. Mike from across the hall was standing in front of him, a six-pack in his hand, a smirk on his face.

He whistled when he saw Stephen's mouth. "How's the other guy faring up?" He pushed past Stephen and strolled over to the kitchen area as if he owned the place.

Stephen followed Mike into the apartment. "Sorry, Mike, now is not a good time. I'm just after a run, I'm not feeling like drinking …"

"Think your bottle opener is right …" Mike grabbed the magnet opener from the fridge door, "here." He busied himself uncapping two bottles. He turned and slipped one across the counter to Stephen, taking a long drink of his own. "My God, that's good!" He crossed the room and sat on the sofa.

Stephen picked up the bottle and drained half of it. "I called last night, you didn't answer."

Mike took another long drink of beer, his eye on Stephen's laptop. "I was busy. You're not the only person with things to do, Stephen." He leaned forward on the sofa. "Who's this? Cracking-looking girl, isn't she?" He peered closer. "Hang on, is that who I think it is?"

Stephen walked over and shut the laptop. He scooped up the device and tucked it into its sleeve.

Mike leaned back on the sofa crossing one leg over the other, a smile playing at the corners of his lips. "That's the girl, isn't it?"

"Sorry?"

"The girl you told me about? The one you met in Castle Cove?"

"I don't know what you mean." *Christ.* He must have told Mike about Grace, that night they had got pissed drinking neat whiskey.

Stephen searched the fridge for ingredients to start dinner, hoping Mike would take the hint. "Look, Mike, I'm just back after a long run, and I have to prepare dinner – can we do this next weekend?"

Mike stood and sauntered over to the kitchen counter, leaning against the edge of one of the stools. "Yeah sure, I'll just finish my beer while you cut your vegetables, then I'll be on my way." He took another drink. "Grace? Wasn't that her name? Grace Doran. Instant attraction, you said?" He gave a low whistle. "Mind you, I don't blame you, she's hot."

"Nothing happened between us." Stephen grabbed his beer and took a long drink. He needed it.

Mike laughed. "Ah, that's not what you told me, now is it, Stephen? You said you guys were all over each other, you couldn't keep your hands off her on the beach. That's what you said, she was gasping for it, you both were. She was young, and ready and crying out your name!" Mike laughed.

Stephen swung around, the knife in his hand. "*Shut up, Mike. I'm warning you. Just shut up and get out.*"

Mike held his hands up in the air. "*Whoa*, sorry, Stephen, didn't mean to piss you off. I just thought you might want to talk about it. Can't be easy keeping a secret like that from Andy."

"I'm warning you, Mike …"

Mike picked up the photo of Stephen and Andy on their wedding day. "Mind you, she probably has good reason not to trust you. I mean …" He pointed at the photo. "Take a look at this shot of the two of you – neither of you look happy, do you?" He laughed. "You, Stephen, *you* look like someone has hung a noose around your neck. As for Andy, she just looks like she arrived at the wrong party." He put the photo down on the counter. "She probably looks at this image every day. Doomed from the start, if you ask me." He grinned as he put his beer bottle to his lips. "Drink up."

The room started to spin. Mike's head divided in two. His grinning mouth doubled, disrespecting him, mocking him. *Prick.*

"You OK, Stephen, mate?" Mike's voice sounded strange, slow and slurred.

Stephen inched forward with the knife and fell heavily on the counter. His breath quickened and his eyelids felt heavy. He could just about make out Mike's voice repeatedly asking if he was OK. He felt himself slipping down the counter onto the floor, like a rag doll, bringing the board of chopped vegetables with him. The last thing he remembered was the sight of peppers and carrots pirouetting in slow motion across the kitchen floor.

44

Grace had been awake for hours. She lay in bed, perfectly still, until the morning light made the room appear brighter. She'd had the same dream again. She was steering the boat, she couldn't get the wheel to straighten, and she was heading directly for someone in the water. The only difference this time – there was a face: Erin's. Her beautiful blue eyes wide open with fear as the boat gained speed. Just before impact, Grace woke up, drenched in sweat and gasping for air. She stayed as she was, lying on her back, until her breathing returned to normal, trying to make sense of it all. She concentrated on what the dream might mean. Was she, Grace, the one in the water and did someone intentionally steer the boat towards her? Or was she the one at the helm? No matter how hard she tried, she just couldn't remember what happened that day. *Come on, Grace, remember.* Memories don't just leave your brain, the right trigger can bring them back. After she had taken her drink up onto the deck, someone came back, she knew that much, but who was it? Maybe Sarah would have answers. She was due to arrive at Grace's house later that morning, and Grace was still not sure how she felt about that. Lana's request had come as a surprise – though, she was aware that she would have to see Sarah at some point. Once she hired an investigator, she knew this day would come. She would have to see all of them, but she wasn't expecting it to happen this soon.

Erin reassured her that she would be there with her the whole time. Erin had held her hands and told her she was much more resilient than she gave herself credit for. Grace hoped Erin was right, she would need all the resilience in the world to get through the next few months. But, she was determined that she was going to find it from somewhere, because there was one thing she was sure of – someone was responsible for her accident, and she wanted to know who that person was, and, more importantly, why.

She heard movement out in the hall and then a gentle knock on her door. She smiled inwardly at her sister's attempt to respect her privacy. Erin had seen Grace at her lowest and most exposed these past few months, yet she still knocked on the door and waited to be asked to enter. "I'm awake, Erin!" She called out.

The door opened and Erin walked in, fully dressed and ready for the day. "Come on, let's get you sorted!"

They set about their morning's routine, Erin helping her into the small bathroom tucked under the stairs, so Grace could brush her teeth and have a light wash. They returned to the bedroom and Erin assisted her getting dressed. She then prepared breakfast while Grace applied face cream, light make-up, and brushed her long dark hair, down over her shoulder, pushing it back over the left side of her face in a vain attempt to cover her scar. She wanted to feel good about herself for this meeting, not to appear weak. If there was one thing she had hated these past few months since she woke up in the hospital, it was the look people gave her when they realised the extent of her injuries. The tilt of a head – she couldn't stand seeing the pity in their eyes. Nobody in this world wanted to be pitied, and Grace would not be, not anymore.

She wheeled herself down the narrow hall to the kitchen and rolled her chair under the table. She noticed the photo album was where they had left it the night before. Erin and she had looked through the collection of photos for hours after their grandmother had left, dissecting each and every one of them for a second time that day. Earlier, their grandmother had gone through each image slowly, describing who was who and where they had been taken. Photos of both their fathers growing up in the house next door, with each other, on their own, with their dad and mom, all through their younger life, into adulthood. There were photos of the boys in school uniforms, T-shirts and denims in summer and duffel coats and woolly hats in winter, strange haircuts. Pictures of their mam with Erin's dad and then one of their mam standing between both brothers, linking arms, everyone smiling for the camera. And then another one of the three of them on their mam's wedding day, her groom on one side and his brother and best man on the other. Rosie, James and Michael, the bride and the two brothers, their smiles brimming with happiness. A few years later, one would be dead and the other would be on the run, a fugitive of sorts. The prints had stopped, twenty-five years ago when Grace was two and Erin was five. The irony was that Erin looked exactly like her dad James, with red hair and pale skin, and Grace looked exactly like her dad Michael, dark-haired and sallow-skinned. Neither girl bore any resemblance to each other, or to their mother.

Grace checked the wall clock, it was just after ten – Lana should be here by now. She said she would arrive earlier than Sarah, so they could go through their questions together. Grace nibbled on a piece of toast that Erin had put in front of her, but she had no appetite. She pushed her plate away, sipping her tea instead.

"Penny for them?" Erin asked from across the table.

"I just wonder where he is. Don't you? After all these years, why has he not shown any interest in meeting me? I mean, he clearly loved my mother, our mother. Enough to have rekindled his relationship with her, and risk his bond with his brother. Surely he would be interested in me?"

Erin shrugged. "I don't know, Grace. He did kill my father, even though it was an accident. Maybe our grandmother is painting a nicer picture of him than there actually is, you know?" She hesitated. "I mean, he had an affair with our mother while she was married to his brother. OK, our mother isn't entirely innocent here, I get that."

Grace shook her head. "But they were childhood sweethearts, Erin."

"Mam was terrified of something. When she told me about him, she looked afraid … no … she looked petrified …"

"She was just overreacting – you remember what she was like."

"Let's change the subject, we have to prepare for this meeting."

Grace glanced at the clock on the wall again: it was quarter after ten. Where was Lana? She should be here by now. She felt the build-up of anxiety tighten in her chest. Sarah would be knocking on her front door any minute.

45

Stephen was lying on the beach with Grace. He was sifting hot sand onto her naked body as she dozed beside him. He felt her fingers flutter as they covered his hand and he traced it over her skin towards her breast, slowly. The nipple hardened and he felt his arousal. He wanted her, again. His breath quickened as his hands moved all over her body, his fingers kneading roughly into her soft flesh. She started sinking into the sand. He tried to hold onto her but she was sinking deeper, her eyes wide with fear, her hands reaching out to him as a silent scream escaped her open mouth. He woke up trembling, his heart racing as he tried to catch his breath – he was drenched in sweat. It took him a moment to realise that he was lying on the sofa in the living room of his apartment, a grey blanket tangled around his body. *What the fuck?* His head throbbed, his mouth was dry and he felt a gag reflux as he tried to sit up. The radio was playing some summer tune about a heatwave. There was no sign of Andy. He glanced around the empty room and tried to remember how he had ended up on the couch.

He had gone to the gym, to confront Declan, hadn't he? And Harry had been here. They had a fight – he felt a dull ache in his jaw and his lip was throbbing. Had Harry said something about

Declan and the news? Where was his laptop? He slowly swung his legs over the side of the sofa. He was still wearing his jeans and T-shirt from the day before. What the hell had happened? Why hadn't he changed his clothes and what was he doing sleeping in the living room? He wondered where Andy was. She had been working at an exhibition and mentioned something about doing the clean-up. Had he passed out before she came home? Was she the one who put the blanket over him? He had been dreaming about Grace Doran, their afternoon on the beach. It wasn't the first time he had dreamt about Grace. He ran his hands through his hair. He needed a shower, but when he tried to stand, a wave of nausea took hold. He sat for a moment, taking several breaths. It was Sunday, wasn't it? Or, Monday? His laptop wasn't on the coffee table, and there was no sign of his phone.

He slowly stood, and the room swam as the nausea took hold again. He staggered to the kitchen and made his way around the island to the fridge. He grabbed a bottle of water, noticing two empty beer bottles by the sink. Had he only had two? Two beers wouldn't cause a hangover like this. *This* was something else. He spotted his wedding picture on the floor next to the dishwasher, the glass shattered. He frowned as Milo slipped his skinny body between his legs. "*Fuck sake, Milo!*" He grabbed the cat and flung him across the floor. The creature cried out, scuttling down the corridor towards the bedroom. Stephen was sweating profusely and he tore off a wad of kitchen towel and wiped his forehead. He opened the water bottle and took a few tentative sips. Once he felt sure the liquid wouldn't come back up again, he drank some more. Where the fuck was his laptop? He had a vague memory that someone was in the apartment with him last night. He was sure it wasn't Andy. He glanced at the time on the digital oven clock. It was coming up to ten.

He slowly made his way down to the bedroom, holding on to the wall for support. The bed was made, Milo curled up on Andy's pillow, scowling. He glanced at his reflection in the mirror, noticing a cut on his lower lip. He splashed some water on his face in the bathroom and brushed his teeth. Feeling a little bit more human, he took his drink into the living area and started searching for his laptop. He pulled the grey blanket off the sofa and rummaged behind the cushions. But there was no sign. His head was pounding, he could almost hear the whooshing sound as his brain reverberated around his skull. He heard a key in the lock and, a moment later, Andy opened the door. She carried a bag of groceries and wore a forced smile, her blonde hair hanging loosely around her shoulders. She regarded him for a moment before continuing to the kitchen.

"You're up," she said. "Must have been one hell of a night."

Her tone was even, but there was a hint of something else, coldness, he couldn't be sure.

"Gala was so busy, bank-holiday busy. But I got the last pack of their special bacon," she announced as she laid her purchases on the counter. "Bacon and eggs, what do you think?" She was acting normally, but there was something different about her – her movements were mechanical.

He watched her as she busied herself around the kitchen. "Andy, I don't think I can eat …"

"Oh, dear. Have we a bit of a hangover? Well, perhaps just a couple of eggs?" She pointed towards the stool. "Sit. I'll cook. And you can tell me all about your night."

"Well …" Stephen began. "There is not much to tell, really. I came back here and had a beer or two …"

"Ah, I think it was more than that, Stephen." Andy laughed. She drizzled oil into a pan and added seasoning, breaking in two eggs.

His stomach churned.

"Hey, remember that weekend last year when I went to visit my sister and baby Izzy?"

"Yeah?" *Tread carefully, Stephen.*

"What did you do again?"

Stephen shrugged. "I worked, didn't I? On a work presentation." Why the hell was she asking? He glanced at the broken picture frame on the floor.

Andy followed his gaze. "Yeah, I was wondering about that too."

"Did I … did I break it?"

Andy shrugged. She flipped the eggs and slid two slices of bread under the grill. "Beats me, Stephen. I came home to find you lying on the kitchen floor, surrounded by vegetables and a smashed-up picture frame of our wedding day."

He was incredulous. "What? But, how did I get …"

"If it wasn't for Mike, I wouldn't have been able to get you onto the couch on my own." She shot him a glance. "He helped." She grabbed a plate from the press and began dishing up.

Alarm bells started firing up inside Stephen's head. "Mike was here? When you got home?"

She nodded. "Yep." She pushed a plate of food across the counter towards Stephen. "Eat up." She took a knife and fork from the drawer and placed them beside his plate.

"Andy, I can't eat …"

"Yes, you can, Stephen."

"I don't feel well, sorry …"

"*Eat. The. Fucking. Food. Stephen!*" she said through gritted teeth. She held the spatula in her hand as if it were a weapon.

What the fuck was wrong with her? He had a hangover, so what, it wouldn't be the first time. He picked up a piece of toast and took a small bite. His mouth started to fill with saliva and the gagging returned.

Andy handed him a piece of kitchen towel. "Are you OK, Stephen?" she asked, her gentle tone returning.

He pushed the plate away. He ran to the bathroom, barely making it before vomiting into the bowl. When he finished, he cleaned his teeth again and washed his face. He stole a glance in the overhead mirror – the whites of his eyes were lined with tiny red veins. His skin was flushed. He looked like shit.

"Feeling better, Stephen?" Andy called from the living room.

"Yeah. Be out in a minute." He took a breath before leaving the bathroom, passing a glowering Milo on the way. When he re-entered the kitchen, Andy was sitting at the kitchen counter, his laptop open in front of her.

"Were you looking for this?"

He went to grab it.

"No, no, not so fast." She held his gaze as she turned the screen towards him, revealing an image of Grace Doran. Recognition dawned. *She knew.* "So, Stephen, I'm going to ask you again. Do you want to tell me what you were doing last year while I went to visit Cathy?"

46

There was a knock on the front door. It was twenty-five minutes after ten. Erin and Grace regarded each other, not sure what to do. Neither of them moved. The clock ticked. The knock came again.

"I'd better answer it." Erin slowly pushed back her chair and stood.

Grace grabbed her by the arm. "No, Erin, it could be Sarah. Lana isn't here yet, I'm not ready to see Sarah."

"Maybe it's both of them arriving together, Grace. Don't worry, I'm here with you." She held her hand. "You can do this, Grace, trust me. You are much stronger than you think." Erin squeezed her hand and left the kitchen.

Grace could hear her footsteps retreat in the hall and then the front door opened. She strained to listen, unable to make out whether there was one voice or two. The scar on her face began to itch and she resisted the urge to scratch her skin, instead carefully placing her hair around it, smoothing the skirt of her dress over her absent leg, the other one hidden under the table. She told herself to stay calm, *breathe*. She sensed someone behind her, watching her. She hoped it was Lana or Erin. She heard a phone ring in the hall.

"Grace?"

The tone was gentle – Grace recognised it immediately. She felt her heart beat a little bit faster in her chest, and she instinctively straightened her shoulders, in order to control it. She swallowed hard as more footsteps approached.

"Grace, I'm just going to ring Lana, OK?" Erin's voice sounded concerned. "Sarah said she has been trying to reach her all morning. I think that might have been her ringing just now. I won't be a minute."

No, no, Grace didn't want Erin to leave. Before she could say anything, she heard the kitchen door close. What was Erin doing? She had promised that she wouldn't leave her!

Sarah walked around and stood in front of her, but Grace refused to look her in the eye. She imagined Sarah's sorrowful expression, the angle of her head, the pitying look in her eyes. Grace longed for Erin to return.

"Grace," Sarah said again.

Grace stole a quick glance at Sarah. "I think we should wait for Lana."

Sarah was standing no more than two metres from Grace, her perfectly groomed, glossy hair, her pretty smile too much to bear, while Grace sat there, ruined. Sarah perched on the chair that Erin had just vacated. *Too close.* Grace sipped her tea. The clock ticked.

"So, how have you been?" Sarah asked.

Grace sighed. What a stupid thing to ask!

"I'm sorry." Sarah must have realised her mistake. She tried again: "Alex started school."

Grace rubbed the side of her cup with her thumb. Neither of them said anything. A dog barked somewhere outside. The clock ticked.

"Do you mind if I get a glass of water? It's so warm today. Do you want a glass?"

Grace ignored her.

Sarah stood, took a glass from the draining board, turned on the tap and filled it with water. The clock ticked. *It's so warm today. Do you want a glass?* The clock ticked. *It's so warm today. Do you want a glass?* Grace narrowed her eyes, her brain scrambled as a memory tugged.

And Grace remembered.

* * *

"Sorry, I didn't mean to frighten you. God, it's so warm today. I need a glass of water. Do you want a glass?"

Grace made her way down the steps towards the cabin and Sarah followed her.

"Where were you guys? I thought you were on the beach with Stephen, but I couldn't see you when I came back up from cleaning the toilet. Oh my God, Sarah, I can still smell Declan's vomit, he really needs to apologise. It's so disrespectful to do something like that. I mean, he must have realised he spewed all over the toilet, right? And he just walks away?" Grace opened another bottle of red wine and poured some into a glass, handing it to Sarah, before topping up her own. "We are out of white." She held up her glass, grinning. "It's not so bad though, I'm on my third! Cheers!" They clinked glasses. "Thanks so much for inviting me, Sarah. It's been the best day ever." Grace beamed as she sipped her wine.

"You've cheered up." Sarah took a drink of wine and climbed up the steps towards the deck. Grace followed her.

"Yeah, sorry about earlier. I just, I don't know what happened to me, I panicked a bit, the way Declan was behaving, I just got a bit freaked out, but, you were right, I need to chill. I mean, look at this place?" She gestured towards the view in front of her, the sea shone like crystals where the sun hit the tips of the waves.

Sarah didn't reply.

Grace turned towards her. "Where is Stephen?"

"He went after Harry." Sarah didn't look at her – she had a distant expression in her eyes, her mind was clearly elsewhere.

"Sarah? What is it?" Grace asked gently.

"Nothing." Sarah sipped her wine.

"Come on, what is it?"

"Just leave it, Grace!" Sarah warned.

"What's going on?"

"Just leave it, I said."

She sounded hoarse, her throat catching on her words. Had she been crying? Grace was taken aback. She reached out to touch Sarah's arm.

Her friend pulled away. "I said leave it." Her tone was angry.

"Sarah? It's me, Grace, you can tell me, whatever it is."

Sarah wiped a tear from her face. "What's wrong with me? I mean, why do I keep making the same mistake? Over and over and over?"

Grace frowned. "Is it Harry?"

"I just get disrespected, Grace!" She sniffed. "Men just use me, they get what they want and they just throw me away, like a second-hand object. Again, and again and again. I mean, what the fuck is wrong with me?"

"Sarah …"

Sarah laughed harshly. "Harry! Turns out he's just not that into me." Her voice was filled with sarcasm.

"I thought he was into you, Sarah …"

Sarah shook her head. "No, he's not. He's just like all the rest, Grace. He's out for a bit of fun, and then he'll ghost me, after this weekend."

"What happened?"

Sarah shrugged. "He's texting some other girl. I just saw a message on his phone, he left it on the beach. Something about bringing some girl to the World's End tonight. I mean, he finds out I have to go back, and he's immediately moving on, replacing me. Stupid idiot, can't even hide it for one weekend."

So, Stephen was right. He said his friend wasn't the type to commit, but Grace hadn't thought he would lose interest that quickly. She put her arm around Sarah's shoulder. "Sarah, what did you tell me when we were coming down here? You said, this weekend was a bit of fun, remember? Lighten up, you said?"

Sarah turned towards Grace. "I'm tired, Grace. I am tired of doing everything on my own. When I close the front door in the evening, it's just Zack and me. I'm so lonely, Grace. I just wanted someone in my life, someone I can trust. Why do I always pick the wrong guys? Do I have 'mug' written across my forehead or something?"

"Don't be daft, Sarah. You are better than all of them, and you know it. Jesus, Stephen was clearly right about Harry."

Sarah sniffed, frowning at Grace. "What do you mean? Stephen was right about Harry. Right about what?"

"Just that earlier, he was saying that Harry moved from one girl to the next."

Sarah observed Grace as she took a sip of her wine. "And you never thought to tell me?"

"I didn't really believe it, Sarah."

"You are supposed to be my best friend, Grace." She loosened her arm from Grace's grip. "I thought I could trust you, Grace, but you know what? You are just like everyone else." She pressed a finger into Grace's chest. "You put on this stupid act, 'I'm so scared all the time', so people will like you, and it is so irritating, Grace, did you know that? You are so irritating. You are a stupid bitch!" Sarah practically spat the last few words in Grace's face. "I think I'm done with you." She forcefully pushed against Grace before stumbling down the steps towards the cabin. Grace didn't know whether it was the wine, or the heat from the sun or Sarah's push, probably a combination of all three. She lost her footing and fell, hitting her head off the seat corner. She felt dizzy and disorientated. Dazed, she grabbed onto the edge of the seat and tried to stand. She staggered, losing her balance, and tumbled over the boat's edge into the cold water. The side of her cheek bounced off the jetty before she hit the water. She felt her skin rip, the taste of blood in her mouth, nausea rose up inside her, and her head felt as if it was going to explode. She tried to cover her face with her hands as she submerged, but the boat shoved her against the jetty, trapping her movement. With all her strength she pushed at the boat and managed to slide out from the wall and break the surface. She glanced up at the jetty, but there was nothing to hold on to, no stepladder, just a round metal rope hook. Had she seen a ladder on the other side of the boat? Her head throbbing, she swam around the boat. The ladder was there, attached to the rim, but it was too high. She pushed her body up but she couldn't reach the bottom rung. She thought she heard voices — shouting, and then a moment later, the boat shifted as someone jumped on. She called for help but the sound was muffled by the sea. She heard the engine roar. She cried out for help again, but she could barely hear her own voice. She swam around to the front of the boat, hoping someone might see her. The vessel started to move, and she heard the *swish of the propeller coming towards her. She tried to swim away from the boat and felt something sharp slice through her legs. Excruciating pain. She turned to see Stephen, Harry and Declan standing around the helm, clenched fists, furrowed brows, tense jaws. Nobody saw her.*

With every bit of strength she had left, she swam away from the boat. She screamed and waved her arms, but nobody could hear or see her in the water, the sound of the engine drowning out her voice. Her heart was hammering so fast in her chest she could barely breathe. She thrashed her arms towards the jetty and looped her fingers into the metal hook in the wall. She felt so tired. She counted in order to stay alert. "1000, 999, 998, 997, 996 ..." She had to get out of the water. She turned towards the beach. She could make it. She had to try. The others would come back for her, once they realised she wasn't on the boat. She swam as hard as she could, though her legs weren't of much use, tasting salty water, the waves fighting against her. A short time later, she felt the rough sand beneath her. She crawled her way up the beach, turning over onto her back, exhausted. She dared not look at her legs. She knew there was something terribly wrong with them. The initial excruciating pain had changed to a tingling sensation – now, they just felt numb. She hoped that her friends wouldn't be much longer. She felt herself floating, she just wanted to sleep.

The next time she woke, she was in the hospital, it was three months later, and she couldn't remember a thing.

She had been dreaming about herself. This whole time.

* * *

Sarah was now sitting beside Grace.

"I thought you were on that boat, Grace. I swear to you, I had no idea you had fallen into the water," she pleaded, her eyes brimming with tears. "I fell asleep in the cabin. We had arrived back to the harbour when Harry came down to the cabin to wake me and he wanted to know where you were. He went ballistic. Declan had told him you were with me. Harry started losing his shit with Declan, shouting his head off about him being a complete fuck-up and how he couldn't trust him to do anything right. It was horrible. I thought you were on the boat, everyone thought you were on the boat, I swear to you." She started to cry, tears running freely down her face. "I'm so sorry, Grace, I'm so sorry. I thought you were on the boat."

"Why didn't you go back for me?" Grace still couldn't look at her.

"When we got back to the harbour and I realised you were not on the boat, I begged Harry to go back for you. He said he would talk to Gary Duke, the guy who hired out the boat."

Grace was incensed. "Why didn't you alert the coast guard?"

Sarah shifted in her chair. The clock ticked.

"Harry is involved in something, was involved in something, I don't know, it was something illegal," she finally said. "That afternoon, when Declan walked up the beach, he wasn't just going for a stroll, he was meeting a boat. Remember Harry went up the beach to find him? He was really going to help Declan with something. Harry didn't know we had to get back to the harbour because we had to catch a bus. He was pissed …"

Grace narrowed her eyes. "What was he involved in?"

"I don't know."

Sarah answered too quickly. Grace knew she was lying.

"Harry couldn't risk the Gardaí coming to the World's End. They agreed to take the *Karina* back out to the island after dark to look for you, but when they got there they couldn't find you. Harry told me they spent hours over there. Everyone thought you would be on the beach."

"Who?"

"What do you mean?"

"Who went back over to the island?"

Sarah shrugged. "Harry and Declan. Gary Duke."

"Are you serious?"

"Why does it matter who went back? They tried to find you, Grace. It was dark and …"

"You stayed in the World's End with Stephen? While I was out on the island? In complete darkness, on my own?"

Sarah shook her head. "I took the bus home. I had to get back to Zack, remember? And Stephen left immediately."

"You just got on with your day?"

"I didn't know you had fallen into the water, Grace!" Sarah protested.

"You left me out there, all alone, in the dark, and then you didn't bother to look for me? You let a couple of strangers search for me? Guys who didn't give a shit whether I was dead or alive?"

"Grace, it wasn't like that! I had to get back for Zack. Please, you have to believe me?"

Grace pulled her hair back from her face, revealing the long jagged scar, the new shape of her jawline. Never taking her eyes off Sarah, she wheeled her chair back from the table and pulled up the hem of her dress. Sarah recoiled in horror. She couldn't hide behind the tilt of her head now. She cupped her hand over her mouth in a vain attempt to mask her shock. But she couldn't hide the horror in her eyes.

311

"What took them back to the island, Sarah? Because it wasn't me – what was so important that they could risk leaving me behind?"

"I – I can't tell you, Grace. I'm so sorry, *Jesus*." She started crying again as she looked up and down Grace's damaged body.

Something dawned on Grace. "They paid you, didn't they? They paid you to stay quiet. About whatever it was they were doing? Whatever sordid business they were involved in, they paid you to say nothing, and you sacrificed me. Your friend? *Your best friend?*"

Sarah shook her head.

"You took me there, Sarah, to the World's End, and that weekend was the end of my world." Grace shook her head in disgust. "I think I'm done with *you*, Sarah."

"Please?" Sarah begged.

"Get out." Grace pulled at the wheels of her chair.

"Grace, I'm sorry …"

"*Get out of my house!*" Grace screamed.

Erin came rushing into the kitchen. "What's going on?"

Sarah staggered a few steps back towards the kitchen door, wiping her wet face with her hands. She couldn't take her eyes off Grace's body.

"I'm so sorry, Grace." She turned towards Erin, pleading for her to understand.

"You'd better go, Sarah, you are not welcome here," Erin said, evenly.

Sarah ran out of the kitchen and pulled open the front door, letting it slam against the hall table, knocking the red phone onto the floor. She ran out into the street and, a moment later, Grace could hear a car door close, an engine start. A clock ticked. A dog barked, somewhere.

Epilogue

Lana noticed the sign for Castle Cove as she drove into the small fishing village. Slowing her pace, she passed the white cottages on the cliff's edge. She took a left towards the harbour and parked near the boat hire kiosk. The cabin shutters were closed. There was no sign of Gary Duke or his nephew Danny, nor were there any hire boats moored along the harbour. The summer season was over in Castle Cove and only a few locals meandered along the harbour, wrapped up warm against the autumn breeze. She sat in her car for a moment longer, not wanting to leave its warm interior. The seawater appeared dark and murky and she thought about the last time she was here, and everything that had happened since.

Grace Doran had moved to Canada with her grandmother where she was re-introduced to her birth father, Michael Doran, for the first time in twenty-five years. A man she had thought was her uncle. Michael had been living in Vancouver for years, and he had done quite well for himself as a hotelier. The details of why he had left Ireland were hazy. Grace had a different father to Erin, the man they thought was their uncle. Curious, Lana had searched the national archives and managed to get a hold of the Dorans' family records. She discovered that Erin and Grace's documented birth father, James Doran, had died around the same time his brother Michael had left for Canada. Lana thought the timing of Michael's relocation was coincidental, but she decided not to investigate any further. Whatever it was that Grace and Erin were hiding, she thought it best to leave well enough alone. The girls had suffered enough.

Her phone rang. Lana glanced at the screen to see Erin Doran's name. She pressed answer. "Hi, Erin! It's good to hear from you."

"Hello, Lana, how are you holding up?" Erin asked, her tone gentle.

"I'm doing OK, thanks, what about you?"

"Alright, I guess, missing my sister, but I'm happy for her."

"Have you heard from her?" Lana asked. She watched as a colony of seagulls flew towards Mutton Island, forming a perfect triangular shape in the grey sky.

"Yeah, I spoke to her this morning. It was coming up on dinnertime over in Vancouver. She had some promising news actually!" Erin sounded excited.

"Go on?"

"My uncle, Grace's dad, set up a meeting with a world-class plastic surgeon and he wants to start working on the reconstruction of Grace's face as soon as possible. The specialist also thinks that Grace's leg is strong. The surgeons took the pins out and the limb is holding up well enough on its own."

"That is amazing news, Erin."

"It is, and Grace is showing interest in her dad's hotel. Hospitality is in her genes, she says. Who knew?" She laughed.

"What about you, Erin?"

"I'm going to stay in Ireland, for now at least. I started college last month, social care."

She would be good at that, Lana thought. "Erin, you are a born carer, but, it's time to be kind to yourself. You have been through so much."

"That morning Sarah came to our house, I really didn't want to leave Grace alone …"

"I know you didn't, but I couldn't be there with you. My mother, she needed me. I wanted you to leave Grace and Sarah alone. That's why I called you, and I know you found that difficult."

"Yes, but it worked, didn't it?" Erin replied. "Grace remembered."

"Seeing Sarah in person unlocked her memory."

"Thank you, Lana, for everything."

"You're welcome, Erin. Make sure to stay in touch, and give my regards to Grace."

"I will, take care of yourself." Erin hung up.

Michael Doran had written many times to his daughter, via his own mother, but Grace's mother had banned the older woman from her home. When Rosie Doran moved into a care home, Grace's grandmother had attempted to visit without the girls present, but Rosie always refused to see her. Rosie Doran had locked her secrets into a box and she had buried that box. Erin had laughed when explaining this set of circumstances to Lana, that they had different dads. "Things are complicated in our family," she had said.

Stephen hadn't been found guilty of anything in the end, if you didn't consider the fact that he had behaved like a proverbial asshole. Nothing could be proven, neither his presence on the island, or at the summerhouse. His wife had stuck by him, *for better or for worse*. It turned out they had a creep of a neighbour. The couple installed cameras after Stephen suspected someone had been inside their apartment, and it seemed the guy living across the hall had been paying regular visits. Of course, this was also Stephen's fault – he had given the neighbour a key to their apartment so the man could feed their cat.

Lana scrolled through her contacts until she found Ella's number. She hit the call button and a moment later heard: "Good afternoon, Ella speaking, how may I help you?"

"That's much better, Ella!" Lana laughed.

"Lana?" Ella sounded anxious. "Is everything OK?"

"Yes? Why wouldn't it be?"

"Just, that car of yours …"

Oh Jesus. "How do you like your new office, Ella?" Lana changed the subject.

"*Em*, it could do with some plants around the room, some colour…"

"Is it more comfortable? Quieter?"

Lana could almost hear the girl smile on the other end of the phone. "Ms. Bowen, it's so peaceful here, I love it. I can get so much work done."

"Good!" Lana was pleased. She had given up the unit she was renting in the city and set up an office space in her mother's home. She heard papers shuffling.

"Hey, I just got a call from Garda Donal Mulcahy!"

"Go on?"

"Well, he informed me that the Gardaí are preparing a file for the DPP concerning Harry Reddan and Declan Slattery. The two men are deep in trouble – money-laundering, bogus investment companies, drug-smuggling, not to mention their more recent venture, human trafficking. And get this, they now have strong evidence connecting them to the missing girl, Eva Mroz."

"Eva Mroz?" Lana asked.

"Remember the girl from Estonia? She went missing last year."

"Linked to the Criminal Assets Bureau investigation?"

"Yes." More shuffling of papers. "It turns out the young girl's laptop showed up a history of discourse on a private platform for messaging, with the premise that she was connecting with an employer in Ireland. The receiver of this correspondence deleted their conversation, but Eva Mroz didn't. Declan Slattery sent the messages."

"*Bingo!*" Lana replied.

"Yes, Ms. Bowen, and he also told me that Sarah informed the Gardaí that Harry and Declan had planned on throwing a big party the night that Grace ended up in the water, that a boat had ferried girls on to the island that afternoon, and Declan had walked up the beach to meet that boat." Lana could hear Ella tapping away on her keyboard. "I hope you don't mind but I did some investigating. So, we know that Slattery Holding's owns the World's End and that the company belongs to Declan Slattery, right?

"Go on?"

"Sarah thinks that Declan arranged for clients to come to the party that evening so he could display the young women, like merchandise, for a price. Only, the girls didn't make it onto the island, or if they did Sarah doesn't know what happened to them. The family of Eva Mroz are pushing for a murder charge, but without her body to prove such a crime it is looking unlikely. For now, she is still listed as a missing person. "

"Thanks, Ella. Any update on the boat repair?"

"Yes. Coleman boat repair look after all of Gary Duke's vessels. They have no record of a repair either before or after the long weekend of May 2018."

"So, the *Karina* never made it to their workshop?"

"No. The lad I spoke to, he said the *Karina* is a low maintenance cuddy boat. They rarely cause problems."

"Can you call Mulcahy back? He might want to get a forensic team out to look at the *Karina*."

"Will do, Ms. Bowen."

"You did good, Ella, thanks."

"You are welcome, Ms. Bowen.

"Anything else I can help you with?" The girl was incalculably enthusiastic.

"Yes, there is one thing."

"What is it, Ms. Bowen?"

"Please, call me Lana." Lana smiled as she ended the call.

It had taken a while, but her assistant had grown on her. The girl was immensely positive, and Lana needed that in her life right now. She ruminated on what Ella had just told her. So, Sarah was helping the authorities with their enquiries, a small peace offering, and maybe too late to save her relationship with Grace. Sarah admitted to a struggle that resulted with Grace ending up in the water. The Department of the Marine carried out a full safety check on Gary Duke's boats and found that the boats did not comply with safety regulations. Subsequently, they shut him down. Grace had an insurance claim against Gary's Boat Hire citing gross negligence. The Gardaí were also looking at Gary for other misdemeanours. Someone was working closely with Harry and Declan, supplying a boat with intent to aid their transgressions. There was no proof as of yet, but Lana felt sure that the authorities had their eye on Gary Duke.

Sarah was back in college. She had made several attempts to repair her friendship with Grace, but understandably Grace was finding it hard to trust her again. Sometimes, broken relations just can't be fixed – the damage irreparable.

Lana stepped out of her car and opened the boot. The container was still in the same position, tucked into a cardboard box, newspapers pushed down the sides to hold it in place. She carefully lifted the jug from the box and closed the boot. Glancing down the pier, she could see Lukasz on his boat untangling his nets, his head bent low focused on the job. The fisherman glanced up then, as if sensing her watching him. He smiled and waved. She smiled back and walked towards his boat. The wind picked up and she stopped for a moment, placing the pot on the path so that she could fasten the zip on her jacket. She needed both hands to carry the container. She continued along the harbour until she reached Lukasz's boat – noticing Peter's was empty. Lukasz stepped onto the quay.

"Hello!" He embraced Lana warmly, pushing the vase into her stomach. "You are early."

Lana hugged him back before putting the vase down beside her. "Traffic was light."

Lukasz looked confused.

"Light?" Lana offered. "Not heavy?"

His expression didn't change. She shook her head, amused. "Come on, Lukasz? How long have you been living in Ireland? Your English is really good!" Lana laughed. "Traffic was light? It means there was not that much traffic on the road?"

"Then why not say that?" He grinned and she pushed him playfully. He regarded her for a moment. "I like your hair. It suits you."

Lana self-consciously felt the short brown locks around her neck. She had been trying to grow it out again and it had reached shoulder length. "Thanks."

"Would you like a coffee? I have a pot I just made up in Nora's cabin?"

The good stuff. Lana remembered the last time she drank Nora's coffee.

"I would love some."

Lana picked up the vase and Lukasz helped her onto the boat, gesturing towards one of the storage boxes for her to sit. He poured steaming hot coffee into an enamel cup and handed it to Lana. She sipped the hot liquid, savouring the nutty roast. Coffee had never tasted this good, she thought. He poured a cup for himself and they both sat in silence watching the sea. Lana smiled at the sight in front of her, the picture-perfect postcard.

"It's just beautiful. Even in the autumn."

Lukasz nodded in agreement. The water lapped gently against his boat. Seagulls made shapes in the sky.

"My friend did some investigating for me, Lukasz." She stole a glance at him, making sure that she had his attention. "Your old boss, he is in prison."

She heard Lukasz's intake of breath.

"He was caught with sizable quantities of drugs on his boat, not long after you left Poland. He was offered a plea bargain if he gave the names of his accomplices. He complied, but when the authorities were unable to locate the men, the plea bargain was withdrawn. He has served three years of a twenty-five-year sentence without parole, and he is almost sixty years old now. It is doubtful he will step outside a prison again."

Lukasz looked confused. "What does that mean?"

Lana gave a small smile. "It means you can go home, Lukasz, to visit your mother. It is safe."

Lukasz's eyes watered and he turned towards the sea, shaking his head.

"I can't thank you enough, Lana. I love it here, but I need to see my family. My mother, she is getting older. Family is everything to me."

Lana smiled sadly. She understood – family is everything.

Lukasz stood. "Forgive me, I must go to Nora's cabin, to make a phone call."

She watched him step down from his boat and hasten up the harbour toward the small cabin. She held onto the vase as she sipped her coffee. Sensing movement behind her, she turned to see Peter standing there.

"Ready?" he asked.

She nodded, yes. She set down her cup and handed the vase to Peter. Then she climbed from Lukasz's boat and onto Peter's. He started the engine and steered the vessel out along the buoys, turning at the World's End. She hugged the vase close to her chest as they maintained a steady pace towards the island. The sun was high in the sky as Peter steered, his strong hands gripping the wheel, his jaw set as he concentrated on the sea.

They made it across and Peter jumped onto the jetty and tied the boat. She carefully held on to the vase as he helped her down onto the pier. When she landed, she lost her balance and he held onto her waist to support her. His blue eyes searched her own, a small smile playing at the corners of his lips. "Think we've been here before." He grinned.

She reached into her pocket and handed him an envelope. He closed his fist around the document that contained his brother's coroner report. Death by drowning. The sea had positioned the young man behind the rocks – an enigma. Peter had wanted to blame someone for his brother's death, but there was no one responsible. She left Peter sitting on the pier.

Lana strolled up the beach. A short time later, she arrived at what felt like the edge of the world. Lifting the lid off the urn, she carefully placed it on the sand. Lana's mother never did wake up after the night she had found her lying on her kitchen floor. She had been suffering from cardiovascular disease for over two years, but she had not told Lana. The doctor had said her heart had failed and that she most likely had no idea what was happening to her.

Shielding her eyes, Lana made her way to the water's edge. She opened the vase and scattered her mam's ashes into the sea spray. The wind picked up and the powdery residue dispersed in front of her. She heard her mother's words echo in her ears. *If March won't kill, April will try …*

Wiping her tears with the back of her hand, she slowly returned to Peter, who was engulfed in a sadness of his own. She shoved her hands into her pockets. "Drink?"

Peter tucked the envelope into the inside pocket of his jacket. He held out his hand. "Sure thing, Nancy Drew. If you're buying." He grinned.

Lana accepted Peter's warm hand. "Don't call me Nancy Drew."

Peter laughed.

"Seriously," she said.

They climbed onto the boat and made their way back to Castle Cove.

THE END